Cody Wallace is an archit..d.
He's been on one of those year-end benders that can get you kicked out
of *Gentlemen's Quarterly*. His wife Peppi is a movie actress, and she's hot,
and she's gone AWOL. Cody figures it's New Year's and her place is beside
him, linking arms and singing Auld Lang Syne.

Reska DeWoers, big-time film director and big-time lesbian, has other
ideas. Her production is in trouble – though no one is admitting it –
and she reckons she needs Peppi even more than Cody does. When Cody
busts into her Bel Air eyrie he blunders into a tense sexual drama involving
strip poker, fetishism, controlled substances – and another game altogether,
played for the very highest stakes, in which Peppi is a mere chip . . .

By the time he's finally caught up with her he's been treated like human
garbage – literally: shot at, chased from LA to the Napa valley to Palm
Springs to Mexico. And what the hell are those Cubans up to . . .?

Low Mean Men is a high-anxiety tinseltown suspenser that is a worthy
successor to Rowland Morgan's highly regarded début, *Tall Dead Wives*.

LOW MEAN MEN

ROWLAND MORGAN

BLOOMSBURY

First published in Great Britain 1992

Copyright © 1992 by Rowland Morgan
This paperback edition published 1992

The moral right of the author has been asserted

Bloomsbury Publishing Ltd, 2 Soho Square, London W1V 5DE

A CIP catalogue record for this book
is available from the British Library

ISBN 0 7475 1174 8

10 9 8 7 6 5 4 3 2 1

Typeset by Hewer Text Composition Services, Edinburgh
Printed by Cox & Wyman Ltd, Reading, Berkshire

When I was in jail I heard a lot of stories. Guys gather in little groups . . . Someone will come up to you and say, 'Hey, Art, take me on a trip.' And so you tell about something you did, something that happened to you, the whole thing, you paint a picture. On the street nobody will listen to anyone else for more than a minute, a couple minutes at most, but in jail people will listen, if a guy can talk, for two or three hours straight without ever saying a word.

Art Pepper

THIS TRIP IS FOR PRISONERS

<u>From the makers of The Slave</u>

VISIONVILLE STUDIOS PRESENT

LEONARD KERRY WILLS*PENELOPE HARMAN

A RESKA DEWOERS FILM

THE SPIRIT THAT MOVED HER – MOVED MOUNTAINS

Leo Kempinski PRESENTS   IN ASSOCIATION WITH Visionville

A Carl Carmody PRODUCTION OF A Reska Dewoers FILM

Leonard Kerry Wills   "CHI"   Penelope Harman

SCREENPLAY BY Nevil Rayner   MUSIC BY Harry Myers

STORY BY Nevil Rayner & Della Lemuel

PRODUCED BY Carl Carmody   DIRECTED BY Reska Dewoers

© VISIONVILLE | ORIGINAL SOUNDTRACK AVAILABLE ON OK CASSETTES | ▷◁ DOLBY STEREO IN SELECTED THEATERS

LOW MEAN MEN

ONE

1

ON AN AVENUE of lonesome homes in high Bel Air I clambered out of a cab into tepid drizzle. Mauling my face with a sleeve, I watched my ride accelerate away into the night and took stock in the light of a distant streetlamp. DeWoers's entrance was an imperial affair left over from some forgotten millionaire's demolished estate, the gates twelve feet high, made of iron hammered into creeper and flanked by granite pillars topped with five-foot gryphons sitting up to beg. Dense yew hedging stretched away on either side, and the gates were closed.

Before wrenching the bars open with my bare hands, I unbuttoned and took a piss against one of the pillars, which was lousy manners, but in character with my jealous-husband outfit of sweat-stained T-shirt, rumpled chinos and beat-up deck shoes. Emptying my inflamed bladder onto the architecture, it was funny to think that last time I'd seen these gates the Wallaces, man and wife, had swooped through them in a limousine to attend a crowded garden party, me in a midnight-blue tuxedo, giving the limp-wristed wave to a braided commissionaire. Highly funny. Funny puke.

Tires were whispering somewhere down the street, so I zipped up and shouldered my way between the gate and the dripping hedge. The prowl car's fan had a worn bearing and it squealed as they stopped and flashlighted along the hedge, forcing me to shove myself further into the scratchy dark. The light skimmed over my head. Probably nobody'd ever tried it before, but the brush gave way and allowed two hundred pounds of bruised, whiskey-reeking cuckold to squeeze between pillar and thicket out onto the bouncy turf of DeWoers's deer park, which made me part of a movie director's private property and none of the security industry's business. I fell down.

Fan screeching, radio squelching, the prowl car's flashlight beam danced over the hedge, picking out a million streaming droplets of drizzle, then glanced through the gates, throwing a baroque pattern across the paved driveway. Bel Air's noisy sleuths couldn't see me, so after a minute or two they cut the light and the whole rackety outfit eased away to other pastures.

The half-pint bottle tucked into my belt was warm, like the whiskey in it. On my back, it was easy to pour. I lobbed it away empty and wiped off, taking care to spy round as I got up and moved downhill, because if any dog interfered I intended to use my drop-kick to crush its trachea.

A few acres of night remained to penetrate, but I recalled the layout; it wouldn't take long to get to the front door and barge it down. The drive crossed a ten-acre breast of hillside, curving through clumps of eucalyptus to a sprawling glass bungalow which cantilevered out over the valley. I would cross the park, punch a hole in the house, take hold of the the director's neck and stretch it high. Then I would capture my wife, twist her tangerine hair round my paw and drag her kicking and screaming back to Santa Flora for New Year's.

The eucalyptus foliage overhead fluttered in a high-beam and without warning a turbo engine came whizzing peevishly along the hedge. Seconds later a solenoid snapped inside the automatic latch of the entrance, setting electric motors humming. Clumps of brush chased each other around as headlights bucked across the grid of a Texas gate. I slumped into the nearest shrubbery and peered over a clump of lavender. Hard to tell anything about a car when it's a shadow behind a shaft of light, with an engine tone curt and spoilt and husky like the MGM lion. It faded towards the house, and as I lay listening in the wet undergrowth the drizzle gently stopped and a disk of moon sailed out to spook the ten million human souls recumbent in the valley.

LOW MEAN MEN

The moonlight felt warm and its lucid fingers twined round my frame, coaxing me on. I uncoiled and clambered upright. Out on the paving lingering fumes of scorched racing oil tickled my throat and I snarled.

2

THE SPREAD SEEMED bigger than before. No sign of life showed through the woods, and behind, towards the street, the tree trunks resembled cell bars against the glow of the far street-lamp. Rottweilers, Dobermans, pit-bulls were valuable. Clearly their handlers had seen Cody Wallace coming and fled.

A little later I emerged from the trees and halted. The tiles on the low-pitched roof of the house, turquoise by day, shone silvery like a choppy lake. Interior lights glowed up the tinted-glass walls, and strips of dim green showed where the slatted shades inside were uneven. A row of carp ponds played mirror in the foreground, and the patchwork tinsel of the valley lay beyond, a twinkling answer to the lonely disk of moon.

Carp never sleep. I went down and checked them and the highway equipment nosing up to the ponds: an MV Agusta bike, hunched and coiled like a jet-propelled hair dryer, a late-model Ferrari with red pinpoint lights flickering warningly inside its cockpit, a Porsche 911 Turbo beside a polished antique one, some BMWs, and a white ragtop XKE Jaguar, open like a four-point-two-liter banana split. All of them certainly pre-owned and candidates for repossession. I stood swaying beside the squad of crouched automobiles, a special-delivery piece of bad news waiting to be delivered.

One of the car engines clicked, and the hood of the E-type was cool. At the rear of the collector Porsche a chrome grille was warm. The plate said HONKY 1 – which meant so-called Hunker, DeWoers's Afro-American idol, had dropped by. I kicked a dent

in his door, limped over to one of the places where the slats were
out of place and took a look inside.

It was a good view of the command deck of the Starship
DeWoers, beaming south over the sparkling ley lines of the city. A
card game was in progress at an island of green baize under a green-
shaded lamp, featuring DeWoers, the producer Kempinski, lawyer
Craven and Walrus the gofer, with his Wyatt Earp mustache.

All eyes were on my wife, who'd evidently just got up from the
game. Her chair was pushed back and she was giving handsome
Hunker a big welcome consisting of full-crinkle grin, European
cheek-kissing, bicep-squeezing and a load of animated chat. His
yuppie pinstripe suit seemed to be new, the way they pawed it and
flashed eyes.

Beyond them, two lanky model girls in stonewashed jean suits
were nestling on a fifteen-foot black-leather couch, nibbling celery
sticks. A sinewy Hispanic-looking youth came out, bare-chested,
from behind the bar, wearing black briefs, plenty of eye makeup
and a tray of coffee and sandwiches.

The players threw in their hands and sat back for the catering,
Hunker moving to say 'Hi' all round, allowing me a full-facial on
Peppi, on the luster in her eyes that said *peak experience*, the all-over
burnish on her face and naked shoulders, the athletic shape under
a sleek evening dress, the charisma she gave off that was going to
take her into such a high price bracket once I'd smashed DeWoers's
skull to bloody pulp.

The window-glass helped to cool my forehead. In a little while
I reopened my eyes and after some blinking could see again.

At the table DeWoers was listening to a wafer-thin cordless,
frowning. Saul Kempinski, hunchbacked with shrewdness, was
working at another phone, compulsively tapping the horn-rimmed
glasses up his beak and scraping a fingernail on his baldy fuzz.
High-browed silver-templed attorney Munro Craven was tucking
shamelessly into a multideck BLT, and Hunker was talking up
a storm with my wife, who kept smoothing her haircut because it
was new – or because it sent her undoctored breasts colliding.

Long, strong Walrus, in a Harvard sweatshirt and heavy silver
bracelet, was leaning on the back of the davenport discussing

French affairs with the clothes racks. One of them pointed to the side table in front of me, where a black videotape case lay. Walrus padded over the two-acre rug, tall, with thigh muscles that bulged against his cotton slacks. He kept tugging and stroking the shag that hung from his nose, but when we locked eyes, he ceased all movement. It lasted a second or two, and a lot of plot development was packed into our visual collision. He turned and headed off stage-right through a pair of bamboo-paneled doors.

Looking at where he'd stood, you thought how his kind summed up the futility of it all: the musculature, the cheekbones, the cheek, all shackled up in a lousy step'n-fetchit job at a few hundred a week live-in. Air-freighted from France in the name of cinematic art and a racing motorcycle that he didn't have to wear a helmet on.

My lip must have been curling as I turned. He was on the doorstep, near the prow of the E-type, wearing a black leather waistjacket which had one hand pushed into it, *à la* Napoleon.

''Ow you get een?'

The floodlights pronounced his cheekbones with an accent as unfavorable as his own. Flattering myself he might recognize me, I leaned off the window, moving with hands spread to show no weapon, and deployed the truth:

'News for Penelope Harman.'

Luckily Walrus had no idea who Cody Wallace was, and there must have been a borrowed car on the forecourt, because he stood warily aside, examining the vehicles, leaving the plate-glass doors in the portico wide open for unexpected visitors to stride triumphantly into the conservatory-atrium. It had a rock pool with a bronze dolphin that gushed at the mouth, fan palms in sarcophagus planters ranged round superfluous expanses of marble checkerboard, and a blue-period Picasso worth a billion yen hanging on the main wall in a quartz-halogen glade. Across from it was a de Chirico depicting nude women with smudge faces and hairy pussies among classical ruins. Next to it were the bamboo-paneled doors. With Walrus on my heels, I threw them open.

3

A CHRISTMAS TREE twinkled in the corner beyond the game, competing with the one stretched out for thirty miles across the plain. The players were clustered in silhouette against the galaxy of the city, with everybody turning to look except my wife. Kettledrums of blood pounded in my head, and I strode far onto a huge Persian rug, shouting.

'Okay! Everybody out! My beef's with DeWoers!'

Walrus gripped my arm from behind and frisked my crotch.

'*Pas d'armes. Il est fou, non?*'

DeWoers was back-to-the-window, controlling the room like a smart stud player. The attitude she took was laid-back and wry as hell.

'Got a problem, Cody, apart from ethyl poisoning?'

'Rip your head off – save the world from any more porno-political garbage.'

The owner-director of Visionville laid her cordless on the baize, leaned forward out of the shadows and showed me the face under the lamp. It was a bad one in magazine pictures, worse in person. Having nothing to work with in the way of looks, she jazzed herself up by overrougeing a thin mouth and skagging her hair out in a frizzy, pink and blue exploding space mission. The kohled sockets holding her glittery eyes were gouged out of a twenty-aspirin-a-day studio complexion made of pizza dough. Her mouth was thin and active. She'd cut a lot of brush to the stump where she was, and her attitude indicated Peppi's spouse was no more threat to her than a pimple on a baby's backside.

'What d'*you* know about porno, chum?'

Seeing her fright of a face took me back to the one time we'd met during *The Slave*'s flush of success, under a party marquee in the lush smell of hot canvas, turf, cigars and organic venison, with Peppi at my side. Cunningly, I switched to a mocking, cynical tone.

'Enough to buy my wife that dress. You like taking it off?'

Things stretched tauter and DeWoers heaved a sigh.

'Listen, I'm making a twelve-million-dollar picture, and as of two days ago the *entire* shoot has had to be rescheduled in a new location.'

The news registered; I took it and hit back.

'Step out here, lover girl. I'll break yer elbows.'

She checked a platinum nugget on her wrist and glanced across at Peppi, who was keeping her back to me, leaking neutrons. Something passed between them, and the director pressed on with a reasonable manner.

'Cody, look, you come here to play cards? Or you intend to upset my star at a difficult moment in a costly production?'

I aped her coaxing tone.

'Tarzan no play poker with ritzy dames in bungalows, DeWoers. Mr and Mrs Wallace have a date for New Year's at home.'

DeWoers wrinkled her nose.

'That's nice.' She shook the bizarre coiffure. 'Tsk, this is what I get for giving the security guys a coupla nights' Christmas break, huh?'

Hunker chuckled just the once: 'Heh,' and attacked his sandwich.

I lunged at the weak spot with a jeer.

'When's shooting start again, huh?'

DeWoers shrugged one of the shoulder pads of her furry sweater and adjusted the posture of her head. The tectonic pattern of the room seemed to shift in accord.

'You're not here to talk shop.'

'I'm married to the merchandise.'

Another stillness, filled with a kind of mourning, Peppi's back nakedly hostile.

DeWoers murmured in a singsong voice, 'Had a little husband, no bigger than my thumb,' to Hunker's sniggering. Then she threw up her hands and used a chiding, persuasive voice that hit all my weak spots. My mother'd cooed to me the same way, back on the ranch in heaven – that's Heaven, Pinewood County, Arizona, Pop. 12. 'Hey, Cody, remember the green-eyed monster, how it mocks the meat it feeds on, huh? Come on, man, journeyed far and long? A little tired and emotional, are we? Why don't you chill out, get into a clean bathrobe and a fresh pot of coffee? Doncha think? Huh? Listen, I mean, *really* . . .'

Vapor of coffee became noticeable, and the Wallace belligerence faltered. A natural aristocrat and proven scholar, I'd married into this racket. The model girls were watching from ringside, perched on stools at the bar with the houseboy. I took a deep breath, grinding fillings, and gritted the words out.

'Malt scotch. Large – and *not* cut with ice.'

DeWoers twitched a grin and nodded towards the bar. Glass clinked against glass, the phone burbled, and as if by magic the tension ebbed. So this was how you made movies.

'No *problema*. I like people to drop in on a game,' the director said, adopting protocol to ease the room back into gambling mode. 'You met these people? This is Saul Kempinski.' The producer nodded curtly, listening to the phone. 'This is my attorney Munro Craven.' Craven shifted his presidential head and raked silver locks at his ear. 'This is –'

She was about to introduce God's answer to black acting, so I cut in, 'Yeah, yeah,' and addressed my wife's rigid, deeply cutaway spine. 'Peppi, let's you 'n' me have a talk.'

Peppi moved nothing. I moved nothing back. The houseboy handed me a tumbler of malt and Kempinski laid down his phone, picked up the deck of cards and tamped it on the baize. One of the models – the sandy-haired one with the sphinx face – gathered plates and whirred a hand vacuum over the table. She had what they call a figure, and the business end of it was near Hunker's nose. He ran a hand up the inside of her thigh and leered at Peppi.

A hawser broke, and I lunged.

Immediately, Walrus's forearm clamped against my larynx, jerking me back, and Hunker loomed up, making abrupt hissing noises. But I was mistaken, the hissing came from me fighting a cramped windpipe. The actor smiled with his thick lips curled down, his eyes distant and pretty as he mangled the T-shirt under my chin. DeWoers called out directions.

'Take it easy, boys. Hunker, *sit down*. Walrus, get the husband another drink, he dumped it.'

Hunker dusted off his hands, giving me the wink and the cold leer, and sat down. Walrus's arm went away to pick up my tumbler. Peppi stared at the baize. DeWoers flicked a finger at the brunette model, and she flowed towards me with a motion of the spray-on jeans that seemed to treasure her genitals. Her accent was thick, but the husky way she expressed it, you forgave anything.

'Mebbe you like to tek you dreenk in the bathroom and wash up.'

'Solid marble, Cody,' DeWoers prodded from the table. 'Amaryllis'll pour a tub and spin your clothes. We'll talk later.' The phone burbled and she took it, grunting and listening, cutting me out.

It meant more hesitation, me being riled up that Peppi might have discussed my thing about marble bathrooms. The players waited to be dealt. Kempinski poked the deck towards Peppi, who reached out to cut. Hunker said something cute to the producer that made her sneer, and Walrus gave me a fresh malt. The way he veered his head away made me aware of my reeky clothes.

Amaryllis touched my arm. Her wavy chestnut hair cried out to be mussed, and warm black eyes under slanting hoods appealed in a way that both mocked and welcomed. I liked her raggedy outfit of bleached jean cloth and chrome chain accessories. She had no shirt under the jacket, but the sleek plunge of her breasts would do. I let her steer me out of the room, across the entrance hall where the dolphin never stopped throwing up, and along a white corridor past more spotlit pictures – Miró, Braque, Chagall, Hockney's dappled swim-pools – to another set of bamboo-decorated doors.

12

We entered a thirty-foot vault built out of Carrara rock, its window wall hung with slatted shades, the ceiling speckled with halogen spots. Amaryllis shut us in, went to a liver-shaped imperial bathtub and unleashed a torrent from a stone lion's head while I placed my drink on a polished rockface vanity. When she'd adjusted the temperature lever, she straightened up with a flush on her cheeks and went to the door.

She sensed my pang of regret, and hilarity danced in her eyes. She pouted and curled the pout, shrugging.

'I tek you clothes.'

The hand towel just made it round my waist. When my bundle came over she pincered it by the fingertips.

She was due to go but still had something to say.

'You lucky tonight.'

'Yeah?'

'You say 'bout breaking Senōra DeWoers's elbows?'

'Uh-huh. So?'

Bright horizons raced recklessly away as she smiled, glancing down at my loincloth.

'No so easy. Senōra DeWoers a strong lady.'

Amaryllis let herself out, leaving me shaking my head, cursing youth, and counting.

At five my patience ran out. I went to the door, grasped the faceted glass handle and twisted.

· 4

THE HALLWAY WAS a wide flow of Persian rugs that felt silky against the feet. One side of it groaned with shelfloads of hundred-dollar art and motion-picture books. Amaryllis was rounding a corner in the distance, and the dolphin was still spewing. The next address, a good way down, was unlocked.

It was a split-level bedroom suite bathed in moonlight, with the spackled ceiling subtly reflecting another expensive view of the city. On the upper level was a suite of velvety couches with screenplays and goofballs scattered on a low glass table. Down a pair of steps on a glassed-in terrace was a circular bed, its satin sheets irradiated with a silvery sheen. Opposite me, the shades were open and a herd of ghostly antelope stood watching with ears and antlers pricked.

Footfalls in the hall sent me into the nearest doorway, which was a dressing room, lined on three sides with fitted closets. Some of the louvered shutters were ajar, with soft garments spilling down in shafts of strip light. An inner doorway gave off a memory of bubble bath, damp towels and cologne from its darkness. I waited, and went out.

The prospect of Babylon made a man dream. I crossed deep-pile carpet to the steps and went down to the edge of the circular bed. No vibrator, no stains, no dildo, only glossy pillows strewn about. My fingers brought one of them to my face. Some of the scent was unfamiliar, but Peppi's was there, mingled with another's. I turned away and gazed far out across Point Vicente towards Santa Catalina and eternity.

A swish of sleek fabric occurred at the door, as if summoned by my busted dream, and a charge of anxiety took my attention off the view. Light from a recessed spot in the hall played on her head and shoulders and floor-length gown. The apricot hair had been cropped short and oiled back with a parting, and a large crystal button clipped to a lobe flashed as she glanced around to see what mischief the guy'd been up to. Her words didn't ring a welcome; the voice just couldn't help sounding that way.

'Look at your gut over the towel. Why did you have to show atall?'

She used the unique timbre with controlled ferment, making no gesture, one hand resting on the doorframe, her skin uncannily glowing.

The pillow fell away as my hand explored the waistline.

'Christmas is a lousy time to be fucked up.'

'You got consolation – about a gallon of it. And made a fool of yourself.'

'Had to finish the job you started. Come home.'

''N'hug a bottle? I'm working, Cody.'

'Studio's dark.'

'Reska's rejigging the schedule. She wants to finish the picture out of state.'

'You believe that?'

'Yes, I believe it.'

'I don't.'

She got out of the doorway.

'Cody, what d'you think you're doing in Reska's bedroom?'

The question bounded around, gagging me.

She stood impervious to irony, bleakly watching. The steps were a ravine, without so much as a rope bridge or a twisted vine. The sobering effect was rapid.

I spread my palms.

'Our second Christmas.'

'That's not fair, you know how busy I am.'

'Poker's busy?'

She gave a little stamp of a silver-pumped foot.

'Reska's heavily stressed. We try to keep her up, but you saw how it is.'

'There's people missing. Where's Carmody, f'r instance? He's the money man. DeWoers is no producer – Kempinski'll clean her out. Maybe the rats know something about the sinking ship you don't?'

Mention of Visionville's head of production balked Peppi for a moment. Some of her force seemed to ebb, and she caught sight of the deer. I broke away from the thrall of the bed and moved up the steps.

'How much d'you *know* about Reska DeWoers? Did you know *Gash* was made by her, for example? A picture so gross that Marilyn Chambers, of all people, took her mouth off a dick, walked naked off the set and broke contract?'

Peppi curled towards me.

'Don't start with your poison.'

'Or that she made *Let My Ocean Come*, which had Oakland whores fucking with dolphins off the Truk Islands?' I clenched an invisible rope and tugged it to my chest. 'Peppi, you don't get where Reska DeWoers is in pictures by having any scruples, surely you realize that?'

My wife looked hard at me, anxiety at work in the muscles round her eyes and a hand wandering over her haunch, which was obviously naked beneath the silk. She flared her undoctored nose and looked away.

'Big deal, you looked her up in a *Variety* annual. So she made a couple of tacky movies. People have to. Making love with dolphins doesn't sound so bad, and anyway, *Chi* was good. Reska made it, and she hired me for it.'

My line was: Yes, *Chi* was a fine picture, and you were good in it. Instead I said: 'What else does she pay you to do? Or does it come free?'

Peppi pulled untied the halter at her neck with a barging motion.

'Get out, I've got to put underclothes on.'

'Keep the lingerie in there, huh?'

She ignored me and went into the dressing room. But the thin thread of confusion I'd sowed in her temples still linked us. She added strayly as she moved out of view: 'Reska wants me to play strip.'

Light from one of the open closets threw her shadow warped against the wall opposite the doorway. The gown slid up a slanting torso. One of her breasts threw a cupola shape onto the ceiling.

'Strip? I don't get it, these people're real gamblers. At least, Kempinski is.'

A pause while the angular shadow did contortions with an elastic bra.

'This time they stake money, I stake clothes.'

'Why not stake money? She paid you for *Chi*.'

Long shadow-legs stepped into a scanty garment. Her half-muffled reply slid lethally out from behind the doorway.

'Hunker's horny.'

A pause, while that sank in.

'Hold it, the guy's straight.'

She reappeared, a silhouette within filmy fabric, her shadowy features edgy, slightly alarmed, uncertain but determined: the state of mind you have to be in to commit hurt. She glanced at me and away, not so much ashamed, more like repelled. Perhaps by me, perhaps by herself. Possibly by both of us.

'Reska likes to watch.' So saying, flaring another darkly defiant look, she showed me the door. 'D'you mind leaving the room? And while you're at it, how about leaving the house? It's not just you and me, there's other stuff happening, business things, very heavy. Promise I'll call you.'

'So they *are* haggling over the picture. Has to be Carmody. What's up?'

She took a step back, indicating the door.

'Who knows? Actors get a page at a time – you're talking commercial secrets. There's a game waiting.'

I plunged forward and seized her arm.

'Peppi, you don't have to buy this shit, it's not part of the package.'

She tolerated no orders. I wasn't giving any, but the flash of fury in her face said she took it that way. She twisted her arm out of my grip and backhanded me hard across the bridge of my nose with the butt of her elbow, one of her street-theater tricks. Tears spurted into my cupped hands along with my gasping noises. She hissed at me viciously.

'You fucking racist!'

The perverse accusation tore the hands off my face and dragged words out of me in a rush.

'Nowhere is it written you have to ball the director to make it. And even if you ball the director, nowhere is it written you play director's whore.'

Her face was a skull with holes for eyes. Her right came out of nowhere accurately onto my septum and my body reeled onto the wall, with my lips mumbling, 'Shit, don't hit me that hard,' into my palms.

Several strong hands grabbed my wrists and I got manhandled away down the corridor, jostling and objecting but half glad to be rescued. By the time my vision cleared, they'd hustled me into the same bathroom where Amaryllis had looked away while Peppi's drunken man undressed.

Walrus stood by the door glaring and tugging his whiskers, flexing his knuckles as if he wouldn't mind a workout while the houseboy in black briefs poked accurate left-right jabs into my gut. I stood it for long enough to sense their enjoyment, then followed my towel onto the floor like a lopped jack-pine. A temple struck marble and the pain hung round for a second or two, then turned into a great dim light, which went out.

5

NEXT THING WAS a remake. Same roles, weirdly different players. It was still a stone sepulcher with a baptismal pool and a stone lion's head, but I didn't know what it had to do with me.

An elegant chicano woman was kneeling over my naked form, offering a view down her jean jacket into fragrance and enticement. She brought up my head and cradled it against a tight denim thigh, anointing my brow with a damp washcloth. As she moved, her chains clinked.

'Wha' happened?'

'Hose heet you.'

'Huh?'

'Hose *muy malo chico*. Señora DeWoers mad at heem.'

'Hit me? Why?'

'Walroos hear a shouting. Señora say find out wha' happen. Nest theeng, he tell her you in the bathroom weeth a headache. She get mad.'

I built a dangerously tall and precarious human edifice, helped the woman fix a towel round its waist, and steered it delicately to a highball tumbler waiting on a long marble vanity. As I grasped the drink the guy staring off the wall caught my eye. He was a big craggy hunk in need of major bodywork, a long, slow battery recharge and a valve regrind. I ran a paw through his tawny locks, letting my fingers stray across a tender lump on the temple to a spreading blue stain under the left eye.

'Who gave me the shine?'

19

In the mirror Miss Mexico came up behind with a quizzical look.

'You wife.'

It seemed strange that this tall hombre could've got slugged by his wife and brained by someone called Hose. He picked up his drink and took a sip of whiskey without enlightening me.

Nurse was holding out a dry T-shirt.

'Hand wash. Is quick-dry.'

The hot clothes she handed me were pieces of a jigsaw which fitted Cody Wallace together again. The man in the looking glass was me, the architect with the waterfront place up-coast in Santa Flora, who lived with Penelope Harman, the actress who didn't seem to live with him any more, and he'd spent Christmas drinking the pain away – until his strength gave out and his patience snapped and he drove through the night to Santa Monica, checked into a Travelodge, and took a cab to Bel Air to rip the head off Reska DeWoers. We nodded in dawning agreement, the guy in the mirror and me, viewing the woman with new eyes.

'And your name's Phyllis, right? Dylis?'

'Amaryllis.'

'Ri-i-ight.'

The sound of her name fitted the last missing neuron back into the puzzle of my cortex and the corridor appeared, stretching away to the altar bed, with Peppi side-lit in the dress, the doubt on her face, and the cruelty that came with it. Amaryllis bent to work the bath-plug lever, which drew my eyes back to her.

'Work at Visionville?'

She stood up, flushed.

'No this week. Shut down.'

'Will it ever open up again?'

She picked up my discarded towel, which bloomed her cheeks rosebud pink.

'Sure, why not?'

'Y' know what they're saying.'

She shook her head beautifully, so I told her.

'They're saying the picture's way over budget. They're saying it's a dog and the studio's folding. They're saying the break's really a strike and Reska DeWoers is in shit. Now she tells us the whole shoot's s'posed to be going out of state.'

Amaryllis leaned past me to tighten a dribbling gold lever at the hand basin. As her hair came by it crackled. When it fell aside, it revealed a swan's neck.

She turned and went to the door.

'I don' know.'

I shrugged.

'It's your life.'

'You gonna play poker now?'

Oddly elated, I felt married again as a result of our row, and if jealous, also more cunning – it was worth considering.

Amaryllis added: 'Señora DeWoers want you to, tol' me to say.'

The room and the green glade at the table beckoned. In my pocket was a wallet containing a few hundred dollars and a folded Santa Flora Mutual Savings & Loan checkbook. Not much of a roll, but my brains were back, and a flutter in my gut was driving me towards that green baize circle as surely as it had goaded me out of a beach house earlier in the night. I let Amaryllis take me on the trek back.

The city vista made a glittering tapestry across two sides of the wide room. Nothing much had changed, only now there was a new player at the table, a raven-haired woman with a haughty profile. No sign of attorney Craven, or Walrus, or the houseboy called Hose who'd used me as a punchbag. The sandy-haired model was snuggled on the floor with her head against DeWoers's knee, and the director was idly stroking her muzzle. You wondered if it ate Lassie or Pal.

Amaryllis put my tumbler on the bar and went away. Stock prices were displayed on a screen, and it was all concentration. One of the phones burbled and Kempinski angled forward out of the shadows to pick it up, muttering. Peppi had the dress stripped down to her waist, and not much of her torso hidden by a flimsy French bra. Kempinski was dealer, and three cards were out, two face up, the players intoning their mantra, pushing forward neatly folded hundreds with their bids. All except Peppi, who had no roll.

'Kings bet.'

'Two.'

'In.'

'Kicking it two.'

'And another two.'

'Three and a half to me and one more.'

The fourth card; nobody looked my way. Kempinski held their nerves in his dealing hand, but something was brooding under the lamp besides the attention of the gamblers. Peppi's skin had lost its glow, her posture was wrong, and her upper lip glistened.

Steered by Kempinski's steady sheaf of fingers, each card made its narrow twist onto a meld.

'A four to the kings, a queen to the possible, a nothing to the threes, a ten to the kicker and dealer shoots himself a red nine. Still kings.'

'Kings check.'

DeWoers had the kings, and she sat impassively with a hand resting behind her roll, ready to finger bills forward.

Peppi had the threes. She gnawed her lip and came back with a raise that Kempinski would record, but naming a puny amount which seemed to feel its way uncertainly towards the kings like a blind man's cane. The kings uttered back, kicking the cane away.

'A grand.'

Peppi kept too still, watching as the bills were counted out. Nobody'd ever seen her hating anything so much, particularly undressing.

The three other bidders dropped out by brushing their cards away. Peppi hardly moved her mouth when she spoke.

'What's a thousand buy?'

DeWoers said: 'Dealer names it.'

There was a pause, during which Kempinski kept his eyes on the deck in his hands. He was the unglamorous cash-register end of the cinema, a hunched, burly cove turning sixty, bald-pated with a black tufty hedge over his ears, thick horn-rimmed spectacles and a tanned – or maybe dusky – disk of a face with a parrot nose, hairy at the nostrils. Decision-making was right up his street and he bristled with it. When it came, it came firm as a china turd.

'The dress.'

Peppi hesitated, knowing three treys could not beat three queens. Confirming there were three queens, in spite of the remaining card to be dealt, with its further chance, would run her the risk of sitting there in bra and panties like a hooker, two garments away from being a naked object to be ogled by the stranger in black seated beside DeWoers.

The stranger was sleek with preening and intellectual smugness. Her raven hair was plastered over her cranium into a tight chignon and the long brow, nose and muzzle made three classy ski jumps to a determined chin. Her eyes were appropriately sunken, shadowy and, when they condescended to survey things, aloof. Stuck into a superior pair of lips she kept a Balkan Sobranie which matched her tangled designer sweater. Her bony shoulders were paper-white where Peppi's were honey. She was like New York night to Peppi's sun-bronzed day, and I longed to switch her lights out. But even in this stripping charade, protocol was law. I kept swallowing back the urge to bellow a protest, upend the table and rescue Peppi from her bummer.

Beside the pulp priestess, Hunker sat, waiting till the underwear came off. I studied his cropped frizz, the back of his thick neck, his spotless white shirt and the midnight-blue pinstripe jacket slung over his chair. His name was Leonard Kerry Wills and he was one of the offspring of the new generation of black rulers, a privileged boy brought up on the shores of tainted infinity in La Jolla, and he was rapidly making good as the corporate Afro heavy that producers had long been looking for. This was DeWoers's find, her lucky gamble. Untried, unbankable, he'd got half a million more than Peppi out of *Chi* thanks to a psychotically greedy agent, and the rumors about his points in the new picture were fat.

Peppi cleared her throat, and everybody knew what it meant, even though her face studying the cards was deadpan. It was no good bluffing DeWoers, or trying to read her puffy, painted face in this game with stakes much higher than money. A long hand with my wedding band on it appeared from her lap, put a fingernail under the treys and turned them over.

Kempinski raked in the kings, carefully keeping the blind card down, and everybody waited while Peppi sent a bleak look across the model girl's doting head to an expressionless DeWoers. In response, DeWoers pushed the model away, and she left.

Grey in the face, Peppi rose and pulled the dress up and over, dropped it behind her and sat down again.

As the dress went up the stranger in black hungrily ogled Peppi's sleek belly, just-right hips in cutaway satin panties, and the amazing Cindy-doll legs.

Kempinski said to DeWoers: 'Break?'

DeWoers shook her head.

'New player.'

The producer briskly nodded assent and let me take the place where Craven had been earlier, between the stranger and Kempinski. DeWoers detached a chubby hand from her cards.

'This is Della Lemuel. She storylined *Chi*.'

'Cody Wallace.'

The writer acknowledged the nothing name with a curt nod, not even granting eye contact, while I blundered into holding her profile too long, because her name had been in the news for swinging history's biggest-ever advance on a novel. The publishers had been quoted somewhere saying something like: 'It had more sex, more graphically described and more frequently featured than we'd ever seen before.' You wondered how the author would ever show her face in public, and here she was, brazen as hell, loaded with money, helping to turn out my wife.

Kempinski peeled the wrapping off a new deck, murmuring for my benefit: 'This is a game of five-card stud, one-bill ante, no limit, dead in the water has thirty minutes to raise a roll outside the game and get back in.' He added as a rider: 'Special stakes apply for Ms Harman,' and there were no smiles. At the edge of my vision Walrus eased into the far end of the room through the double doors. He leaned against the wall with one hand in the Bonaparte position, and I sensed him eyeing my meager bundle of hundreds as it went on the table.

DeWoers impassively cut the deck, and I took a squint at Leonard Kerry Wills, the man known as Hunker. She had cast him as a West African slave-dealer trading in Caucasians, and mainstream producers had ignored the controversy and scouted him as an enforcer, an agent of the illuminati, who possessed authoritarian charisma under a valuable brown skin. It seemed that for all his privilege he'd been court-martialed out of ROTC at some Eastern prep school, and since his hit role in *The Slave* had increasingly made a fetish out of humiliating people. He sat blandly studying the baize, puffed up with celluloid success, although a rhinoceros would have felt through its hide what I was transmitting. My gut rolled over and over, making oral acid squirt up. After a buzz of shuffling, Kempinski started dealing, expertly propelling each card to the point where he wanted it, just short of the players' stacks of bills. The up-card went round with a machine-like repeater action, and I caught a deuce, with a four in the hole.

'Nine, queen, ace, trey, deuce and dealer turns a red six.'

I threw my hand in.

Peppi looked at DeWoers's up-card: an ace of hearts.

'Ace bets.'

DeWoers shoved bills forward. 'Five.'

Hunker folded. Della Lemuel folded. Kempinski scooped up his cards. They wanted the strip game over. Peppi said low and flat:

'What's five hundred worth?'

Kempinski didn't reply right away. He let it brew, and said: 'The pot.'

Another pause, during which Peppi and DeWoers exchanged unspoken information by glances and nervous radio. Peppi seemed unconsoled.

'How much pot?'

Kempinski poked the horn-rims up his beak and fingered the top of his head, as if he wanted to rein in the game, keep it within boundaries he could handle as dealer and decision-maker. He shifted on his seat and sucked through a tooth.

Peppi was perched on a cowhide director's chair, hands interlaced, wearing a heavy glare and light underclothes. Hunker in rolled shirtsleeves resembled a go-go young executive photographed in the pages of *Fortune* magazine. DeWoers was Buddha-faced under the shock of pink and blue hair. Della Lemuel posed heron-like, sending a lone plume of carcinogens up through the cone of light. Time stretched tight.

Kempinski flicked his mouth.

'All of it.'

My wife looked over the view of the city and back again at the green baize table. Her complexion was perfect gallows. The gamma rays beaming at her from the Lemuel woman were tangible.

With a mortified expression, Peppi folded her cards, stood up and crossed her arms to pull the bra over her head, but Hunker was up placing a restraining hand on one of her breasts. Peppi stared at him, defeated but fuming, and let her arms fall to her sides. Hunker slipped a flat pink palm round her nape and drew her face towards his – at five-eleven each, they were eye to eye. She stared back with a smouldering resentment which I knew was real but he evidently interpreted as a come-on, because with his other hand he goosed her crotch and jolted her by it, shifting her away from the table and causing her to whimper. Her spirit was brave and wild, not the type to be turned on by humiliation, but she was too proud to break away in front of Lemuel, and too ambitious to upset DeWoers. They'd trapped her, and the little sob of surrender she gave caused the fingernails to cut into my palms.

DeWoers and the Lemuel woman linked hands on the table as they watched Peppi submitting against Hunker's shoulder. We sat listening to tiny, intimate noises. Nobody made any movement until Hunker had steered my wife past Walrus, who made with the door and saw them out. Then Kempinski said: 'Cut?' and DeWoers reached out a scarlet-varnished claw for the deck. My hand intercepted.

'Hold it.'

6

DEWOERS AND THE Lemuel woman stared. Their nightmare complexions were flushed, suggesting they would not have minded following Hunker and Peppi into the bedroom, but DeWoers was a gambler and she observed poker code. It wasn't clear what Della Lemuel would do.

Kempinski's handset burbled and he picked it up, turning away. Many calls were happening at 3 a.m. Maybe the shoot was moving to central Asia. He muttered 'Yeah, yeah, yeah,' and put the phone down.

'You taking thirty?'

I eyed DeWoers.

'We're both taking thirty.'

DeWoers considered my small bundle of bills, smaller by a hundred than it had been, and moved the cold look up to me.

'Okay, talk.'

'Kempinski goes.'

'Why?'

'Kempinski goes. *She* goes.'

It didn't matter where she went. Possibly she'd distract a piece of Leonard Kerry Wills.

DeWoers shook her head and got up, showing that her sweater was tucked into a pair of white ski pants that packed no spare subcutaneous baggage.

'We were booked fer a talk, so okay, we'll talk – in my office.'

She brought Walrus over to frisk me again, and led me into an

27

adjoining room. The Victorian table lamps she switched on as we entered brought up a tidy, masculinely conservative den lined with glass-fronted bookcases and large, brutally charcoaled sketches of naked women with big tits and shaggy crotches. There was a reference library that included a leather-bound edition of Katz, along with books of movieland lore by the likes of Kenneth Anger and Otto Friedrich, but I was in no mood to look closely. On a bureau were various obscure trade trophies in front of framed posters for *The Slave* and *Chi*. At each end of a wide red-moroccoed desk stood several shoulder-high stacks of typescripts. Pithy marquee titles were felt-tipped onto their spines, like *Cain's Walk*, *Panama Red*, *Gaucho Woman*, *Heartbleed*. Opposite the desk was another window wall, shaded with wooden slats. A cigar box-sized computer lay open on the desk, next to a girl figurine who sprawled forward displaying a pert, polished can. DeWoers hung a buttock on the desk and ran a hand over the soapstone backside.

'Before that phone goes, switch it off, or whatever it needs.' She spilled it over with the back of her hand, tapping a slippered foot on the whorled Chinese rug. My thumb jerked over my shoulder. 'What happened out there was convincing. You displayed your power. She did your will.'

The director shrugged.

'She lost.'

I motioned the comment aside.

'She didn't have a chance.'

'Not true. I staked her. Kempinski recorded. She could've made money. Only, when she lost she didn't pay in bills.'

'In strip you pay in clothing, not in *shtump*.'

'It was the terms Peppi agreed.'

'Freak terms, for a civilized card game.'

DeWoers looked off along her shoulder and back at me with her face cocked in a humorless grin, which combined with the hair completed Le Look Deranged.

'Go to Vegas much?'

'Why? Still making gash movies, DeWoers? How did you fluke a good picture? How did you luck onto Peppi? You don't deserve her. You haven't changed.'

She cleared her throat exaggeratedly and folded her arms.

'So that's why everybody's trying to interfere with me making this picture. Because I make meaningless shit.'

'It's probably because the way you operate makes Sammy Glick look like Saint Francis of Assisi.' She pulled a face of mock amazement, so I persevered. 'Yeah, you're all the same: one hit picture's all it takes and suddenly the human race is there for your convenience, like little kids who take insects apart for fun – pull a wing off, see if it flies sideways. Taste money and power and you pull people apart to see how they work, then leave them around in pieces, broken ...' DeWoers stared imperviously, one eyebrow at an angle. I pointed at the door we'd come through. 'Something *sordid* happened to Peppi out there, DeWoers.' My arm came forward, jabbing a trembling finger at the director, and my voice cracked. 'You *degraded* her.'

DeWoers came back with braying authority, punching fists into her hips: 'Hey, has-been! You some kinda nigger-hater? You think Peppi's never been laid before? *You've* laid her, *I've* laid her, half of San Francisco State's drama department's laid her. Hunker's just another dork squirting in the donut. Try to be color-blind, country boy. Get up to date. Now tell me your business: I have no time for you. You intend to stay in the game?'

'Yes – yes, I do.'

Suddenly I was ice.

DeWoers took her weight off the desk.

'So what's with the tête-à-tête? Raise your roll outside of the game. No juice from me.'

'I wouldn't take your money. What I want to do ...' An inspiration for getting even fell into place, along with the nerve to execute it. 'What I want to do is fix special stakes, like you did with Peppi. This is her husband speaking, and he wants parity.'

The director sank her backside against the desk, folding her arms.

'Special stakes, huh? Talk about it.'

'My attorney – name of Frank Delius – lives in Santa Monica near his office. He has the title deeds of my oceanfront home in Santa Flora, San Mateo County. Thirty-five hundred square feet on twenty acres. With outbuildings –'

I stopped, unable to speak of the stables, or the white horses, or of who rode them bareback on the beach at dawn.

The director eyed me speculatively. 'Put my deeds and yours in escrow?'

'You got it. They're the ante.'

'Best of how many hands?'

'Can't work with stud. Has to be one hand.'

Her eyebrows went up.

'One hand!'

Fresh adrenalin hit me. I'd reached her. Now we knew each other. Know thine enemy. And let her know thee. Then it's sweeter.

She narrowed her eyes, glinting at me.

'And Kempinski . . .'

'Kempinski mustn't know.'

'He deals straight.'

I wiped the issue away.

'Straighter my way.'

She considered the telephone, muttering.

'Well, my dad spent half his life jumping off cliffs testing hang-gliders, which was pretty dumb for a Dutchman, seeing's how there aren't any cliffs in Holland.' She righted the handset, pondering, then picked it up, keying in digits and addressing me aside. 'Munro can hold, he's an insomniac and lives two minutes away.'

'Forget Craven. We use someone neutral.' I named a notorious divorce attorney everybody knew. She nodded.

'Munro'll have his private number.'

She tapped digits again.

In twenty minutes the stakes were fixed. My deeds and DeWoers's were in cabs bound for Brentwood Heights. Craven had come and gone, drawing up a deed of covenant and placing it on DeWoers's desk ready for signature and witnessing.

We went back to the view of the sparkling City of Losers, had coffee off the warmer, and sat down at 3.35 a.m. Della Lemuel appeared in a change of outfit: she'd removed the long black sweater, revealing a crimson sequined tank top draped over pointy breasts like goat udders, and a flat little can in elasticated denims. She didn't mention where she'd been, or look at me. The sight of her made my mind wander. It wandered down a certain corridor towards a certain pair of doors, and my gut skidded hard before the doors could open.

DeWoers put an ante bill in the pot and looked up from under her eyebrows. I did the same, for Kempinski's benefit. Nothing was said about the one-hand decider. We were inside the thirty, so Kempinski asked no questions. Nobody mentioned the bedroom.

The producer handed me a deck sealed in celluloid with the tag of a Chicago stationer and we passed it round. When it returned to him, he peeled it open, removed the jokers, shuffled a few times and chivalrously placed the cards in front of stony-faced Della Lemuel, who cut with fingernails that were painted black. Kempinski took back the deck, carefully concealing the underside, and shot out the hole cards with the rhythmic accuracy of a rotary lawn spray. I copped an ace of spades. The magic of it cooled my turmoil like morning dew.

As agreed, DeWoers and I played a straight game, bill for bill. The other two sat out. Nobody bluffed or chased anybody out. It could have been the first tentative hand in a long session headed for dawn. DeWoers played as impassively as before, moving only her eyes to view the cards and her long painted fingers to poke forward hundreds with a clink of bangles. We minded our own business, murmuring responses to the dealer's litany. The slumbering city glittered beside us, at one with the mood.

They say more than two and a half million possible poker hands exist in a deck, and out of that number the odds on being dealt a straight flush are forty. That's forty in two and a half million. Or one in sixty-two thousand five hundred. During the cold hour before dawn on Yerba Buena Drive, the mathematics of probability allowed one of the exceptions that prove the rule. Kempinski shot me a ten of spades. And a king. And a jack. And a queen.

Reska DeWoers had three nines on the table and a lethally

bored expression fixing them which prefigured a fourth nine in her hand. The others watched, and she called me.

My hand flipped the hole card to show a royal flush in spades.

As I locked with the shock and suspicion in DeWoers's eyes a scream penetrated our silence from the direction of the bedrooms.

7

I'D THROWN MY chair aside and got a few yards towards the doors when the Lemuel woman tripped me, Kempinski achieved a throatlock and the combined weight of both of them on my back crushed my sternum against the Persian rug. The bare forearm under my chin was hairy and surprisingly hard. The breath near my face had sour coffee on it.

'Let's play poker, lover boy. People enjoying themselves; you wouldn't wanna break up the fun.'

'You're no pervert, Kempinski. Get off my back.'

He wrenched my neck further. Creaking noises came from the Wallace windpipe. A Nike sole pressed on my splayed-out hand. Walrus's Parisian drawl said: 'Where you wan' 'im, Reska?'

Her voice came back jeeringly: 'If he wants to go so bad, take him in there!'

'Innair?' Walrus echoed.

I got one shoulder up and some leverage. The other Nike stood on it.

Walrus said: 'I use zeess?'

'Show him.'

A black plastic cosh came down near the rug.

'Fi' t'ousand volt.'

It hummed. I squirmed.

'Give him a taste.'

When it touched my neck, the convulsion was like epilepsy. A mean, fusing ache lingered.

'Okay, get him up.'

DeWoers came and stood there as I dusted down and worked my neck. She was small, wired, and in control – like a detonator.

'Look, Cody, why don't you go home, huh? This here's the independent sector of the motion-picture industry, we're kinduva strange breed, y'know? Anarcho-dipshit tendency. Not *politically correct*. F'r example, I got a lotta pressure happening; I have to unwind. I don' mind how *you* unwind, unwind any way you like, go fishing, walk the dog, whatever – I'll unwind *my* way. My way's different, okay?'

There was another remote scream, followed by muffled male shouts. Della Lemuel took DeWoers's arm expressionlessly and moved her towards the door. DeWoers elbowed the writer away, watching me.

I spat venom at her.

'Get off my property, DeWoers. You're trespassing.'

The others stared.

The effort at reasonableness drained from the director's face, leaving a nasty deadness in her eyes.

'Yeh, you lucked in that time,' she said. 'But we'll see who makes out in the best of three.'

That brought the bile spilling around my gums. My tongue made a blowpipe and gobbed it at her feet. Buckling my voice down, I said, 'One hand decided. We agreed.'

She shook her head.

'Best a three.'

'But like I told you, best of three means nothing in stud poker, You have to match the cards in each game –'

She cut in flatly.

'Nope, take it on wins.'

'But you can't bet that way, on three games. If you change the deck there's no combinations. If you don't, you have to match the hands across the set.' My voice got shriller. 'I told you! It had to be fixed on *one game*!' The others gaped back at me and I grabbed at a straw. 'Craven wrote it up.'

DeWoers hefted the prod.

'Nothing like that in the agreement, as I recall.'

'That's a lie!'

'Nor about when we have to play the games.' She patted her thigh twice and handed the prod to Lemuel, who took it and eyed me. 'Really, now, so that you can go home feeling good, I want you to check for yourself Peppi's okay. Go right ahead.'

She waved me towards Walrus, near the door.

I held my ground and jabbed out the words.

'Double-crossing bitch, you'll pay for this. Peppi stands by dealer's law, and you break it.'

She veered aside irritably.

'Oh, go fuck y'self, small-time.'

I rounded on the producer, who seemed to have damaged his horn-rim frames and stood fiddling with them myopically.

'You're my witness, Kempinski – a royal flush won the game, and the game was for this house.'

Kempinski ignored me, putting the glasses back on.

'I want to show you the clause! In the office! *I want to sign the deal – now*!'

Walrus came over and dabbed at my jaw repeatedly with his knuckles, like a Parisian poseur having a workout. More muffled shouts came from the hallway and Kempinski and Walrus grabbed my arms, jostling me out into the entrance hall where the fountain played. Wrenching an arm free, I whipped round and hit Kempinski solidly between cheekbone and jaw, bringing my knee up as he bent into his cupped palms. With Walrus clambering up my back, I grabbed DeWoers by the scruff of her bra and hustled her, off balance, to the edge of the ornamental pond, scattering koi. Her calves hit the rim and she back-flopped into the water with a heavy splash. As I bent down to pick up her ankles, Walrus poked fingers into my eyes and an electrical convulsion occurred in my cortex, flexing my leg muscles with enough power to send both of us into the air and me face-down onto marble under him.

Somehow I shielded my bruised temple and as the stunning wore off Walrus had time to haul me upright and manipulate me up the hallway, with DeWoers squelching behind, blustering about voltage and frying my brains. More muffled screams reached us. We stumbled past pictures and art books as far as the master-bedroom doors, where I wedged a knee against the jamb. My larynx was dry and I was pleading.

'Leave me outta this, DeWoers, I don't deserve it.'

The Lemuel woman leaned over me and worked the glass handle, exhibiting her veiny white udders and pushing a door open. I whispered at her tassel earring.

'Right, bitch, we get even.'

Walrus shoved me sprawling onto the deep-pile carpet, overlooked by moonlit holm oaks.

My head came up, and the scene registered before I could drop my face back onto the shag.

She was down on the round satin island, stretched out naked, with her knees splayed open. Hunker was reprising his role in *The Slave*, standing stripped to the waist at the other end of her with his back to the city, brandishing a flail. He brought his fist down, laying a plaited whip across the length of her torso, which made her writhe and gobble like a frying egg.

Cold plastic touched my nape and pond water dripped on me as my head was yanked back by the hair. Della Lemuel came by, pulling off her glittery tank top and dragging it along the floor. Hunker noticed her and raised the whip again. I was dragged onto my feet and pushed towards the steps. It was like sleepwalking, to watch my wife crank her head round and try to focus.

'Hi, Zella, vavy.'

She slurred the stupidly blithe greeting to her topless rival, absently touching one of the weals which ran from her rusty pubic tuft to just short of her droopy-lidded smile.

DeWoers shouted from behind me.

'Fer Crissake, Lenny! She has nude scenes!'

The director made no more art-direction comments after my backhanded chop landed sweetly across her larynx. She fell away, dropping the prod. Lemuel went to her aid, and Walrus stooped to retrieve the weapon. As he bent down in profile, my instep collided square with his mustache, snapping his head back.

A fresh scream penetrated, the same scream, coming from somewhere else.

I tried to grab the prod before Hunker could use the whip, but the lash cracked in my face and wrapped fire round my wrist. He projected his voice at Kempinski, Shakespearian-style.

'Who the fuck is that screaming – I thought it was Wallace!'

Kempinski was scrambling towards the bedroom door, almost on all fours like a baboon. A shoe came in and stamped his head, felling him. Amaryllis appeared shortie-nightgowned in the doorway, squirming against a throat clamp being held on her by the white-jacketed arm of a big hooded figure who had the barrel of a heavy black automatic pressed against her temple. Blushing and grunting with the effort, Amaryllis extracted an arm from behind her, groped overhead, got a hold of nylon and wrenched the hood off, revealing a swarthy male with puffy eyes, hamburger cheeks, wire-wool hair and a white mustache. He ignored the unmasking, kept the barrel of his automatic pressed against Amaryllis's temple, and called over his shoulder in Spanish, getting answering shouts from behind. Somebody threw Hose into the room, and when his shoulder hit the carpet, it stayed there.

Rising from tending the choking form of DeWoers, totally oblivious of the intruders, Della Lemuel scooped up the prod and lunged at me. I grappled with it, but the dildo-like black knob veered too near my neck and a jarring convulsion threw me away into fresh, uncorrupted darkness where no cityscape glittered.

8

CODY AWOKE ON a mattress curiously warm and lumpy. When he shifted empty cans clanked, and under his fingertips he could trace the bellying shape of a capless Perrier bottle. The migraine he had was so different he briefly panicked about having gone blind. But there were chinks of light which stayed when he watched, and he could gradually decipher the geography of his uneven bed.

My brain, the brain of Cody, slowly analyzed information and issued a report: that I was in a dumpster half-filled with garbage, that my clothes were damp and I had my watch on.

I lay decoding the recipe of a sweet, nauseating odor. Festering animal, menstrual waste, rotting exotic fruit, ant-infested cereal cartons, dreggy champagne magnums, sour ashtray relics, stained panties, fermenting tofu, and the rest. It was a warm, wealthy whiff, life-giving to portly maggots and worms. Small, leggy creatures were inspired by it to forge new trade routes across the uncharted skin of my back, making me feel comfortingly part of the scene. I was garbage. High-class garbage.

A world did exist elsewhere, part of it was dimly visible overhead. A concrete rafter, right angles of piping, insulation-clad ducts – and a gaping chute. I sensed a connection. Abruptly it seemed feasible that other rejected articles like me could spew down the aluminum tunnel: bucketloads of putrid offal, families of drowned kittens, tin cans with jagged edges.

It brought me upright and able to see over the rim of the dumpster.

I was a piece of garbage sitting in an empty triple garage, which was poorly lit by portholes in the up-and-over doors. I vaulted out of the hopper, tried to save myself on the way down, and belly-flopped against the streaky metal side.

I limped around. The proportions looked right, and one of the portholes showed a daytime version of last night's view, too polluted to tell what time. My watch said ten. On balance, I preferred Pacific Ocean without carpet of urban sprawl, but what the hell, now I owned both. The thought inspired a picture of Craven's deed of covenant lying on DeWoers's desk upstairs, next to the figurine. I brushed T-shirt and clawed hair. A bit of stubble on the jaw, but I was wearing *eau de garbage* as a freshener. Then another image came up: Peppi's dopy mask, the woozy drawl: 'Hi, Zella, vavy.' The screams. The gunman with a white mustache.

Halfway up the stairs in the corner, I stopped. The door at the top of the stairwell was in darkness. No sound. Another step, praying it wouldn't creak. Still no sound. Five more steps and an ear to the door, still nothing. Try the handle, ever so gently. Locked.

At the nearest up-and-over the handle gave, the door went up silently and I put out primitive sensors for dogs. On the graveled back yard there weren't any cars either, and beyond were paved terraces and a long swimming pool with an orangery, soaring palms like flagpoles and a pergola with puffy furniture ranged on the terrace beneath it. Lawns sloped away from the pool to a fence and a line of cork trees. Beyond the foliage lay a gray-brown city, giving off remorseless thunder.

DeWoers's patrols were supposed to be off, but what if they'd come back on? Who the hell was the guy with the wire-wool hair and white whiskers, with cheeks like steak tartare? Some actor friend of Hunker, brought in to give the sadism a spice of extra excitement? Did some women come harder and longer with black automatics waving around? Why not run for it – put a few miles between me and this bunch of sickoes? No, get that piece of paper and a signature. Then call Rentakil.

On the west side, under where the house cantilevered out, steps followed a ramp up to the main level. At the top, where I'd spied on

DeWoers and her entourage from the side window of the lounge, the gilded mirror-glass was impenetrable.

The carp in the pools took cover under lily leaves in a bored manner. There were no low-slung cars. No motorbikes. The curved portico and its plate-glass portals glinted opaquely, showing me a stooping hobo with tangled hair and crumpled, stained clothes, peering back with hollow eyes, one of them draped with a purple sash. High-tech security equipment was arranged around the area, including a couple of video cameras under the eaves, an entryphone unit and something that looked like a credit-card locking system underneath. I gave the nearest camera a scowl and moved on, stooping close to the glass till I was round the far side. Here the glass paneling had a different texture, as if it was meant to give a frosted effect inside. I was wondering whether it might mean I was outside the porphyry tub room when I noticed a disk of darkness two foot above the ledge. It was a hole, cut in the glass, and it was easy to bend forward and lean in, so I did.

9

THE HOUSE WAS empty. Not just unoccupied, *empty*.

I wormed through the bathroom hole and wandered along corridors, warily fingering doors open. DeWoers had moved out, leaving only fitted carpets, drapes, built-in units and scraps of fluff and paper. Even halogen spot sockets in the ceilings were gutted. Uplighter shields had gone. In the hall the pond was empty, its fountain silent. I bent and felt the mosaic: dry. On the white emulsion of the entrance hall vague outlines showed where paintings had hung.

I paced arid rooms wondering how long I'd spent unconscious in the hopper. A removal job like this could have taken hours. The lounge, giving onto a gassed city, was chilly and lonely, with a gray smell of freshly raised dust.

Recognizing the interior door to the office, I cautiously poked it open, tiptoed in and gazed down at nothing where the tooled-morocco surface of the desk should have been waiting, offering up the paper. No telltale shadow on the carpet, because the Chinese rug had vanished, no arrays of information on the shelves, no stacks of scripts, Victorian lamps, glassed wall cupboards, reference library, trophies, posters – it was blank.

Back through the lounge . . . out of the inlaid bamboo doors . . . across the atrium . . . past the dead fountain, was the kitchen. It had a cooking island with halogen range, a breakfast nook with a condor-nest's double-aspect view, a mile of laminated hardwood worktop, ranks of windowed closets, fitted microwaves, rotisseries, grills, and many plain lower doors which promised concealed fridges, freezers, washers, dryers, incinerators, compactors and who knows what else. I went straight to the set of white sinks and yanked open a closet door: empty. The one next to it was hinged at the base and opened to reveal a square metal flange with a black garbage bag ballooning down. Reaching into the bag, I extracted the sock-end and spilled out light bulbs, bent brackets, fragments of china, bunched-up wire hangers, crumpled bags – the detritus of a removal, but no documents, so I ripped the bag away and peered down. It was the top end of the aluminum chute I had woken under. The flange folded down for disposing of used architects, and there was a clip arrangement for sealing garbage bags and casting them off.

I turned, intending to go back down into the basement, shin up into the dumpster and look around for deeds of covenant. Instead, I sank down into the jetsam on the floor.

It was just possible. Reska DeWoers had her game to protect. If the big-time players she knew heard about grifting they could get awfully hard to meet. To break the code would mean leperdom. Yentzing a sucker like me was not going to do that, of course, but a certain famous divorce attorney was holding the deeds of two properties, and two other attorneys had explained to him why. The divorce attorney was known for his game as well, and if the stories were right, he played with money people who cared about character. They could say nasty things about DeWoers, and next time she was raising funds around the circle some of it might get back to her in the form of a two-letter word. Okay, DeWoers was a woman, the kind that observes no code, only force of nature. But Kempinski was no artist; he was bald, pointy-headed, ugly and needed people, needed his reputation, needed his game. I'd had him kept in the dark about the stakes, but after the fracas at the fountain and the grotesqueries in the bedroom, he must have found out what was involved. He was clearly DeWoers's new investor and in that role one of the few people who could put the arm on her. He would've put it in perspective: Why get a bad name for a property worth only a few mill? Sell a painting and get a place with better security.

So DeWoers had moved out, handing the house over to me. Okay,

I'd regained consciousness downstairs in the garbage, but the two facts weren't incompatible. In fact, my conviction was strengthened that I now owned number 3098 Yerba Buena Drive, because in the dumping me down the garbage chute I recognized the director's sense of humor – no, not humor, *honor*. It was her way of saving face. Her way of handling the crisis of having to deal straight.

I clambered back onto my feet and considered the trip to Reska DeWoers's bedroom.

On the way there I had the idea of calling Frank Delius. Craven might have contacted him about the deeds, or I could instruct him to talk to the divorce attorney. But after taking a long diversion around the baseboards in the lounge all I'd found by way of telephones were empty sockets with thin gray wire trailing away from them.

Quietly, I went towards the master bedroom. Stopping outside the doors and taking hold of a faceted glass knob, the pain on my knee told where it had been wedged against the jamb in an effort to prevent me from being forced in there. The door opened without a sound.

There'd been nothing much in it before, what with the Japanese bare look and the windows being the feature. Down two steps onto the glazed-in balcony there was nothing atall except varnished parquet and the flight-deck view of the city. I looked in vain for signs of a struggle: bloodstains, bullets embedded in walls, dried semen on the floor. In the dressing room the clothes closets were naked and the strip lights inside them had been removed. Beyond, in a shivery marble shower room, on the floor behind the toilet bowl, I found a crystal ear-button that I recognized. Standing juggling it in my pant leg, the way my high school 'shops teacher had jiggled his micrometer in his lab-coat pocket, I melted and the tears welled up.

Peppi would be with DeWoers, and would recover. It was not the first time she'd broken the vow we'd agreed on at a little beach cottage on the north coast of Oahu, taken from Ruth 1:16:

> For where you go I will go,
> and where you lodge I will lodge.
> Your people shall be my people,
> and your God my God.

The brain could renew itself after strong dope. Wounds would mend. Her heart might soften. I didn't know how safe she was with DeWoers, but at least both the people I needed in the world would be at the same address. Right now, I still felt the need for a deed, so I went back the way I'd come.

The layout suggested the stairwell door was the one in an alcove opposite the kitchen. There was no obvious security equipment, only a round handle with a latch in the middle. I swiveled the latch, turned the handle and the door opened.

From the bottom of the stairs the garage looked different, more in focus, more deserted. I was sober now, not delirious on garbage methane. I went down, got a fingergrip on the rim of the dumpster and managed to haul my elbows over, and one leg, so I could roll in.

I was kneeling on stuffed garbage bags which floated like meat-balls in a gravy of loose trash, but I figured Craven's deed of covenant had to be in the topmost bags. Either that or DeWoers had burned it. I hauled a bag towards me, revealing behind it an empty blue-corn chips package, a used bottle of blush wine, a couple of dog-eared graphic novels, a soiled gimme-cap marked with the words *Etak Navigator*, some rotting oranges, and a feminine hand hanging slackly from a wrist.

10

A PULSE WAS going in it. I shoved bags aside and burrowed with my front paws through light trash – tea bags, tissues, damp bread – and soon I could see most of Amaryllis. Nothing on, and breathing.

My mission, should I choose to accept it, was to take a lovely, tall Latino female about twenty years old, whose clothing had been removed, her body smeared with compost and placed in the middle of a Bel Air estate in a basement with no hot water and no communications, and try to get her to my hotel.

First I had to get her out of a garbage hopper. And PS – she was unconscious.

I pondered the problem for a little while. There were no weals on her belly that I could see through the streaks of yogurt, coffee grounds and melon seed. When I dusted an apple core off her dainty black pubic hair she stirred modestly, so I tapped her cheeks with my fingerpads. The eyes came open, interestingly hooded and instantly alarmed.

I said: 'Shsh!'

A diesel was being overrevved not far away. It profaned an oppressive silence, getting louder. Amaryllis moved her eyes, evidently following the same line of reasoning I had earlier. She took in the rubbish and frowned up at the ceiling. It was time to get her out, but she had no clothes on.

'Wait here,' I added, finding my voice, and vaulted over the rim of the dumpster again, making an adrenalin-inspired landing. A porthole in the closed garage door showed a garbage truck laboring up the service driveway. It was grubby green, marked over the cabin DOMESTO-HAUL, and there was an operator inside wearing a fishing cap and blue coveralls. No way was it Reska DeWoers. I went to the open doorway and watched the truck perform a U-turn towards me, its pair of hydraulic grabbers reaching over the compactor and down, ready to scoop the hopper out of the garage and empty it. I waved and the chauffeur saw me in his bracketed mirror, got out and came over. He was Afro-American basketball material with PETE tagged on his left pocket. His eyes flickered up and down my stained outfit and round the garage.

'You the new guy?'

For a moment I thought he meant the new owner of 3098 Yerba Buena Drive, but remembering Walrus and Hose I shook my head, giving him the eye and waving at the dumpster.

'One helluva party – kid got dumped in the swill. Any blankets?'

Pete went and rummaged around in his cab and came up with a ruined sheet he said he'd been intending to tear up for rags. I took it towards the hopper and saw Amaryllis glaring over the rim. Her face was a scream trying to happen and her mouth gulped like a beached cod's. One of her hands was making a frantic movement as if she wanted to push the ceiling off her head. Air sucked into her lungs with a grating sound, but no words came. She grasped her mucky hair and waved at the ceiling some more, and the sheet slipped away from my fingers.

'Get in the truck!'

Up the stairs, past the kitchen, along the corridor to the bare atrium I hared, skidding past the dry dolphin into the lounge. A telephone socket was fixed halfway along the baseboard on the inner wall. Speaker wires led out of it in two directions, one back along the baseboard towards the doors and into a grilled heating vent, the other further along the base of the wall towards the southern panorama window, where it disappeared into a built-in seat. There was a similar setup in the office, and I found another in the kitchen, but hardly bothered. At the top of the stairwell I braked by my hands on the frame and stared over my shoulder at another door in the alcove. Something about it spoke to me. I reached out. It was a closet.

Inside, a dozen filaments of speaker wire hung in a loose arc, joining a junction box on the right with the furnace's electronic timer system on the left.

The stairs took three bounds. Amaryllis was still staring over the rim of the dumpster and when I beckoned her she shook her head and found her tongue.

'They waitin' to get us!'

Pete stared, silhouetted in the garage entrance against the cityscape. There was nobody beyond. I threw myself at the dumpster, got a fingergrip on the slimy rim, hauled myself up and over and reached out to help, but she was boggle-eyed, teeth-chattering scared, and irrationally tigerish in defence of her modesty. Covering her sex parts tightly, she recoiled from my hands, huddling into the heap of bags.

I stage-whispered at her, as if the sound of a voice could detonate the place.

'Amaryllis, you were right. The house is wired. We have a sheet for you down there. That truck will take us away. Nobody is going to hurt you.'

It sounded credible, but again she vibrated her head from side to side. I lunged, she fell back, and I pinioned her, raising a fist to tap her jaw. She thrashed her head aside and my knuckles rammed painfully against an olive oil canister. She wriggled over me, banging her pubic mound against my cheek, and I crawled after it. Any other time the sight of such a rear end would not have caused me to reach for a bottle. It was a textbook example of restraint, abundance, daintiness and crude mating imperative. But I grabbed a nearby bottle anyway.

'Hey!'

We both looked down at Pete, who had his eye on the weapon I was wielding in the air like Cain. I dropped it, and caught Amaryllis off guard by pushing her over the side. Eyes bulging, Pete leapt forward.

When I hit the ground he was standing gaping at her cradled in his arms. She thrashed her head, eyes jammed shut, trying to cover herself. We got her upright with the sheet round her and I told Pete, 'Listen, we have to get outta here – structural problems,' jabbing a finger in the air.

He got a contact hit of anxiety and we all ran out to the truck, which was waiting with the diesel idling.

'Hey, man!' Pete shouted uncertainly, blindly engaging the clutch and jerking us forward. 'I got a dumpster to clear.'

'*Drive*!'

Pete accelerated down the gravel trail, which curved round and brought the house into view so that we witnessed it jolting off its foundations on a jagged gust of light, barged rudely upwards by dust and vapor. We watched the golden glass walls burst away, driven by cumulus billows of oily orange, and felt the noise arrive: a deep, rolling thunderclap and a gashing roar which sundered the roof in a fountain of turquoise shards of tile, and launched a fury of flame into the world.

TWO

11

WE FLED IN shock. Pete dropped us off near more garbage hoppers at the ramp in the back of the hotel I'd wandered into in Santa Monica, and I went round to the lobby. Like me, the place had been raised in the ugly Sixties, had lost its convictions and was now well scuffed. Built as a forbidding fifteen-story Bauhaus stump, it'd become a tacky symbol of why I had architect's block and draughtsman's elbow. The periods of refurbishment in the vestibule showed like glacial layers and the junior desk clerk could have been a life form found under one of them. His watery Caucasian face was a map of junk-food under-nourishment, from malformed bones to pocky skin and watery eyes, but the poor eyesight was helpful, because there was no need to explain my own appearance. He took a hundred and dolefully noted down dress size 10, size 8 sneakers and ladies' briefs. He let me spell out b-r-i-e-f-s for him, and stated plausibly that he knew the place to get a deal.

I went back to the elevator and pressed LG. The doors opened onto the usual piss-streaked, dangerous underground lot. Amaryllis stood barefoot, wrapped in her sheet, with the expression of Cinderella after the coach reverted to a pumpkin and two rats. She hardened on seeing my room, with its cigaret burns on the side tables and view of flat roofs with legionnaire's disease air conditioner units, and refused to discuss what had happened at the house.

'Who was the guy with a gun on you?'

She shuddered, gathering the greasy sheet round her.

51

'No!' was all she said.

'Who blew the place up? Him?'

She tossed her head and showed me the back of it.

I took her ear and brought the grimacing face round, talking close.

'You're part of the racket.'

Her eyes widened and it was the expression she'd had on her face when white-whiskers was pushing a gun against her temple, so I let go. Her expression burned with wounded dignity. The glossy chestnut hair was tousled, she had nipples erect and belly and bush and thighs that contoured against her wrap. It was very flamenco-passionate. The lady's proud resistance hinted at hot, turbulent surrender, and I could remember the feel of her fighting me, naked. I showed her the way.

'You need a bath.'

She surged towards the bathroom door, so I blocked it.

'Just one thing. Where's my wife?'

Her warm black eyes shone, and there was a prompt change in the air which came from getting round to Peppi. Things were better round Peppi. When I found Peppi all this trouble would be over.

Amaryllis's tears spilled over. Sight of the bathtub through the doorway had humanized her. Her face worked as though she was reliving the nightmare in the bedroom. A trembling lip and two brimming eyes did their magic on my arms, wrapping them round her shoulders for me.

She rested her brow on my arm, her hair wafting up *eau de garbage*.

'The woman heet you with the electric.'

'What about Peppi?'

Her head rolled on my shoulder.

'Mmmmnnnstmn fffnmmm –'

'Hold it, I can't understand.'

The face came up, streaked, eyes pressed shut.

I said: 'Is she okay?'

The head shook.

'Don' know.'

'Did they give her a jab, too?'

'Mebbe.'

'That'd make three of us. How about DeWoers?'

The eyes squeezed tighter, and her voice was hoarse as a vixen barking.

'*I don' know!*'

'Take it easy, honey.'

Amaryllis had probably been raped as well as doped, the condition she was in. She most likely needed a doctor and a hospital ward, so although there were plenty of questions left to ask, I got out of her way. Soon the bathroom door was closed and she was behind it, at one with the healing waters.

The answering machine at our home in Santa Flora failed to deliver Peppi's message: *We're up to our eyes, up to our ears, up to everything except taking your call.* The poop-poop, poop-poop, poop-poop tone played across two hundred miles like mockery, cheating me of her voice and bleating futile questions about my power outage.

Frank Delius sounded guarded and unsympathetic. No gambler he. I didn't mention the explosion. An attorney was retained to reason clearly and maintain orderly files, not for sympathy.

'Without a contract of exchange your claim on the deed is tenuous. Why didn't you sign the deal before you played? Then all you'd need would be witnesses to the win?'

'Frank, I was uninvited, there were kinky sex things happening, Peppi was giving me mental cruelty, the idea of staking the house came to me like that. My main motive was keeping DeWoers out of the bedroom where humiliation was being administered to my wife.'

'What if you'd lost?'

'Look, I was ready to die. A house was nothing.'

He took a moment to absorb that.

'What's Peppi say?'

'What d'you mean, what's Peppi say? I got knocked out and thrown into the garage. Where Peppi is I haven't a clue.'

'Is she still with DeWoers?'

'Maybe, maybe not. I think she broke with her last night.'

'Why?'

A deep breath came and went. What tired oxygen it brought helped a little.

'For Peppi, the affair with DeWoers is to do with glamor and power and ambition, not sex. Peppi's very loosely bisexual, for her it's part of being a free spirit, but DeWoers is hard-core bent. She played a brutal game with Peppi last night and overreached herself, partly because it was for my benefit. Peppi understood what was really happening when it was too late.'

The beatific, drugged face rolled silently in front of me for a moment.

'She could be back, then.'

There was a pause.

'Should be. I still love her.'

'Better forget the house. If DeWoers won't honor the deal there's not much you can do.'

'Legally.'

'Okay, legally.'

'Some of the big players would be disappointed to hear she'd welshed on a wager.' I named the divorce attorney for one.

Frank agreed.

'I guess there's a remote chance she might be talked into letting you have the place. It seems unlikely. I don't know her, but she has a reputation. What was her picture again?'

'*The Slave*, Frank.'

'That's right, yeah. Well, she went through all three majors making that one, got points on the gross, handled the outcry, rode the wave of a hit. Since then she's set up a studio of her own, and you simply don't do that if you're not a Japanese transnational. I think you may find her hard to handle, Cody.'

'You mean, out of my league.'

'How much is the place worth?'

I nearly said: Now it's burned? Instead I blurted: 'Five mill?' And added for accuracy, 'Just the lot would fetch four. About ten acres on Yerba Buena, with the view.'

'And how much is DeWoers worth?'

'Who knows? Ten? Twenty?'

54

Frank's tone changed from prosaically practical to tunefully dubious.

'I wonder,' he said. 'I wonder.'

'You heard the stories too?'

'Munro Craven called.'

'He did? When?'

'After you did, last night – this morning.'

'What'd he say?'

'Wasn't giving away much, just his tone, y'know? We confirmed the arrangement and he muttered, kind of lawyer-to-lawyer, "She's gotta be crazy, Carmody's at her throat". That's all.'

'"Gotta be crazy"?'

'Gotta be crazy.'

'Suggesting she couldn't afford it? Would explain why she was ready to play.'

Instead of going into the bedroom.

'Who's Carmody?'

'Her chief of production.'

'And he's at her throat already. Okay, I'm an attorney, but we all know making movies defies logic. It's a co-operative process where few people co-operate and many versions of what's happening tend to collide. Watch out.'

With DeWoers's phones burbling and flashing again in a replay, I thanked Frank and called imformation for Munro Craven. He was unlisted.

My hand was taking up the phone to call Frank back when it rang. Pimples was on the line, from reception.

'A busload just arrived on the New Year's package.'

'People come to this city for New Year's?'

'Sure, only reason you got a room was Christmas closed out yesterday. New Year's starts checkin' in today.'

'Okay, thanks.'

'Hey, you want your hunnerd dollars?'

I did, but couldn't bring myself to say it.

'Hang onto it, kid, and keep an eye on me.'

The voice glowed.

'Betcha, sir!'

Mr Big-Time hung up and went and knocked on the bathroom door.

'Yes?'

Amaryllis was lying neck-deep in the bathtub with her eyes shut, her shape warped and spangled by sudsy water.

'The organization won't stretch to buying an outfit. I'm going to step out and see to it, okay?'

She nodded, so I went through a lobby that was crowded with Midwesterners and turned south towards Wilshire looking for a J C Penney. There wasn't one, and Amaryllis was a nice-looking woman with limbs that deserved it, plus I'd just acquired wide pastures in Bel Air, so I charged four hundred twenty-seven thirty-five in a couple of boutiques. A silk shirt, kilted skirt, bikini briefs, poncho-type coat, tights and pumps.

It was a big swag to hump back to the room. When I got there I dumped it on the bed, not without a certain pleasurable anticipation, and tapped on the bathroom door again.

No answer.

The bathtub was full of suds, but there was no husky-voiced chicano woman in it or anywhere else. The bedroom was easy to check, there was only the queen-size box with chocolate-shake counterpane, long Formica vanity with circular drink stains, patchy shag carpet, the hanging closet next to the bathroom door, and the sealed and grimy windows that looked out onto tar and gravel wastes. I checked again that the bathroom was still empty, and peered once more into the dark of the clothes closet. I almost got down and deeked under the bed, but pulled back with a curse. A naked woman had walked out of my bedroom into the city – or had been removed from it. The courtesy sachet of foam she'd used in the bathwater perfumed the air, the only proof of her presence. It brought with it a sudden towering weariness and I gazed at the hollow expanse of mattress, but forced back the urge to keel over.

Amaryllis leaned naked out of the garbage hopper, gesticulating in a silent scream.

Freaking out because she'd awakened in a garbage heap with nothing on? Or had she *known* the house was primed?

The corridor was straight and long, with signs for fire exits at each end, the set of elevators recessed halfway along. Neither direction offered any immediate ideas, but when a cleaner wheeled her buggy out a few doors down, glancing at me in a guarded way, it drew my attention. She was chicano, taller than most, and about Amaryllis's age. She saw me coming and backed into the room she'd been doing, but I got a foot in the door, rammed the buggy aside and seized her by the lapels of her nylon housecoat.

'Did a woman just borrow clothes off you?'

She was all soulful Indian impassiveness, and her wedding band came up for display between my forearms. With the other hand she scooped a silver cross out of her V-neck and held it in front of my nose, huge-eyed. Who knew what she'd been told about me? I let her go and swung out down the corridor, loping past the elevators to the far end of the tower, where I hauled open the fire door and leaned out over the stairwell.

The concrete steps were dusty and littered, giving a faint aroma of urine and drains. A toc-toc-toc of lightweight shoes reached me from four or five storeys away near the ground floor, and I made like an ape-man with the steel handrail.

Unlatching a push-bar of the emergency exit doors, I barged out into the street and caught sight of a leggy brunette in a skimpy frock weaving away through halted traffic near a busy intersection. She rounded the corner, where there was a shoe market with ranks of footwear displayed on the sidewalk. When I made it to the shoes she'd blended into the lunch-time workers spilling out for freedom on the street.

Instinct steered me back to the hotel. I was harassed and angry and lonely and hungover, and it felt better than sex to flop onto a rented time machine and let my personality dissolve.

12

I VOYAGED FAR on the bed and awoke partly refreshed, in a mood to have lunch and take action. A call to Pimples on the desk got them working on my order of two Heineken, scrambled eggs on brown, sirloin rare and a green salad. The crushbag I'd left in the room revealed no toilet kit but somehow I'd drunkenly thrown together a windjammer, chinos, tennis shirt and lace-up moccasins, so I took a shower and a shave with the complimentary disposable razor and got fresh. While I was pulling on the Lacoste shirt, a pinhead-sized red mark showed on the inside of my left forearm and confirmed a conviction about why I'd spent six hours snoring in a heap of garbage. Somebody'd meant me to stay under for a little while longer – long enough to awaken floating down in little wafers of fried bacon high over Mount Wilson. It made you wonder. Would somebody really go that far to evade honoring an IOU? Even a woman like Reska DeWoers?

There was a knock at the door. A room waiter brought in a lunch and took out a ten-dollar bill. The first Heineken tasted like a glass of Roederer Cristal. The second tasted better. The scrambled eggs had the creaminess and the steak had the juice, with a pat of butter melting on it. The lettuce was loaded with chlorophyl.

Frank Delius rarely lunched; he gave me Munro Craven's details and I put in a call to his private number. There was a taped reply, so I called his partnership in Burbank. A girlish voice said he was not expected in all week and could they take a message? So it was

58

down underground to start up my 1961 bottle-green 3.8 Jaguar. The upholstery squeaked and the smell of old leather and varnished walnut gave me comfort: we needed some.

Traffic was light among the soaring palms between UCLA and the LA Country Club, attendance at Acapulco and points south being *de rigueur*, and life was even sparser than usual in the rarefied habitat of Bel Air. A Fire Department Land Cruiser was nosed up to the closed gates of 3098 Yerba Buena Drive, and a blue and white patrol car was parked the other side of the street. The yew hedges stood tall, the gates were blocked and there was nobody to pull up beside and ask casually: 'What happened, officer?'

Munro Craven's place was about a mile away on a wooded slope overlooking part of Glen Aire golf course. A brick wall round the estate had spiked railings on top, and the high entrance gates were closed, framing a lane which wound away through pine trees. One of the gateposts had a video camera fixed to it; the other was fitted with an entryphone. Craven answered my call, and neutrally assented to letting me in.

Turning a corner after a hundred yards and seeing the house looming ahead prompted a memory of another Craven celebrated at college, a Julius Craven who'd given his name to a library of the cinematic arts in Palo Alto. I'd not used the library, only sketched it: Frank Lloyd Wright was a hero. Now my car was losing power as it approached a bravura example of Wright's prairie style, so brutally imagined that it could have been a shogun's palace.

Two hundred feet wide, Craven's residence stepped down in flanking wings from a central stronghold, creating shadowy terraces roofed with shapes like aircraft wings. Long bands of shaded windows under these gantries were leaded in intricate geometric patterns, and you imagined the patterns of colored light they projected inside. My tires crunched to a halt.

Craven was on the first-floor deck, leaning with his fists on the parapet, wearing a panama hat and light sweater. Through an opening in the fortress-like perimeter wall was a graveled square leading to a deeply recessed entrance. After a moment one of the hammered copper doors drew back and Craven, hatless, admitted me to a long, sunken hall, checkerboard-tiled and gloomily paneled in dark oak. Wordlessly he turned and led me past a bare baronial fireplace and through wide double doors into an eighty-foot galleried library worthy of a mid-sized Ivy League college. He took up a position silhouetted against a view of woods fringing a splash of velvety parkland. In the distance a group of eyeshaded gnomes were staring down at a green. The attorney appeared unperturbed, but that was his job.

'See you picked up a black eye last night.'

'Not the first, counselor.'

Hundreds and hundreds of law books had their backs to me.

'Who won?'

'Does it matter any more? Where's my wife?'

'I have to confess, I don't know.'

It was quiet as a crypt in the Craven family library.

'You did hear about the place going up?'

'Of course. Crazy, isn't it.'

'Crazy, man, crazy. Where's Peppi?'

'I wish I knew.'

'You're stalling, counselor. Why?'

Craven smoothly delivered a line about his duty to the studio, his vows of servitude and brain paralysis and whatnot, and my eye wandered along the shelves to an enormous gilt-framed oil painting which occupied most of the end wall under the book-lined gallery. It portrayed a long room like an extension of the library, but done out in ocean-liner Deco with pillars and uplighting, bare of furniture except for deep armchairs which were fitted flush with the walls on each side.

Craven trailed off with his ear-candy, seeing me staring. He affected a Harvard accent that played down the Rs when it came to naming the family treasures.

'Parlor car, Central Pacific Railroad. They traveled in style.'

'Was your father associated with Leland Stanford?'

'My grandfather.'

'Julius.'

The neutral voice warmed just a little.

'Why, yes. It's rare people show any knowledge of the history of our state these days.'

I let it ride.

'Heard from DeWoers?'

'No, she'll be seeing her personal attorney about this horrific accident. I'm purely corporate.'

There was a pause while his perfect self-analysis blended into the suffocating atmosphere. Something nauseating about Craven prevented me from mentioning Peppi again.

'That's all?'

'Why? Is this about the game?'

'You sound like it's the last thing you'd expect it to be about.'

'Do I? I wonder why?'

'Me too.' We locked stares. Immobile in his sweater, plaid pants and deck shoes, the Visionville attorney seemed to be melting into the surroundings. There was part of him wide-eyed and available, but the rest was in a safe. I poked something at it. 'Frank Delius told me about the conversation you had.'

He looked away, raking silvery hair past his ear.

'Oh yes. It wasn't much. I don't really gamble, and incurred disfavor by quitting the game three hours after my bedtime instead of five or six. No sooner had I dropped off than Reska called. Frankly, I don't remember much.'

'Frankly, I don't believe you.'

He looked at me speculatively, as if I'd abruptly switched to a rare language he understood. His response was concise.

'Stay out of studio politics.'

'Men with automatics?'

The cool voice took on a hard edge.

'Obviously you're upset about the poker game and your rash stakes. If you lost, I suggest you leave town for a few weeks and see if it blows over.'

'What if I won?'

He didn't blink.

'Look, Mister – Mister –'

'Wallace.'

'Yes, of course . . .' He pushed his hands into his pockets and stuck out the presidential chin. 'It wasn't a game last night, it wasn't a deal, it wasn't a wager, it wasn't anything like that.' He gave me a hard blue raying. 'It was an ugly bust-up between ...' The mouth compressed itself. '... *Lovers*, Mr Wallace.' He frowned, as if fighting back tears of regret. 'In show business we have to be extremely broad-minded about these things. Creative people ... well, they need latitude. Reska is a brilliant artist and a Renaissance genius. Unfortunately, she has plenty of Machiavelli to go with it, not to speak of Lucrezia Borgia.' He puckered his mouth smugly at the Craven wit. 'All of us on the management team have tried to talk her out of getting involved with the staff, and actors *are* staff, they have to come and go. But ...' He pulled out his hands and scooped air over his shoulders helplessly. '... The Reskas of this world have been tangling with actors ever since Lasky opened in a barn on Vine and Selma eighty years back. It must be the climate. If I were you,' he added coaxingly, 'I'd head up into the high timber and wait for the little lady to find her way back to the cabin, y'know? She will sooner or later, and more likely sooner. Okay?'

He was all candid blue eyes, but I'd noted something ratty and gnawing about his front teeth. There was a pause, during which I held and fondled the hint that he might be capable of delivering Peppi. But again, I didn't mention her.

'I understood the high timber was where DeWoers was headed, along with the production.'

Craven twitched his mouth and composed his gaze.

'Whatever you've heard, forget it. The making of a motion picture is rarely a smooth ride. Like I say, walk the other way.'

Cody walked, but not the other way. I went closer to the painting of the Pullman car and its vision of the high era of continental rail travel, flanked by portraits of noble-browed grandees in wing collars and whiskers.

'Weasel words from a descendant of this caliber of stock, Mr Craven. They look like big men who did big things.' I turned and faced the golfing showbiz attorney. 'How about making a gesture in the family tradition and telling me where my wife is?'

Craven patted down the situation with splayed hands and a lurid grin, which quickly dissolved into a darkly sincere glare.

'She's fine, Wallace. I don't know where she is exactly, but you can take my word for it that she's being well looked after. After all . . .' He allowed himself another anxious, dimpled smirk. '. . . the picture she's contracted on's not finished shooting. I don't know whether you have any idea of how much investment is riding on the final cut? I mean, it's an incredibly complex business to dub and use stand-ins for a star who has –'

He bit his lip, and his eyes went vacant.

I moved again, this time towards the living Craven portrait, frozen on its words. There was no substance in his vicuña sweater and silk shirt, so I took a tuft of short hair behind his ear and pulled it as well.

'Look, brother, a house blew up. Last time I saw my wife, she was in it, stoned out of her brain on pethidine, thorazine, or smack or Christ knows what, and an unattractive man was waving a big-gauge automatic. Today, she's not around, get it?' I shook, and he clawed at my hands. 'I sure hope for your sake that two and two make fucking five.' His head jerked at me and bounced the bridge of his Roman nose off my upper brow.

He slumped down onto his knees, whimpering into my fly.

One of the dark-stained oak doors at the end of the library opened and a tall young woman with superb bone structure stood there clutching her cropped apricot hair. She was wearing a white toweling bathrobe and pom-pommed step-ins. She threw out a hand, Lady Macbeth-style, and glanced back over her shoulder. Then she stared at Craven and where his face was.

The attorney fell away. Peppi watched me approaching, the way a woman might who was sinking in her car after driving off a pier. When I was a few feet away she picked a little stainless-steel revolver out of her robe pocket and showed me the business end of it in a steady sort of way that slowed me down until I stopped. The words seemed to be spoken through her by fear.

'They're here. I saw them.'

The gun barrel was cool in my hand as I worked her warm grip off it, corralled her and docked our solar plexuses. The fronts of us fused in a fierce exchange of energy, as if they knew each other better than we did. Her forehead gently tapped against my clavicle in secret acknowledgment, then she was staring at me again, working herself free.

The forearm appeared as a shadow on her cornea, a dark shaft across a tiny reflected library window; a second later it was round my throat, the radius bone cutting into my bruised larynx and throttling it. It reminded me irritatingly of Kempinski's arm. I raised a revolutionary fist and brought the elbow down hard. Craven hawked and slumped against the doorjamb behind me, wheezing.

'Peppi went by and grabbed his wrist, hissing the words, 'I think they got into the house.'

He clambered onto all fours, spitting repeatedly at the parquet floor. Ptew, ptew, ptew. I rounded on her.

'Who did?'

She looked up from tending Craven.

'There's been trouble at the studio.'

'Are they it?'

'I don't know.'

Craven took a deep breath, got up embracing his gut and walked past us into the mock-Tudor hall. We followed him over the checkerboard tiles to an arched door with a ring handle which he twisted, lifting the latch with a clack. He switched lights on and we went down a turning stone staircase into a cellar where there was a console with monitor screens on it. Craven worked controls on the console and the tubes brought up monochrome images of passages and furnished rooms. The remote cameras panned slowly, jerked, and panned back. As we watched, the scenes switched from screen to screen.

'Men here all year,' Craven croaked, peering. 'All year except now.' He wiped his mouth and backhanded the controls. 'Where's the Police Department? They can earn my taxes.' He scooped the handset off a telephone. Peppi gasped from behind us, freezing him in mid-jab. The dial tone in his hand was all we could hear as we watched two shadowy, hooded figures moving across the far end of one of the televised corridors.

13

WALLACE IS NO hero. I grabbed Peppi's hand and towed her out of the house, into the Jag and out of Bel Air, watching the rear-view mirror all the way. We didn't speak until we were on Wilshire, crossing the LA Country Club course, where the palms were high. At least somebody was.

'So who the hell was in Craven's house?'

Peppi'd looked into the mirror on the sunshield and ferreted a pair of dark glasses out of the dash compartment; they glinted as she glanced my way, speaking with precision.

'Cody, I'm naked except for this bathrobe.'

I dug in my pocket and handed her the crystal ear-button.

'Are they the people who broke into DeWoers's? Blew the place up?'

'I have no money, either.'

I dug in my pocket and handed her coins. The dark glasses made two shots of me at the wheel. In the windshield area there was a forward view and a rear view. I watched both.

'They come into your room? You get a good look at 'em?'

'No.'

'How did –'

'I was in the bathroom. There was no towel, so I looked in the bedroom and I saw two men on the roof.'

'On the roof?'

'There's a terrace opposite with a pagoda-type roof. They were on it, crouching down. At first I thought they were installing a TV dish.'

65

'Did one of them have crinkly hair, a white mustache, pocky face?'

The glasses came round onto me.

'They had hoods on.'

'Who *are* they?'

'I don't know.'

'Trying to sabotage the picture?'

She shrugged.

'I guess.'

'Why would they want to do that?'

'I don't know.'

In awe, I glanced at her profile. The presence still shone out in spite of it all. She could screen-test in anything. Which made it worth mentioning an important detail.

'They sabotage Peppi Harman, they sabotage the picture.'

She chewed her lip, staring resolutely ahead.

'D'you have your credit cards?'

'Peppi, could you get scared again, please?'

'I'm too far gone.'

'What did Hunker give you last night?'

'Don't bring it up. It wasn't his idea.'

'Did he dope Amaryllis? Or did they?'

Her face whipped round.

'Where *is* Amaryllis?'

'I got her out. She took off. Haven't seen her.'

Peppi moaned, and muttered lines.

'The time is out of joint; O curséd spite that ever I was born to set it right.'

'That's appropriate. I think these guys want it to be theater in the park again for Peppi Harman.'

'Like, next week.'

'How much d'you remember?'

'Let's not talk about it.'

'Where's DeWoers?'

My question echoed as we scooted under Sepulveda, surrounded by unfurling ramps of expressway. It could have been any old twenty-third century city. Keep the sun to the left, I'd make it

66

to the coast – if the coast was still there. Stores were appearing, square rocks in lakes of parking.

'Cody, we have to find Reska. Stop and buy me an outfit. You'll get paid back.'

I checked the mirror.

'We can't stop.'

'All I have is this robe of Munro's and a pair of step-ins some woman left.'

'He has women?'

Many cars were behind, many ahead. Machines in hangars burped them out every few seconds. Mothers strained and dropped drivers for them as fast as they could. In the toxic brownish light, windows were mirrorized. Any car could conceal a hooded man taking aim with a high-powered rifle. A shot, a car peeling off into an exit, Peppi slumping.

Her hand touched my arm.

'I'm sorry.'

Her apology so weakened the muscles of my neck that my head almost bowed down onto the wheel.

'Sorry's something. Guess I am too.'

The hand gently withdrew and she looked south towards the airport, where a jetliner was gliding slowly up a gentle gradient over Santa Catalina island, and addressed the world:

'Reska, where *are* you?'

I said: 'Was she at Craven's? Where the hell do we look for her? The studio's shut down.'

Peppi gazed at the spiritual desert of a cityscape. I recognized some of Santa Monica's addresses and started to believe I might make it to the Travelodge, figuring perhaps I should drive there a strange way, maybe put the car in Palisades Park and walk back. Good to walk. Particularly away from automobiles. When Peppi spoke I didn't catch it.

'Huh?'

'I said, she's probably in Canada. I'm supposed to have a bed scene with Hunker scheduled as soon as the set's built in Toronto. Maybe Monday.'

My knuckles went white on the wheel.

'No way.'

We went into a routine we worked together.

'It's a job. I'll handle it.'

'No way.'

'Cody, don't.'

The car steered rigidly beside the center line. If the road had turned, it might have ploughed across into a building.

'There's no way you're going on with the shoot, Peppi.'

'Cut it out, okay?'

'You don't seem to understand. Try *thinking*. Try thinking about what those people at Craven's were doing. Were they out to pump him for case law? Were they looking for lost golf balls? Did they want to share his electric racing cars?' My fingers clenched and unclenched the wheel, she got stonier and stonier. 'Did they want to pull his shorts down and play with his winkle?' There was a red light right ahead. I kicked the power brake and we hit the top in a wrenching squeal of rubber. 'They're after your ass, Peppi!' I shouted as we landed.

She sat massaging her temples and a patrol car eased up on the inside. The officer driving, a battery-fed surf Nazi, examined my passenger and gave me the hard eye.

Peppi looked at the patrolman, got out of the Jaguar without taking too much care with her bathrobe and stalked over to a crowded Pizza Hut half a block long with many entrances. As she walked away, squarejaw kept a very cold gaze on me, and his partner had no sense of humor either, but the scenery up Peppi's legs had clearly saved me a citation. I prayed for the green.

There was a space thirty yards ahead. After the patrol car had dawdled away I burned rubber into it and hurried back to the restaurant. Peppi was on a stool in the window, not going anywhere, so I went in and leaned on the beige plastic counter beside her.

'Peppi, we're both confused, but get this: I happen to have *clothes* ready for you in a hotel room about three blocks from here on Colorado.'

She said nothing.

'Listen, consider this: you're a sitting target for anybody driving by.'

She appraised the scene outside, and slid off the stool. I steered her by the arm out of the fug of cheese and toppings. On the sidewalk she snatched her arm free.

'Which way.'

'Along here.'

We headed south, abandoning my car to many tickets. None of the people passing by took a second look at a five-foot-eleven orange-crew-cutted beauty walking along the street in a white toweling bathrobe and bedroom slippers. Each car that came by without incident allowed me to breathe a little easier, but the street was crowded with them and oxygen was short until we made it into the Travelodge lobby.

The people on the desk were being besieged by a busload of prairie folk with string neckties and blue rinses. When we got into the room Peppi said: 'Christ!'

I kissed her shoulder.

'Forget the interior design, feel the privacy.'

Suspiciously, she started pulling things out of the boutique bags and I went into the bathroom to splash water against my eye. When I'd done that enough I found her flaked out across the bed, breathing deep and slow. It was time to tell her to get dressed, ready to leave town, but it came over me how bad everything was, how Peppi must feel, how wrecked my own head felt, how probable it was that these hard cases were professionals who would perform their contract in full whether we got police protection or not, and I said nothing. Instead, I pulled out of my pocket the Lady Smith .38 I'd taken from Peppi at Craven's, leaned back against the bathroom wall, slid slowly down it and sat watching the door.

14

ABRUPTLY I WAS awake, knowing that I'd been not awake. And not awake had lasted longer than it felt, because I was laid out across the bathroom dooway, one knee drawn up, one hand under my cheek and a throbbing ache behind my eyes. I fought against five gravities to get my head up and around to scan the rest of the room and at first sight it seemed right – the place was empty, including the bed. Life was a replay of the disappearance of Amaryllis, until it became clear that I had run out into the street after her already, and since then I'd been to Munro Craven's prairie-style palace, and Peppi'd been on the bed.

A closer look at the mud-colored counterpane showed no long lovely lanky woman atall. No bags of boutique clothes. Bags, yes, thrown down there on the floor near the window. Clothes, no.

Message?

Yes, written with a discarded Travelodge ballpoint on the flyleaf of the Gideon Bible. The wide, confident flourish of my wife's handwriting took center stage on any paper. The message resembled Tagalog, Sanskrit or Serbo-Croat. Gradually it turned into Ps. cxvi: 11. It lay before my visual equipment for a long time, motionless. Engines groaned and bumbled remotely through double glazing.

Then I tore off the flyleaf, stuffed it in my pocket and laid the Bible back on the bedside ledge.

There was a faint savor of Peppi on the counterpane. I crouched over it, breathing, and traced where her hair appeared to have been, finding a couple of short strands.

Staring at the bathtub for a while didn't establish for sure whether she'd bathed while the family dog lay snoring across the threshold. It wasn't clear whether the beads of water in the hand basin were mine or hers. It seemed to matter. To matter how long it'd taken her to leave. To matter whether she'd done her hair, taken a leak – gotten *ready* to go.

My fingers checked for the automatic – yes, warming beside by my pecker – and Frank Delius's secretary answered my call. He was in court. I called Munro Craven's partnership. They'd not heard from Mr Craven, did I wish to leave a message? Information gave me a number for Visionville. A security man with a speech defect replied. The studio was closed for the holiday period. No, he didn't know when it would reopen. I could call his area manager.

At the residence of Cody Wallace in increasingly faraway Santa Flora the line rang for a long time. The messager was not responding.

My tennis partner Roark Manners in Salinas had a recording machine which worked. It told me he couldn't deal with my call right now, but if I'd care to leave a . . . and memory volunteered he'd flown to Maui on Christmas Eve, after urging me to fly too before dialysis was required. How come the birthday of Jesus cleared the place like a Scud missile attack?

Friend and would-be lover Clara Butt gave no reply, either. She had no truck with gadgets, often failed to pick up a ringing phone. I imagined the ringing in her studio on the beach, littered with silvery cedar and hemlock driftwood, Indian silver work, Mexican rugs and sculptures, Arizona blankets and her hard, cynical presence against the white pounding outside. It was me calling, the only one she trusted to reveal her secret soul to. On the side of the bed, holding the handset to my skull, I lost count of the rings.

Abe Levene snatched up his handset the usual way, directly he heard it start to ring and before I heard a tone.

'Yep?'

'It's Cody.'

'Alive or am I hearing you over the ether?'

'Alive, I guess.'

71

'Borderline, huh? Where are you physically?'

'LA.'

'Drinking?'

'Not any more.'

'Peppi?'

'She was around.'

'Not any more?'

'Not any more.'

'What's with the picture?'

'Trouble. She says they're moving the shoot to Canada.'

No answer.

'Abe?'

'Still here, running a few numbers.'

He lived at his desk in front of four computer screens. After making his pile in Manila sock factories, he now managed his beachside condos next door to me and played the markets by keyboard. He and I wine-tasted.

'Abe?'

'Going to cost her mucho dinero – thinka the unions. There's a percentage in Canada, but the waste of plant ... What's it all about? Is her studio going down the tube?'

'Abe?'

'Sorry, that threw me. Sound rough, Cody. You okay?'

'Abe?'

'What is it?'

'Abe ...' Him telling me how rough I sounded made me feel that much rougher. It took an effort to force the piece of paper into focus.

'... Peppi left me a message and I can't figure it out.'

'What is it?'

'It says: pee-ess-space-see-ex-vee-one-space-eleven.'

The line gave static and I waited for it to go dead.

But Abe's bass voice said: 'Is it, uh, some kinda code?'

'I'm not sure, that seems too ... well, too theatrical.'

'She's an actress, Cody.'

'Okay, but basically actors're artists, you know, not crypto-graphers.'

'I've got it up on screen, could run some programs on it, never

72

tried to crack a code before. Hold it, let's check the external evidence first. How did you get the message? Tell me she wrote it on the bathroom mirror with the corpse's lipstick.'

'It was on the flyleaf of the Gideon Bible. She left it open by the bed.'

Silence.

Abe said sadly: 'Oh, Cody . . .'

Peppi's handwriting swam on the ripped-out flyleaf and my voice mumbled: 'Philippians?'

'Psalms, I think you'll find. D'you have it there? Mine's kept under the birdcage.'

Psalms. My lips moved, counting off the numbers to one hundred and sixteen and ran a finger down the verses to number eleven. What was printed there I read aloud.

'"*I said in my haste, All men are liars.*"'

'Is that it?' Abe's voice said richly. 'Psalm one-one-six, verse eleven? "I said in my haste, all men are liars"? Hey,' he chuckled, 'what's that quote about Eve crawling on her belly in the dust?'

I mumbled something deprecatory.

Abe's digital voice dropped an octave: 'Not like that, huh? Poor guy, you better come home and wean on this new Chardonnay they're making about five miles from here, right *inside* the San Andreas rift. Has to be drunk quick, before any tectonic action. Come on home, Cody.'

The Bible opened and flapped like a dove before hitting the window and buckling up in the corner.

'I'm coming, but first I have to go to Toronto.'

Somewhere inside me my own words registered, and I started packing my brains. Abe told me to take care.

'I'll take paracetamol.'

The handset warbled under my fingers. I picked it back up and was going to say 'Wallace', but instead felt a sudden need to say: 'Who is it?'

As I spoke I noticed no cable running to the telephone; the unit was wall-mounted beside the bed. If you answered the phone, you had to go to it, unhook it, and stand or sit in a certain place at the bedside.

These perceptions took a millisecond. My head whipped round. Out through the streaky windows, the flat roof across the service lane registered a movement and my knees gave way. The carpet was coarse nylon tuft and smelled of car fumes, fused static and sour milk, but I held onto it. This patch of carpet was in the lee of the bed. It was precious carpet.

For a few seconds I treasured Dupont floor-covering technology, wondering whether they'd called from a cellphone on the roof of the building across the service lane outside, or from a car on the nearby street, or from the lobby. The handset, hanging near my ear, made a tumbling clunk and went dead.

15

A HIGH NOTE came from the dangling earphone, and I crawled to the bedroom door. Out in the uplit beige corridor I kept the wall against my back and went to stand in the shelter of an overweight unisex couple dressed in garish dancercise outfits and beltbags who stood hand in hand watching the indicator panel over the elevator doors. The one beside me dribble-farted audibly as we moved forward.

Escaping at mezzanine, I went to the fire escape where earlier I'd thought I'd glimpsed Amaryllis. Down on the street, weaving through the consuming, the consumed, the confused and the mistaken who milled there, I felt like a looming, ramshackle dummy tacked together for high-velocity target practice. A cab stopped mercifully and I politely requested the Hawaiian-shirted gypsy minstrel inside to rush me to LA International. His acceleration, pressing my steamy back against Naugahyde upholstery, brought comfort. I unclipped the telephone, gave my card details and called directory.

Carmody Associates had an office on Alameda in Burbank and the number rang for a long time, but there was no hurry. Maybe a passer-by out on Alameda would hear it and break in.

The ringing halted and a deep contralto doggedly repeated the number I'd called. I tried to convey information across the dull madness of the city without overtones of threats or extortion.

'I know where Peppi Harman is.'

The voice intoned a holding phrase and the line went dead. A jingle from 'Eine Kleine Nachtmusik' started piping into my ear and cut abruptly to a curt demand:

'Who's this?'

'Carl Carmody?'

'This is Carmody. Who's speaking?'

'Cody Wallace.'

'Who?'

I had a little surge of Hollywood-husband rage and bore down on it.

'Peppi Harman's my wife.'

Carmody shoved the mating information aside.

'Okay, what?'

'I wondered, are you looking for Peppi?'

A longer silence than I expected followed, as if we'd been cut off. The cab made a left south on Lincoln Boulevard and joined the other alligators in the slow metal mud flow under the yellow disk which lurked behind grime in the western sky. When the voice came, it sounded skeptical, cautious.

'Should I be?'

'Gunmen keep appearing, and they're not in the Screen Actors Guild.'

'I'm very concerned to hear that.'

We were stationary in four lanes of assorted tin-can vehicles, slowly sucking Alaska dry. Somewhere in the vapors ahead the body of a distant wide-bodied jet found a scrap of light and glinted dimly off it as it lazily slid up an escape trajectory.

'You don't sound so concerned.'

'Mr Willis, I've not met you, but I do know Peppi. I'm her production chief. She works for me.'

'At Visionville, right?'

'Wrong. She now works for Carmody Associates.'

Methought he emphasized a tad overmuch.

'Well, how about that. Does Peppi know?'

'Negotiations are under way.'

'She seems to be expecting to work a long way from here Monday.'

'Yeah, 'sright, yeah.'

'You don't sound so sure. Got problems at the studio?'

'There's been a strike, but that should be settled now the new picture's in turnaround.'

I listened hard to the handset. We were being vibrated by the adjacent diesel of an interstate eighteen-wheeler.

'But there's film in the can! Since when is the picture in –'

'The trade press knew last week, but it won't be carried until after the holiday break.' The voice's implausible confidence degraded into undisguised anxiety. 'What's this about people with guns? What's the problem with Peppi?'

'She's alive, is the problem, way I see it. Why's the picture in turnaround? Is it because of all this?'

'All what?'

I bore down on my turmoil until I could speak evenly.

'All this' – I swiped my hand across the hazy view of suburbia we had from the skyway – 'mental torture and gun-waving and striking.'

My faltering note seemed to bolster Carmody.

'The strike is indeed one of the principal reasons the production is in turnaround. I have two lights – tell Peppi to call me.'

'Hold it, Carmody! Someone's interfering with the picture – why? Is Carmody Associates still with Visionville? Are you producing? How the hell can any picture get made with this kind of –'

I was barking rhetorically into a disconnection, and the gypsy was watching me in the rear-view mirror. He was pale and crow-faced, with black curls and sharp, close-together eyes. His voice had the nasal twang that comes from a damaged septum. He was chewing gum.

'That Carl Carmody, the producer?'

I shook my head, sighing. Then I hung up and nodded, deciding to make conversation since we were sharing a cell in a hundred-square-mile gas chamber.

'I seen him. I do the stand at the Bev for my brother-in-law, nights.'

'Uh-huh. I don't know the Bev that well.'

He chomped a bit, reflectively.

'Lotta picture people. A few pretty crazy people.'

I started measuring the distance through the jam-up of gas-guzzlers to the side of the boulevard, scanning round for a side street I could flee down.

''Nother producer, Saul Kempinski – had him inna back a coupla times. Took him up to a place on Malibu Beach not long ago. Two hunnerd bucks.'

We advanced a couple of feet. My head returned to base.

'You know Kempinski?'

'To look at. Kinduva hunchback. Face you could chop a tree down with. Has an account.'

We sat inhaling hydrocarbon compounds together. The crow chewed some more. Another jumbo jet made its getaway. Being spoken to bothered me. My head was attracted to the tinted window-glass to pound against it, spatter gore there. I looked down at the soft part of my elbow, where I figured the man with a poxy face and a white mustache had risked my immune system. Then something else the squinty chauffeur was saying tuned me back.

'Come again?'

The black eyes checked me keenly.

'You mentioned her, right? She was in that picture *Chi*? My girlfriend liked it a lot, called it a three-hanky job. I don' buy the weepies, but she was good in it, yeah, I could see that.'

'Who're we talking about?'

'Penelope Harman, right? She your ol' lady?'

'You drove *her*?'

'Like I said, to Kempinski's from the Bev, 'nother time. I know it was her 'cos I asked, right out. The new faces, they like to be asked, them and the old ones. The big names, no. Like, you wouldn' say to Nick Cage, "Hey, man, you Nick Cage?" know what I mean? Not in a million years, no way. So I asked her. Uh-huh! She is one beautiful lady. 'Course, y'get all kinds. Had Lucille Ball inna back only two weeks before she died.'

'When?'

'I dunno, whennid Lucy die?'

'When did –' I bore down on myself some more. 'When did you drive Peppi – Penelope Harman?'

He considered the array of robotic transportation streaming past us in the opposite direction.

'Hard to date it, must've bin around – maybe – I guess –'

I leaned on the back of his bench, digging in a pocket.

'Not today, right? Listen, hang a yewie, please.'

He glanced over his shoulder at the folded hundreds I was holding there. His eyes searched mine.

'You wanna go to Malibu now? Think she may be there, huh?'

'Now.'

Car butts waved for miles ahead. A couple had already broken loose and doubled back, and Peppi's effect is potent. The gypsy could get behind it. Also, the cab was not his property. Its wheels hit the median with a bone-jarring bang, the oilpan grounded, and the chassis screeched. Maybe they heard it in the GM plant.

We were on the coast highway when I got through to Ray Mandel at his leafy dacha near Maple, Ontario. Ray was a few hours ahead in a drinking day and bellowed a greeting – we corresponded but hadn't met for two years since he'd contacted me on a script-development trip to the coast and we'd talked up a picture book about the heyday of studio sets, a project he'd not forgotten.

'Sold *The Plasterbuilders*?'

'Lousy name wasn't it? Never could think up a better one. But I'm not calling about picture books.'

'You have a script. Let me guess. Fashionable architect sells out to Japanese, moves upcoast, rebuilds Stonehenge in Big Sur, violates blonde virgins on altar at dawn, gets strung up by righteous Mennonite mob – moral: prophets must die.'

'Listen, Ray, I'm in a cab on the coast highway – with a problem.'

He picked up on the stress – we'd been pals since squash team at Stanford – and his voice sobered down.

'What's going on?'

'You know Peppi's working for Reska DeWoers?'

'Sure, I saw *Chi* – wrote her about it. Wunnerful.'

'Forget the letter. Reska had problems at the studio which're getting totally out of hand. Someone Semtexed her place in Bel

Air this morning. The whole house went up, right in front of my eyes. Keeps replaying in my head.'

A whizzing noise came out of the handset.

'Wow!'

'Peppi hid out at the studio attorney's place 'n' a couple of guys broke in after her wearing socks on their heads.'

'*Wha-a-a?*'

'I got her away, but she took off looking for DeWoers.'

Big squinty eyes drilled me in the mirror. I moved out of their view. Ray took a moment to absorb what I'd said.

'These goons, who are they?'

'I think it started out as a union hassle.'

Ray made a derisive noise.

'Sounds more like Colombians – maybe they need a studio. Where's the money coming from?'

A pause. This time it was me thinking across two thousand miles.

'Saul Kempinski's involved. They're supposed to be shooting in Toronto on Monday.'

'Where, I wonder?'

'Visionville's being picketed, they must need sound stages. The phones were going all night at her place.'

'That could be a problem up here.'

'The locals won't approve of strikebreaking?'

'Yeh, this isn't LA.'

'Even in LA, film crews looking for a pay deal don't blow up people's houses, do they, Ray?'

'Source the funds, is my advice. Want me to sniff around? Shouldn't take long, there's not many sound stages.'

We signed off. I pressed cancel and got another number. Again, Peppi's recording failed to play. Abe gave no reply either. We passed Will Rogers State Beach, a strip of desert against battleship-gray sea and soiled-washcloth sky. My palms refused to rub dry. Many other things were dry, like my tongue, like the driver's wit – he was talking again – like the rocky hills round Topanga. I huddled, cringing away from the world, hovering on the edge of sleep, building new houses on Yerba Buena Drive and seeing them go up in oily flames . . .

My gypsy guide was still drawling ten miles later.

'They should bulldoze these places under, man. People think they own the ocean, y'know that?'

'They c'n have it.'

We drove some more. Perhaps he stopped talking. Anyway, then I heard him say:

'This is it. Now three doors along, you're lookin' at –'

I didn't hear which big cheese was the neighbor. We were pulling in on the inside lane of the coast highway beside the choicest section of the long strip of beach houses, where they stood shoulder to shoulder giving directly onto the highway, offering only sealed carports, tightly enclosed porches and grilled windows to the passing world. Spears of palm jabbed out from behind a tight patio at the number the nasal voice indicated. The place was tall, heavily wire-screened and freshly sprayed pastel pink.

'Drive by.'

'Okay.'

There was security equipment round the patio door, which had a hem of spattered dust from the passing traffic. Near a shuttered upper window was a striped alarm box.

'Stop at the next beach access.'

'There's not many on Malibu.'

'Just the next one.'

It was a little way. Like the man said, they owned the ocean. I paid him off with the last of my hundreds, watched the cab make a U-turn, and went into the gas station we'd stopped beside. It was Exxon, but this time I had to let it go. Anyway, I wasn't buying crude like they dumped on eight hundred miles of Alaskan shoreline; I wanted the bermudas they had among the gaudy junk in the store, and I charged a pair, plus some shades, a beach towel and a pair of thongs. The sales clerk lent me the restroom key to change.

It wasn't the ideal day for a swim. The Pacific looked as if Exxon had taken care of it, but an intruder had to live the dream. You blew out a gray day with your garish shorts. You demonstrated your career success by strolling with a roll tucked under your arm downbeach to some neighbor's stoop for chitchat in the tub over a few LA beers and surimi snacks while the workers down in the city got X-rayed at computer terminals. I recrossed the highway to the alley between two blank-walled houses and trudged out onto the western edge of America. Reject construction grit for sand, metallic effluent for sea, climate-damaged sky. Two streaks of unearthly yellow vapor gave a troubled look to the steel-edged horizon. The air seemed too bored and used up to move.

Here on the seaward side the houses bordering the highway were transformed into theater balconies for the daily marine productions. They had a variety of seating areas: terraces, sun rooms, roof decks, open patios, porches with hot-tub installations, sliding doors, French doors – glass everywhere, so much of it in some places the housing looked too frail to withstand a storm. Several places were pink, but Cody'd been in architecture a while and he could pick out the Kempinski address by the patent brand of all-weather sandtex sealant they'd used, hosed on under pressure and guaranteed for far longer than most Malibu owners, or the sealant, would last.

Your ankles ache, wading along in construction grit, and thong soles offer little protection against the needle of a discarded syringe. Movements occurred behind windows, probably cleaners – generally Malibu beach lay under a curfew. Holiday week demanded gaudier shores like Tahiti, Bali or the Seychelles.

Abreast of the house sprayed with pink patent sealant I veered inland. Like its adjoining neighbours, it had a wooden sun deck. Giving onto the deck were sets of French doors fitted with small panes of multicolored glass. Inside was a sun room, with its billowy expanses of woven cane and chintz upholstery dappled in green, blue, yellow and red.

A gnarled length of arbutus bough lay washed up nearby. I fetched it, went back across the bleached teak and started poking panes in. Each broke with a sharp snap and fell without fuss onto the carpet inside. When I'd done enough poking I padded my shoulder with the towel roll and barged open the fretwork with minimal noise, which made it easy enough to step over the bottom panel and wait there until something happened.

No alarm sounded, but it was fair to assume we were wired. In a little while, when my aorta had ceased flapping and the trembling had diminished, I felt more confident about walking through the sun room and penetrating further into Kempinski's property.

A plate-glass sliding door which was supposed to seal the house off from the sun room had been left rolled back, so I moved quietly into the scent of freshly tended soil and early-blossoming mimosa. A humidifier was whirring among the foliage.

Looking round at the tropical garden and galleried landings they'd installed under a big stained-glass skylight two-stories over-head, I momentarily forgot where I was and mistook it for one of my trendsetting early jobs – a plastic surgeon's eyrie in Beverly Glen refitted by Wallace Associates years earlier. By now, the avant-garde Wallace style had spread; you planned a walk-through life on multiple levels and in varying dimensions, with no clear demarcations, so that dwellers moved from space to space with nothing boxing them. The style needed much time and funds for gutting a structure and rebuilding with steel inside the shell. In this house, ramps at soft gradients led away from a palm-treed oasis through glades of rainbow. It was a miracle to achieve such an impression of space in a town-house on a sixty-foot lot.

The kitchen zone beyond was all black vinyl fetishism, its matt charcoal fitted units bare and unfeatured, like a perverse morgue. Idly my finger pressed against a panel and a spring-catched ball-bearing action glided it forward, revealing a tray of Japanese knifeware which looked unused. Nothing must look used. I pushed the drawer smoothly away, and the voice reached me.

At first I thought it was voices outside, amplified by the modi-fications I'd made in the sun room, but through the foliage the beach was a blank. A scarab-like hump was the only feature on the charcoal worktop, and a section of it was removable. As it reached my ear, there was a tiny whirr from the micro-motor which automatically extended the antenna, but I hardly noticed: an actress I knew was talking on the phone.

'Stop going on about these dead people. Talk about *me*, I'm still alive.'

She was talking to a male, baritone, non-American.

'So were they once, and what they stood for has been twisted around.'

A quiet, precise voice, maybe English. The voice of an unknown man, talking to my wife.

'It's all history. I don't give a shit any more. How can you talk about anything except where Reska is?'

She sounded bitchy, querulous, running on empty.

'Stay where you are. Reska'll get in touch.'

'How d'you know?'

'She can't move without me. What would she shoot?'

'God, man, she has people like you lining up.'

'Not with my contract.'

'They sack you and find something in the small print later.'

'I'll call you in an hour. Don't go anywhere. Do you have tickets?'

'Of course not.'

'Okay, look, take a rest, right?'

'Sure, sure.'

'I'm going to put the phone down now, okay? Be strong.'

'Sure.'

'I'm with you, you're deep in there, in my heart. We'll come through.'

'Yeah.'

'Bye, okay? I'm putting it down.'

'Yeah.'

The line clicked. I fitted the handset back and moved quietly up a green-carpeted ramp, made a U-turn and moved up another ramp until an upper lounge came into view which had outsize lime-green pillows scattered on low, designer-gray couches that had wide plate-glass views of the ocean. Staring out to sea, silhouetted against the concrete-colored skyscape, was a tall, elegant-boned woman with cropped peach-colored hair. She swung round and caught sight of me, choked on her breath, and splayed a hand over the front of the silk shirt I'd bought for Amaryllis. Then she ducked her face into her palms, moaning.

Stopping at the head of the ramp, I kept the tone of voice as reasonable as possible.

'First you hold a gun on me at Craven's, then you walk out on me at the hotel. It's time you let me in on this thing.'

She squared the warm, full-mouthed face on me. Her eyes were in a green phase, hollow and shadowy now.

'I didn't recognize you at Munro's house.'

'Walking right at you?'

'You looked like one of his boyfriends. I thought he was giving you head, if you really want to know. After seeing those men I couldn't think straight, and I was afraid when I woke up in that squalid room – I need a ticket to Canada.'

She clasped her hair.

'First, do I need this?'

She stared as if she didn't know what a Lady Smith .38 was. Her voice became small and weary.

'Of course you don't.'

Her hands fell limply at her sides. She inclined quizzically, looking upwards.

I crossed the room, dropping the gun, and caught her as she fainted, clasping the whole of her against my batteries so that she moaned and revived. Our nerves were out on strings and a flame licked up immediately between us like brush fire, stemming achingly from our sex-roots. Her face touched wet and softly against mine. Force flowed out of me into her, and she clung to it, kissing as if feeding. The surging libido wiped the world clean, and I overheard our abandoned, exhausted moans mingling like the sound of nature's engines. Within a few seconds she was sinking with me onto the floor and I was blindly bringing the kilted skirt up, pulling away the little bikini briefs I'd charged near the hotel, cupping my palm over her dainty bush, her legs yielding, opening soft wet flesh, but her moaning changed note and she fended me off.

'I'm all stripy.'

Unbuttoning the shirt, my eyes gave away how it looked, and she made a disgusted face, pulling up her briefs.

I said: 'Maybe a medic should check it.'

'They're only sores, but I thought I couldn't live again after last night.'

My hands brought the shirt together over her lash marks.

'Remember Lahaina? Twin beds overlooking the sunset?'

'Oh, Cody . . .'

'You wanting to make love, me saying no, we get married first?'

'What've I done?'

'Nothing. It's all held in us, no one can take it away.'

'I'm sorry.'

'Let's be together. I'll come to Toronto. Cody's nobody without us being solid. Us as a pair makes life work.'

She crawled away and flopped out on a couch, a glow coming off the sheen of her legs. I arranged her skirt. The bell voice came muffled by a pillow.

'Reska's disappeared.'

'She's probably flown to Canada. We'll find her.'

'Okay.'

It was the okay she gave when she was drifting off – the only time she completely conceded anything – but Wallace felt reborn, and stupidly happy.

'If I lie down by you, don't walk out on me this time, right?'

No reply came, only even breathing that blended with the stillness of the house. The bone at my temple throbbed where it'd hit the marble in DeWoers's bedroom, and a weird electrical blastedness lingered where the prod had worked on my throat. I rubbed the jab mark on my arm, wondering whether to take Peppi home before leaving for Canada, or fly direct. Whether to fly for home or leave for Canada. Whether to leave home. Whether to leave Canada. My brain weighed up the jumbled proposals and came up with FAILED TO COMPUTE. Aching weariness sent tentacles round my waist, reaching up to pull my body down onto the floor and into darkness.

But this vigil I intended to keep without falling asleep. Carrying the revolver, I padded barefoot down to the sun room to press parts of the kitchen and see if it came up with coffee. At the clump of palms somebody grabbed my arm, removed the gun from my hand and jerked my wrist up between my shoulder blades. Three young security men appeared in front of me, one of them dark-chocolate Dravidian, the others Caucasian, one with a squashed face, another long-haired with a ring in his ear.

'Under ten minutes. Not a bad response time.'

'Shut your mouth, sir.'

16

THEY MADE COFFEE and watched me drinking it out of a thermos mug on one of the davenports in the sun room until the client arrived.

Peppi must have called Kempinski earlier, because he came through the front door charged with hunch-shouldered bustle, issuing instructions in his clipped, slightly mid-European accent before I'd made much progress on the drink.

'Keep a man out front,' he told the squash-faced guard who'd twisted my arm, 'put this guy on the deck and wait for the repairman, he should be along right away. Tell your office we don't need the police to attend. Oh, and where's Miss Harman? Asleep upstairs? Okay, she can stay that way, there's no one to look after her anyway. We'll get medical help later. Mr Harman? Will you step into my study?'

'Wallace.'

'Sorry?'

'Cody Wallace.'

'Ah, yes, of course. Tsk, tsk.'

He took a good squint at me relaxing on his davenport near the ruins of the pretty French doors. I returned the compliment. On his own turf Saul Kempinski presented quite a package. When you got over him looking more like a drive-in theater manager than a movie magnate, you noticed the eager poise of his build, his peculiar stooping posture, perhaps related to myopia, but expressing the accumulated force of concentration that focused behind his horn-rimmed specs. He was a man who laid a shadow. I remembered his treacherous silence when I appealed for witnesses. It occurred to me that this was one man who could handle Reska DeWoers. Which made you wonder. I crossed my legs and sipped coffee, a nice Viennese-style dark roast.

'Where's DeWoers?'

He thrust his hairy hands into the pant pockets of his tailored business suit and flapped them.

'Let's talk in the study.'

'I think I'll wait for the carpenter and show him how to put the window back together. After all, I took it apart.'

Kempinski ducked his horn-rims at the mess.

'You owe me a thousand deductible for that, but we'll overlook it. I realize you've had a difficult day.'

'A difficult night.'

He nodded gravely.

'Yes. That too.'

'What exactly's been happening to me, Kempinski?'

He rasped his chin with a coppery hand and sighed, pacing to the aerated French doors and back again as he spoke.

'The studio trades are going apeshit. Reska tried to launch Visionville without them, which was a bad start. They organized the place last year and she fought it all the way, so there was plenty of bad feeling. Still, the first picture went into orbit –'

'*The Slave?*'

'That's right. So everybody got over it and things looked okay for the new one –'

'*Chi?*'

'Yes, and that made a profit in the art houses –'

'They general-released it here and in New York –'

He touched the fur on his dome with a fingernail.

'Mmm, well, we arranged a deal on it – distribution is the toughest part for us, of course. In fact, the *Chi* deal led in to this picture –'

'Which is?'

He came to a halt and faced me, joining his hands behind his back.

'Confidential information in this case. Working title is *Can o' Beans*.'

'Listen, pal, I nearly woke up dead this morning in a garbage hopper. Somebody'd poked a nightcap into my elbow and a model called Amaryllis was lying in it with me, also whacked up. We got out, but only just in time. The place got incendiaried.'

He rapped back sharply.

'Where's Amaryllis?'

'Remember her now, right? Who cares?'

He shrugged, rolling the hunch once.

'Well, I guess Peppi needs her.'

'Peppi?'

'Amaryllis, you know, sees to her. Answers the phone, pours fruit juice, fetches the Kotex, that sort of thing.'

'On the payroll?'

'Sure.'

A pang of envy made me grin bitterly, which hurt. Kempinski glowered.

'For a man in trouble, you look pleased with yourself.'

'Trouble? Hey, I thought I was out of it now, or are you going to call the police and make a B and E complaint?'

He stayed motionless.

'Why wouldn't I?'

'Because I took sanctuary here.' I held up a pair of crossed fingers. 'Pax.'

Kempinski raised no crossed fingers.

'It was a manner of speaking. We can overlook it. You broke in here because you figured a reasonable place to look for your wife was at her producer's house, although why you didn't press the doorchime, I have no idea.'

'Maybe that's what those Hispanic guys should've done at Reska's place last night. Dumb of them, wasn't it, waving round automatics when they could've knocked on the door? And fancy climbing all over the roof of Munro Craven's place with hoods on instead of ringing the bell. Ridiculous.'

Kempinski was considering me, the ski-tan draining. He spoke softly, as if reminding me of an embarrassing truth.

'But nobody is interested in you. You're nothing.'

'Strange thing is, they don't seem to be interested in you, either, Kempinski.'

His face was still displayed, but it had blankness behind it. His manner turned testy.

'I've withdrawn from the production.'

'Do *they* know that?'

'Of course.'

'Did you tell them?'

'No, they found out.'

'How?'

'Things get around pretty fast.'

'Know the guys, huh? They close the studio, you buy it cheap?' He studied me hard.

'I won't take offence, that was so puerile.'

'Then who d'*you* think they are?'

He pursed his mouth, leaving a brief pause before answering.

'Marielitos hired by the unions.'

'Cubans? I'm s'posed to believe that?'

Kempinski checked a big investment strapped to his wrist.

'They enjoy the work.'

'They get Craven?'

Squash-face came in and tapped Kempinski's arm and the producer went away, leaving me with the impassive Dravidian. I listened for waves. There were none. I longed for a hurricane. Nothing happened. Kempinski came back cleaning his lenses with the blue silk handkerchief from his breast pocket, a compulsive action which allowed him to show off his eyes, large, penetrating and without comfort. When he put his glasses back on, the room felt safer, and he seemed to have reached a decision – at least he'd checked my name.

'Mr Wallace, I very much regret you getting involved in all this. I've been in touch with Miss DeWoers and she asked me to help you in any way we can.'

His words jerked me onto my feet, setting my coffee down too hard.

'Is DeWoers okay?'

Kempinski stared.

'She's fine.'

'Oh.'

'Now, can I get you a ride home? Security service for your residence will be provided courtesy of Visionville Productions for as long as it takes. Or should you wish it, the studio has a small guest apartment in West Hollywood where you can stay for the rest of the holiday week, if it would make you feel more at ease, although I assure you this labor problem is being sorted out and you're in no danger atall.'

'What about DeWoers?'

'What about her?'

'She in "no danger atall" either?'

'She's at a secure address. Fortunately her house was overinsured and rebuilding will start right away.'

'Ready for me.'

'Talk to her about that.'

'What about Peppi?'

Kempinski poked the horn-rims up his beak.

'Peppi has to fly to Toronto. Shooting starts again Monday.'

'I go along.'

The producer pouted, showing his palms.

'Sure.'

There was a pause. Traffic rumbled out on the highway. I shrugged.

'Suddenly it's all tickety-boo, huh?'

Kempinski made a wry noise and glanced at his watch again.

'The world is a chaotic place. I make my money organizing it.'

'Owning it.'

'That's right. Now I very much want to make your acquaintance – let's have a drink when the new picture opens. Meanwhile, you wouldn't believe how much I have to do.' He gestured the way out. 'One of the guards will run you to the limousine office.'

I stayed put.

'So, are you back on the picture?'

The glare moved off his lenses and the dark eyes sent a little rush of recognition into me.

'I have an interest, yes.'

'DeWoers got you back on board, right?'

He twitched his face.

'Not exactly. Financing pictures is a complex business. Now if you'll excuse –'

'Can I run it past you the way I see it?'

He huffed and put on a long-suffering expression.

'My *time*, Mr Wallace.'

'There's bad feeling about unions at the studio, but the first picture makes millions so the payoff's there and everybody's happy, which means the unions're in, right?'

He sighed.

'That's about it.'

'*Chi* breaks even, so union rates prevail, everybody's still happy. Then the new picture gets going and all hell breaks loose. Tell me, I don't get it – what's the problem?'

Kempinski gestured the way past his little jungle again.

'Go home. Your wife will be through in approximately four weeks, paid handsomely. Maybe she'll buy you a winter together in Paris. You can write that screenplay you've always been meaning to, maybe show it to me after. For now, though, let it go, huh?'

'Funny, that's what Craven said.'

The producer nodded agreement and opened his hands.

'It's the best advice money can buy. Won't you take it?'

He beckoned to the security man.

'Ride Mr Wallace to the limousine office we use. See he gets the best.'

I waved him down.

'Hold it, I want to see DeWoers first, or at least talk on the phone.'

Kempinski studied me for a moment and pointed squash-face away.

'I'm going into my office, please follow me.'

We went down a carpeted incline past the black kitchen area into a windowless room lined with books, typescripts and electronic gadgetry. The floor was white tiles lit from underneath, and the desk was made of chromium tubing and some kind of NASA nose-cone substance. Its sleek black surface was fringed with expensive trinkets from adult toyshops: a realistic 1930s Bentley, a flickering lightning effect in a tube, a Rubik game made of brushed aluminum – I'd barely taken in a few before Kempinski rounded on me from behind them.

'Look, I'll be totally honest with you.'

My mouth involuntarily went into a cynical smirk.

'Sure, sure.'

He gestured me into a hammock-type seat made of tubing and leather. Perching on a swivel throne, elbows on the desk, making shapes with his hands, he let me in on some Kempinski lore.

'My father walked us from Paris to Morocco during World War Two – do you have any idea how far that is? I'll tell you, it's five months on the open road. We were like rodents running from exterminators. Bone-racks, we were, by the time we got to Africa. These young film-school guys in the business these days, they know nothing. They'd call it Third World news, have benefit concerts and make TV specials about it if you were lucky. But not then. We were on our own – literally. My father got shipping connections that took him nine weeks to get to New York. We traveled later, carrying baggage for another family, and it took us three months by sea. My father started out selling roofing materials off the back of a horse and buggy in the markets down on the docks. He died of overwork at fifty years old. I took over where he left off, and now I am where I am. *A Power of Eagles* grossed forty-five million dollars in eight months. May not be top of the list, but still one of the top-grossing pictures of all time.' He laid one hand over the other and fell silent, but there seemed to be more, so I waited. 'The way it's done is very simple: old-fashioned loyalty and honesty. Certain people gave me deals because I stuck with them; other people bought because they trusted me. You, you're loyal. You're loyal to that beautiful woman who's sleeping upstairs, and I respect that. But I wonder how much you know about honesty, because I want you to take something on trust from me.' He pointed two index fingers, like six-guns. 'Are you listening? Okay. It's all in the screenplay, but I can't tell you more than that and you'll have to take my word it's being sorted out.'

'The screenplay?'

'Uh-huh.'

'The unions put a contract out on DeWoers and my wife because of a *screenplay*?'

'That's right.'

'But now it's all blown over. You got out. You got back in with a piece of the picture.'

'That's right.'

I looked down at the illuminated floor, then back at Kempinski.

'And the two things are entirely unrelated.'

'I don't follow you.'

'The arson and break-ins, and you getting points.'

Silence.

'Ridiculous, Wallace. You'd better stop talking that way right now.'

'Take me to Reska DeWoers.'

'Not possible, sorry.'

'What've you done with her?'

'I'll ignore that. She's extremely busy.'

'Take me to DeWoers or I go to the police and report a missing person.'

Silence.

'Okay then.' Kempinski grasped the arms of his throne. 'I'll have one of the security guys run you over there.'

'Peppi goes with me.'

He rolled the hunched shoulders.

'Sure, okay.'

It was suddenly too easy. My mouth felt dry. I went out of the room ahead of Kempinski longing for a drink.

17

TRAFFIC WAS BUILDING outside on Pacific Highway and passing eighteen-wheelers shook the foundations of the house. Instead of obediently walking down a ramp to the street door and getting into whatever security wagon they had outside, I turned up a green ramp and walked to the upper lounge where I'd left Peppi sleeping on the couch.

Squash-face and Kempinski had no choice but to follow, because I had a tiny piece of the mana of *Chi*, being married to one of its celluloid spirits, plus I'd spent twenty minutes holed up with the client, so you didn't twist my arm any more.

Peppi lay in the arms of death's cousin, her face in a trance of peace, and I inwardly begged forgiveness, bending to shake the arm she nestled on.

'Peppi, we're going to look for Reska.'

The beloved eyes snapped open and the security man tested my biceps, with Kempinski giving more orders.

'Cut it out, Wallace.'

I murmured into newborn dilated pupils.

'Peppi, we can have experts look for Reska, and when we find her she'll tell you what to do.'

'Please leave her to rest.'

I took my arm out of the guard's grip.

'Let's go now and find Reska.'

She retrieved reality like a champion, elevating onto an elbow, bringing the legs off the couch, feet on the floor, burying her face in her palms.

Kempinski was competing with me for the steadying, hypnotic voice-of-God effect.

'Peppi, you need the rest. A doctor is coming. We have flight reservations for you. Everything is in hand.'

She seemed to believe what he said and started aligning herself with her employer, but she'd said a big sorry to me only a little while before, and regret builds tenderness, something Saul Kempinski lacked. When I took her shoulders she came up onto her feet, which put both of us a head and shoulders over the guard and Kempinski. They glowered, but I held the product.

'What was DeWoers's number? You just took a call from her right?'

Peppi seized the bait and wailed.

'You had a call from Reska?'

I held the mean look behind Kempinski's glinting horn-rims, speaking at him.

'Yeah, but we have to list her with missing persons, because her whereabouts are corporate information – aren't they, Kempinski?'

Peppi went sailing forward, straight past the producer as he made a 'Stop traffic' signal.

'I have to speak to her, right away.'

We all trooped after the swaying kilted skirt and improbable legs, down the green ramp and onto the black granite tiles of the kitchen area. Kempinski's manner was an anxious mixture of menace and cajoling.

'Peppi, Reska called *me*. There is no way of getting in touch with her right now. She's in hiding, with no telephone.'

Peppi was shocked.

'No telephone?'

I cut in.

'She must've left some kind of contact. What city's she in? Toronto?'

Kempinski picked up a piece of the plastic scarab and poked a finger at it, muttering. I slipped my hands round Peppi's waist and being drowsy yet she swayed with it, so I ran fingers a little way up her breasts, just enough to remind her of what'd happened before on the carpet but no further, wondering how well she knew Kempinski, how much pull he really had on her. Then he was putting the handset down.

'Reska okay?'

He glared at me, and the svelte animal in my arms broke free.

'I want to talk to her.'

Kempinski spread his hands and his eyeglasses flashed off the spotlighting somebody'd turned on in the failing afternoon.

'That was my office, and there's no message. Now if you folks really want to go through the bother of a visit to the Police Department, with the taking of statements and so on, you're welcome, but Peppi, I doubt if it will do your career in motion pictures much good.'

That got my goat.

'Who d'you think you are, Kempinski, Louis B. Mayer, just because you pay off union leaders? Peppi's going to be going up long after you've gone down – into a Forest Lawn lot.'

Peppi stopped my mouth with her hand. Her voice had the usual bewitching effect.

'I'm working for Reska DeWoers, Mr Kempinski, and I think I should see her before I do anything else.' To squash-face and the guy with the earring: 'Could one of your officers perhaps give us a ride to where she is?'

There was a moment of awe over her delivery, fresh from her dreams and sublimely single-minded, before Kempinski recovered and cut the cajoling.

'Sorry, out of the question. If you left this house I'd be involved in litigation with Visionville for the rest of my life.'

I steered Peppi forward.

'Guess it's a cab, then.'

Squash-face saw me with my hands on the waist of a bright new movie player, guiding her towards him, and he backed away, which upset Kempinski. He bunched his shoulders up like a man hefting the globe on his neck and started snarling.

'You go, Wallace, but not her.'

'Why do we have to take your word for it that you've spoken to DeWoers?'

'You trying to wreck this production?'

'Not me, why?'

The producer wrenched the eyeglasses off his face and attacked them with his silk handkerchief, wielding a naked and hunted pair of eyes.

'If you take Peppi away from here, we won't know where she is, will we?' He rammed the glasses back on and poked the handkerchief away. 'And if we don't know where she is, how can we keep the production insured?'

I guffawed.

'Yeah, right, oh man, oh man, I hear you.'

'Cab'll be here any minute,' the earringed guard announced, coming from the sun-room telephone, and I loved him for about a second, until Kempinski dipped a hand into his coat and produced Peppi's Lady Smith, which produced a freeze-frame effect, as if time had caught its breath. Keeping his eye on me and the barrel steady, he carefully beckoned towards the ocean.

'I'm sorry, Peppi, but your husband – Wallace, get over here.' He waved the barrel, but I stayed half-shielded by Peppi. Kempinski's fingers flexed and re-flexed round the handle of the gun, as if he was drooling with the urge to empty it into me. Maybe it was nerves, but my response was hilarity. I used a Bogartian drawl.

'Stow the drill, Saul.'

Peppi giggled, and squealed when I squeezed her. Kempinski's tan reddened.

'This will seem less amusing in a few minutes, when you've been severely hurt. Remember I caught you trespassing. You tried to assault me. I had to shoot you in self-defence.'

'What was that Nazi picture you did – *The Power of Eagles*? Richard Burton raping Serbia?'

His face twitched and he jerked the weapon.

'Handcuff him.'

The good ol' boys weren't too comfortable with gunplay, and us laughing was unnerving. They looked warily from their client to us and back again, fingering the plastic cuffs on their belts. I steered Peppi by.

'Don't worry, guys, we're getting off your hands.'

Peppi ambled uneasily with me towards the exit, not quite sure.

'How will Reska contact me?'

'Call you at home.'

Kempinski shouted from behind us.

'Wallace, I'm warning you, get your hands off studio property!'

Peppi faltered, but I urged her on: no one was going to shoot at the merchandise.

Only, Kempinski did.

The lintel over our heads splintered, and there was a deafening bang as we plunged out of the house, across a little patio and through an open gate into clammy air and a hectic rush of vehicles.

18

WE RAN ALONG the coast highway – the horns that blared were like child's play after gunfire, plus we were half-deafened – half a mile against the flow of vehicles, until Peppi identified Kempinski's scarlet Ferrari hanging a U-turn ahead, and we had to jay-run six lanes.

Peppi outsprinted me, crossing the median strip first and making her own rush at a zigzag gap in the three lanes of northbound traffic. When I arrived she was already grinning and wrinkling her eyes as she thumbed the oncoming drivers, having fun so effectively that a Land Cruiser stopped before Kempinski could get to another junction and redouble back.

We cruised north at a vigilant seventy with one Willis Dorn, who said he worked for the Disney organization as a sculptural designer, which got Peppi interested right away, so the trip fell into shape and the miles slipped by, with me keeping watch out the back, feeling eerily secure in a total stranger's life as he told us about it.

'Starting out in London, one'd finally had it up to here with trying to persuade committees of gray men in shapeless suits that they needed what I had to say in neon tubing and resins.'

He'd made a pile running pine furniture from Paris to London for resale, used the profits to build an ocean-going sailboat out of concrete, docking at Marina Del Ray via Cartagena, so out of curiosity I asked whether he'd imported any powders and got a look from my wife.

100

She refused a line when Dorn pulled in at a picnic site and produced his stash.

'A little *passé* don't you think?' was all I said.

The weariness in my voice stemmed from a mounting regret for Peppi's gun. I could still feel the solid heft of the compact lady's equalizer, and the comfy fit of its rosewood stock.

'I suppose lines have a rather quaint quality now,' was all Dorn replied, flicking at his nostrils and tossing his head. 'Maybe it's why I keep it up.'

I nudged Peppi's chairback.

'Girls in plaid skirts don't do lines.'

She said, 'It's a nice skirt.' Which cheered me.

Dorn made good time to Santa Flora with the help of more snort stops that I dozed through, and departed north promising to take in *Chi* when it was issued on video.

The Wallace residence had never looked better. Its garage ramp sloped steeply down from the highway, a creamy stripe meeting a row of pueblo arches wreathed in palm foliage, with a visionary avenue of orange ocean stretching beyond it, laid by a massive golden disk of sleepy sun. I put my arm round my mate and we wearily descended the footpath, checking the yucca and cacti and arbutus on either side as if we were a relaxed couple returning from vacation. I pointed out how the valerian Peppi'd planted near the wrought-iron gates of the courtyard had grown into a clump, and found the reserve set of keys where Consuela, the help, kept them under a rock. Passing through the gate, we walked hand in hand across the flagstones to the porch with me anxious to get the door open and remind her what a picture pine-fringed sunsets made in the arched windows at the end of the terracotta-tiled entrance hall.

'I'll switch on the tub,' I said when we were inside, leaving her standing there taking the place in as I opened the door of the utility closet where the central switching board was. My finger went routinely to the alarm control and found it off. Flicking the tub switch failed to get a light. Apparently I'd left the mains power off, and the mains switch was in the basement. I crossed the entrance hall and saw Peppi in the reception room. As I came to her side we were bathed in puce light, and the sun descending into the Pacific looked like a blossom you could reach out and crush against your face.

'It's all very tidy.'

'Consuela must've come in today. I kept driving her off before.'

'Have to sleep some more.'

'Should've hit some of Dorn's stuff, maybe.'

Turning to me with sunset in her eyes.

'No way. While we were coming here I worked things out.'

'About DeWoers?'

'No. Us.'

I fingered the ethmoid bone around my eye.

'Could we use some of your rump on this?'

'If you like. I'll nurse it. I'm coming back.'

We had a long, vividly colored look into each other's infinitely strange darkness and felt unspoken understandings, partly about the way the evening could be spent and in which room, but also about a new kind of maturity that was between us, because of the hurts that had been done.

'That is *so* good.'

'There's one condition.'

'Name it.'

Her eyes glistened with pink and orange brine, as if the ocean sunset was welling up inside us.

'You remember Dr Weiss's mantra?'

'Sure! Uh, how did it go?'

'Codeee!' Shaking her head, tipping sunset streaks down her cheeks. 'Acceptance, forgiveness. Remember?'

'I accept, I forgive.'

'Do you *really*?'

'X-ray me.'

She made a half-turn and clasped herself, whispering: 'Hold me,' which I did, inhaling mana from her hair, trembling at the charge passing between us, and muttering at her neck.

'You don't get it. I hold a different woman in my arms – *my* woman, the woman I love. It's as if you're the only one in creation. The other woman, the one that exists apart from me, she's one of thousands. She and I talk, she and I are friends, but the one I love, the one I hold, only exists between us. When it's not us, she isn't there. She's our love.'

Her head rested against my cheek.

'But those lines on my front.'

'They'll fade. Did he rape you?'

'No, I don't think so. He was saving it up – I had to be punished first.'

'Jesus, these people. What did he inject you with?'

'I tried smack once or twice in high school, it could've been that.'

'Demerol, maybe, or Valium. You were dopy as hell.'

'I hardly remember anything.'

We sank onto a couch.

'That's a mercy, but it doesn't help. What'll we drink?'

We had a room-temperature Perrier with a dash of white rum and a disk of lemon, sipping at it and seeking our bearings. She dipped a finger and wetted her forehead.

'Tell me about DeWoers.'

The sun was fizzling down to a vivid orange hump, turning the room a brilliant maroon.

'She's in love with me –' frowning '– but she's convinced if she ever opened up emotionally somebody'd manipulate her.'

'Her? Really.'

'Mmm, hard to believe a woman that strong is so insecure deep down. Imagine what she holds back.'

'Like a walking bomb.'

'Della's to make me jealous.'

'Maybe strip poker was Della's idea.'

'Could be.'

'Would they've watched?'

Her complexion looking into the dying sun made my hand into a caress. *Even Solomon in all his glory* . . .

She brushed me away.

'Crying makes me look a wreck.'

'Sleep, then.'

I got a little glimpse of temperament.

'Cody, there's no way we can stay here – and I need a flight reservation.'

The room reappeared as her mood changed, the way it would to someone waking up. My address still featured in various trade directories. Peppi's could probably be had through the right sources in her union. It was surely among Craven's papers at his house. Or on DeWoers. We had to give DeWoers time to call, if she could. But crazy people could be on their way.

'Let's keep all the lights off and take a tub. We'll give her maybe an hour, not longer.'

The telephone burbled and Peppi pounced, but soon frowned, listening.

'No. I'm afraid she's not here . . . No, I'm afraid you can't . . . No, I'm afraid there's nobody here who could make any kind of comment atall . . . How did you get this number?'

She listened to the answer and put the handset down without signing off, sending a grave answer to my inquiring look.

'Larry Peacock. The *Times*.'

'How'd they get the number?'

'Had his sources. Wanted to know where *I* was.'

The panic glinted in her again.

Directory gave me the number and Larry Peacock barked his name after one buzz on his extension, against a background hubbub of keypads and chatter. When he heard my name and my relationship to Peppi Harman he asked where she was.

Peppi stared as I told Peacock I was in Vegas, had not heard from my wife, was extremely worried by the call I'd just received from my secretary in Santa Flora, and myself needed to know what was going on. Peacock was typically reluctant to switch the one-way flow of information but offered the basics.

'Bel Air home of Reska DeWoers burned flat ten-seventeen a.m.'

'Oh my God . . .!'

'No sign of bodies. Your wife seems to have escaped, if she was there. *Was* she there?'

I looked at Peppi.

'Possibly. I have a sick mother I'm visiting here, and my wife had to stay filming in town.'

A pause indicated Peacock's opinion of that.

'So Penelope's not been in touch?'

'I desperately want to know where she is. Let my secretary know if you hear.'

'I will.'

'Is it a story?'

'Two lines so far, unless it's arson.'

'Where's DeWoers?'

'Police Department'd like to know.'

'Okay, I'll call them if I hear.'

I hung up and pressed play on the recording machine. Nothing happened. Peppi watched bleakly.

'Who next?'

'Have to turn the power on.'

But instead I sat there, sipping rum spritzer, thinking of the trade press, the radio stations, the TV eyewitness crews, the columnists and all the assorted dead-end ghouls and freaks slithering round the western terminus of the USA who'd be attracted to the story if it blew up like the house. Which made me think of the man with a white mustache, and of the hooded men flickering in Munro Craven's security monitors.

'What're the police doing?'

'Why doesn't Munro call?'

'Should we phone in a description of the guy with the white mustache?'

'Description of who?'

'You didn't see him?'

Peppi shrugged, gazing into dreams on the carpet.

'The body lying on the bed was me, but it was like part of the landscape, some earth mother they were all going to fuck and who wasn't going to care because she'd breed and grow and breed and grow till the end of time.'

She rocked with her words, her fingers straying over her brow, and squinted round at me, so I held her close as she sobbed.

'Maybe . . . maybe it's . . . someone who works at the studio.'

'Can you think of anyone?'

She dabbed her nose with the silk shirt-collar.

'No. You say he had a white mustache. There's not many of them – you'd better give a description.'

'Mmmm.'

'Aren't you going to?'

'I am, but I want to talk to DeWoers first – we have business to settle – and so should her leading lady.'

'It's getting dark, how long shall we give her?'

'This is the number Reska will call first. I'll put the power on, it's just . . .'

I trailed off, and Peppi put down her drink to caress my hair.

'Just what, curly?'

'Why did you walk out on me at the hotel?'

Her delicate rakings in my hair faltered and took up again.

'I didn't know who to trust.'

'All men're liars.'

'Something like that. I was confused, needed to stare at something. The Bible fell open on that page.'

'But you trusted Kempinski.'

'You know, business is business. His place seemed safer, I had that change you gave me. When I called he arranged a ride.'

'Made a few calls when you got there.'

'Yes.'

The caresses tailed off.

'Who?'

'Who did I call?'

'Uh-huh.'

'Well, I tried to talk with Mr Kempinski. He said he couldn't spare the time. Desperate for a call from Reska. He must've realized you'd follow and come rushing after me.'

'Who else?'

'Carl Carmody. I only knew his studio number, though, and naturally he wasn't there. Munro wasn't in. I guess he ran for it like us.'

'Who else?'

'That was when you arrived – when you broke in.'

Pause.

'Who else did you call?' Leaning on her knees, Peppi gave me the profile they'd used on the *Chi* poster. 'Speak, oracle. You were talking to some Limey, telling him you were alive. Sounded like he works for DeWoers.'

She sniffed, short and hard, picked up her half-empty glass and stared into it.

'Oh, him. That was Nevil. Nevil Rayner.'

'He of the credit on *The Slave*?'

'Yes, on *Chi*, too.'

For a moment the screenwriter haunted the Wallace household. I was thinking how deep in his heart he'd said my wife was. The way she bowed her brow onto the rim of her glass perhaps she was thinking of it, too. Her neck was hot to touch and she seemed near collapsing again, so I spoke extra gently.

'Better spill the beans, hon.'

She wheezed and jammed her mouth with knuckles. Stroking her back seemed not to help, she was trembling so, then she fell against me.

'Oh, Cody, I don't like it.'

'I better call Clara.'

'No!'

Mauve and pink from the aging sunset, her eyes shunted a load of chill across to me.

'Hey, relax! Clara'll lay you down by her fire, the smell of good driftwood'll straighten you out, get you sleep – it's what you need.'

She unlatched my comforting arm and got up, staring round, working her hands.

'I have to get to San Francisco airport. Oh God, do we even have a car? Mine got left at Reska's place.'

'I didn't see it.'

She wrung the hands at me.

'Do *you* have a car? Why don't you ever have a *car*?'

'1961 Jaguars have moods – as you know. I'll rent wheels off Wayne at the service station, no problem. What about Reska calling?'

She clutched her breasts and kneaded, pleading to heaven through gritted teeth.

'Please God, go get a car! I feel trapped not having one with those guys loose somewhere.'

She oversaw me calling Wayne at the Philips station in Santa Flora. Wayne told me he had plenty of used models I could rent, and would I like him to come round with one?

'I'll run you back.'

'See you in five.'

Hanging up, I appraised a haunted-looking wife.

'Look, your clothes're in your bedroom, I haven't sold them, or cut them up or anything. Why not change?'

Ignoring the suggestion, she came and started poking a number into the handset.

'I have to tell Kempinski to meet me at the airport.'

'Kempinski fired your own goddam gun at you!'

With her face grim and set, she looked up from the phone.

'He shot at *you*, and I'm cast in a production of which he's the producer – I have to be available for work.'

I clutched my hair.

'Christ, Penelope, one minute you're being hunted down by mad Cubans, the next you've got to get down to the goddam office! What now?'

She was angling her head, frowning.

'Cubans?'

'Yeah, why's that stop you?'

'Huh?' Suddenly offhand. 'I didn't know, that's all.'

I threw up my hands.

'Come off it, Peppi, spill the beans! Stop trying to keep the world in the dark about this picture. I know there's script problems, and the writer's cooking something – what's the Cuban angle?'

She eyed me speculatively.

'I don't know, only there's Spanish names in what I've seen of it. My character's called Nardela. They don't tell us much.'

I got up and grasped my wife by her swimmer's shoulders, fighting back the urge to shake the story out of her.

'Shit, Peppi, those guys torched the house. For all we know they may be holding Reska hostage right now, or maybe she's dead. Yes, *dead*. Kempinski could easily be stalling for time. He's got points in the production – he's been in it and out of it like a slippery dick. You c'n bet he's doing some high-speed finagling with his offshore accounts. If the director's dead there's insurance, but if it's union war, or Colombians, no director in the world will take over, and he'll be in the hole for a coupla million. Think about it, the guy even took a shot at you.'

She held onto the phone doggedly, rattled but typically stubborn.

'Not me, you.'

She poked at the keypad.

'And how come Rayner was talking about dead people?'

She gave me a withering look.

'I can't possibly live with anyone who listens in to my calls – hello? Mr Kempinski?'

She turned away muttering, and I set out for the basement to switch on the power, thinking it'd be nice to deek out at the beach, maybe take a paddle, but before I'd got to the door Peppi shrieked up a breath.

I whirled round. Blood had drained from her face and she listened with hollow eyes, muttering Yes, No, Yes, then laid down the handset as if it was infected, turning away to the bloody mess of dead sun, hugging herself. I came up behind and touched her arms. She spoke almost inaudibly.

'They got Hunker.'

'Tell me.'

'They rammed his car, half a mile from his house.'

'Shame. Nice ol' Porsche.'

'He was picking up his plane tickets.'

'Kempinski's insured. You've got other offers.'

'He's not dead.'

'Oh.'

She turned, the eyes fully crazed now, focusing through me and searching agitatedly. Her lips made the words, with only breath for sound.

'*I'm next.*'

The doorbell jangled.

109

19

ALL WE SAW on opening the front door was Wayne's grease-smeared eyes, huge, alarmed and darting about, his voice coming high and strangled.

'I gotta 'eighty-four one-eighty-ess-ell for you, Cody, parked on the highway, din't bring it down. Know how 'tis, starter plays up?'

He nodded frantically, rubbing his Philips 66 coveralls, and Peppi pushed past me, snatching the keys.

'We'll take it.'

She ran across the courtyard out onto the drive with me calling after, but orders never had any effect.

Wayne pointed a finger in all directions and I grabbed him by the wrist.

'Someone up there?' He nodded, gulping. 'With a bead on you?' Gulping, nodding.

I pushed him aside and crossed the courtyard, sliding carefully out of the gate and slipping along the edge of my bamboo hedge to the ramp. Peppi was halfway up the drive, her shirt a luminous blob. Half crouching, I dashed after, Wayne calling me, and being drowned by the approaching noise of traffic on the highway.

High on the crest of the driveway, Peppi was a black skittle against the lights with a waving arm in a bright aura ... two waving arms. My legs pounded and the heart whacked. Hitting the steep part, my soles hammered concrete. Cresting the rise,

I saw Wayne's Mercedes on the hard shoulder with its sidelights on but no Peppi inside.

An interstate eighteen-wheeler keeled round the bend heading south, skimming the Merc by a foot, blinding with its rack of lights and forcing a blast of dust and grit. I reeled, shouting Peppi's name into the maelstrom.

Lights behind the parked Mercedes threw it into black outline and then veered out, bringing behind them a sleek black limousine with its rear window powering down. A second black car appeared behind it, and a face spoke at the open window in a smooth, educated Hispanic accent that got my name right.

'Please step in, Señor Wallace.'

It was a mature, well-dressed man wearing rocket-site shades, with a high brow, groomed black hair, pointed nose, bushy mustache, and a determined chin with a dimple in it. The hand resting on the window rim was dressed in a white kid glove. It went away and the door came open, revealing an all-cream interior like a sheikh's tea party, and the all-white face of my wife. The headlights of passing traffic flashed a nightmarish print of her look, as if pulsed from a distant planet. No gun was showing, but the invitation felt like one. Links with the house strained and snapped. She was mine. They had her. I got in.

We accelerated away, dimly illuminated by downlights under the seating which showed a communications center, computer terminal, TV monitor, cocktail carousel and a bowl of pet food.

The man who'd invited me in had a blue-gray Persian cat asleep on the lap of his pinstriped black business suit, and he stroked it with each of his gloved hands, one after the other, using a voice that was mellow and silky enough to record a coffee commercial.

'Let me introduce myself, Señor Wallace. My name is Doctor Arroyo, and this –' he flopped a proprietorial white hand on its back over Peppi's thigh '– is Señor Gilberto, my secretary.'

The young man seated the other side of Peppi wore another yuppie suit and looked standard IBM material, until you saw the way he'd lost track of the life in his eyes, like someone defeated by an unbearable tragedy. Behind my back a man was navigating the vehicle northwards. Ahead, out the rear window, were the following lights. I tried out my voice.

'So, you guys want in on the movie business, right? Let me tell you on her behalf, Peppi is booked solid till late next year.'

The bushy mustache lifted and stretched; revealing huge slabs of spotless enamel, and one of the gloved hands took enough time off squashing the cat to wave my objection aside.

'I am not so much in the business of making movies, Mr Wallace, as in the business of *not* making a certain movie, and seeing that no one else does, either.'

I looked at Peppi, and she looked a horror story back. I tried to sound hard and determined.

'Listen, Dr whoever, you just committed armed kidnap on a public highway, you're facing a federal rap and a very long investigation of the rules of basketball in a penal institution back east, so would you kindly turn this whorehouse round and take us home?'

He sat there breathing – you could tell by the way he flexed his nostrils.

'Indeed, it is very regrettable that I have to operate in this manner, Señor Wallace. I assure you that were we to meet under different circumstances in some other place we would be able to exchange civilized views on a wide variety of subjects. I am a philosopher, and I believe you might be able to find merit in me, and I in you. Nevertheless, things are as they are. I am a nobleman and a diplomat, and this is how I do business with my enemies. All sadly nefarious, I suppose, but we get into the habit.'

I sat forward.

'So Peppi 'n' I've got positives on you 'n' whatshisname now, does that mean we're dead meat?'

Dr Arroyo peeled the shades off his fleshy face and showed a pair of inspiring black eyes, bright and shiny with a crazy little dazzle. He was one helluva guy.

'Not atall, Señor Wallace, and just to prove it, I remove the glasses I wear against the passing lights. You see, I have immunity, only to be lifted under the most extraordinary circumstances, and

I regret a little road accident involving an obscure architect does not fall into that category.'

Peppi looked hard at him, but not as hard as I did.

'Where the hell're we going?'

Arroyo stared through me.

'We, Señor Wallace, have a script conference appointment at Lago Doncella near Napa, but you, well, you are not involved. You won't be needed.'

Peppi spoke: 'He goes with me.'

We looked down a long, cold passage at each other.

'I go with my wife.'

Arroyo jerked a forefinger up to his mustache, exclaiming, '*Family* people! How very old-fashioned!' and swinging into animated discourse: 'Strange, isn't it, the dual standards that people are able to practice? Could it be connected with our bicameral mind, possibly? The self-hypnotic, half-delirious nature of the hairless baboon? Or is it that humans are obsessive utilitarians who deceive themselves into thinking they are high-minded idealists? Thus' – he flourished a gloved hand at Peppi, who stared bleakly my way – 'we have a woman in all respects decently married and living in holy wedlock with a – Well, we will not call an architect a *decent* man, shall we, Señor Wallace? After all, I am sure you have committed several major crimes in glass and steel on the streets of California. But respectably bound in matrimony, let us say. And this respectable wife, this paragon of virtue, earns her living in a local industry as a motion-picture actor, posing before cameras as someone she is not, blindly accepting the instructions of a director who borrows her body and her brain to *operate* her – like a *Frankenstein!*'

Arroyo's passion was mounting. His puffed-up chest worked, and he appeared to be hurting the cat. I tried to butt in, but he was unstoppable, boosting the marriage v. career analysis into a rhetorical denunciation.

'This alluring monster, this wire-operated freak, is quite prepared to cite herself as a model of marital virtue when it suits her, please note, while lending her person, the temple of her spirit, to another to masquerade as' – a white forefinger poked at hell – 'God knows what, before God knows whom, in God knows which spiritually impotent pseudo-community, in a fiction that, for all she knows, could be the most grotesque *travesty* of the very family values, the very state of matrimony, worth and respect which she takes for granted in her own life, the very *comfortable*, *prosperous* life which she expects to lead as a result of this grotesque *perversion* which she is mindlessly, moronically, brain-damagedly *foisting on the world!*'

Arroyo was halfway out of his seat, cramming the cat against his chest with one hand, poking the other at Peppi and me in turn, his face contorted. Peppi stared aghast. Gilberto looked away. I gulped and attempted to parry.

'What *is* this travesty?'

Arroyo crouched forward and groaned a strangulated name in my face down his finger.

'*Nardela Brú.*'

He quivered behind the poking digit, a red-eyed ball of fury, and sank back into his chair, rearranging the cat and deep-breathing like a boxer, extracting a pump-spray from his coat pocket which he worked in his mouth. I stared at Peppi. She looked wanly at Arroyo and her voice came out uncharacteristically small.

'D'you mean my part?'

Arroyo scratched the backs of his hands busily, rolled his eyes up to heaven and shared a bitter little private laugh with his close pal up there. Then he stopped, jutted the dimpled chin at us mortals and spoke in a tone of withering contempt.

'Your *part*, Miss Harman, is not a *part*, it is the *whole*, and it is the whole which makes the outrage, and it is the outrage which makes a man capable of anything to defend his own dignity and honor, and the dignity and honor of his family. I come from a long line of eagles who fly above your barnyard, your slaughterhouse of values, your camp of no concentration, your Elysium of Nietzschean nonsense, of "all is permitted". No, all is *not* permitted, because I, Luis Arroyo, say no! You people in this city know nothing of dignity, nothing of honor. You are degraded. You are *filth*. Oh God, dear God . . .' He scrunched up his face, banged his fists together toward the ceiling and wailed. '. . . I pray that soon, some day, your redeemer son will return with a nuclear sword and eradicate this stinking Sodom from the face of the earth in a glorious, rolling firestorm of vengeance!'

Peppi stared and cried out.

'What're you *saying*?'

White with emotion, Arroyo explained what he was saying with fervent intensity, scratching the backs of his hands again and jabbing his finger.

'This gross perversion of the truth in which you are contracted to perform, Señora Harman, and which could well be released at about the time a change of régime in my native country causes a major sensation in the United States, this *travesty* depicts Nardela Brú as an adventurer, little more than a whore, who sleeps her way into high places in the entourage of President Fulgencio Batista, finally working her cynical charms on the President himself, and all the while plotting his overthrow with Communist insurgents behind his back. She is depicted as one of these grotesque anti-natures that you spew out from your atomized and destructive society, a ruthless and neutered Lilith, dressed up in the fatigues of a guerrilla terrorist, bristling with arms, swearing like a man and shooting priests and policemen and honest businessmen to death as if she were a hero. *This* is how you intend to depict Nardela Francesca Gomesca y Brú, a woman of the highest virtue, nobly born, daughter of a senior statesman, educated in Madrid, Washington and Boston, and an honored friend of the Free World President of Cuba into his venerable old age.'

He bristled, still scratching his hands.

Peppi screwed up her eyes.

'What *is* it about Nardela and you?'

The cat jumped down and Arroyo rounded on her, clasping an invisible crystal ball near his face and shaking it, staring into its invisible heart as though all God's truth were there, tremblingly reading out a fact of his ancestry.

'Nardela Brú . . . was . . . *my mother*.'

Peppi sent me a flare of shocked understanding that drained into staring alarm.

Arroyo was a fright, but a pain in the neck too, and my voice came out angrily loud.

'This is carrying spoilt-child shit a bit far, Arroyo! You can't hold Peppi responsible and kidnap her because she follows a script that the –'

Arroyo focused across the ball at me, and threw it in my face.

'*Exactly*! That is why, Mr Wallace, we are going to a script conference, and you' – he gestured me to stand – 'are not.'

It *looked* like a gesture to me to stand, but it was Gilberto who rose and lunged across the floor in a kind of football tackle, pincering my skull by poking a thumb into my ear and a third finger into the corner of my eye socket, twisting my head over like that, opening the door with his free hand, shoving my head through it and karate-punching my neck as I fell.

All I managed to grab on the way out was the inside of his coat, where my frantic groping found a purchase on the rim of his inside pocket and ripped it away as I fell.

They must have braked, because my neck didn't snap when I barged onto the hard shoulder, whirled and barged it again, and bounced, over a brink to barge once more, now against gravel, now against steep turf, which sent me into a crazy polka and corkscrewed my consciousness off into orbit, where it could watch my wild, balletic pirouetting, and hear me come to rest with a thud against a slope of sand.

There was no hurry to return to that racked, dizzied frame which lay sending out hundreds of tiny nervous sensors to see what had been fractured – simple or compound – what had been crushed, twisted or wrenched, and what had been torn completely away. There was much work to be done, a big, expensive survey to be conducted down long limbs, through miles of nervous ganglions, chakras, arteries and veins. Two hundred pounds of flesh had to be weighed, assayed and checked for multiple contusions, cuts and rippings. A billion synapses in the brain had to be tested, reported on, rested.

I stayed away, a dark, sightless inventor hovering near its creation, capable only of hearing.

An enormous beast was breathing near me, in and out, with huge restfulness. It was the motionless Pacific Ocean, tipping at its most delicate edge, spreading in a tiny cascade, then quietly withdrawing.

All the wisdom of the whales was in its lapping peace, the love of the dolphins, the doggy happiness of seals, the laughter of gulls.

Also, somewhere overhead, was the purr of an idling engine, with the rustle of feet on grassy tufts, the hush of soles on sand – much closer. Very close.

And a rich, basso, scornful laugh, followed by a rich, basso, scornful comment: '*Necesita un servicio completo.*' Then, over the rush of a passing truck above, a metallic slither and a click-click which sent the nerve sensors dashing back to headquarters, sirens wailing, hooters honking, bells jangling, emergency doors clanging, and waves of lightning crackling down the spinal cord with desperate commands to muscular tissue for instant action.

An extravagant bang echoed into the mountains and pounded something brutal into the grit near the prone man's forehead, stinging the skin there with red-hot grains. All the figure managed was a twitch.

The senses cut out then – even the presence that had been hovering, listening. It heard no sound of the strangers illegally taking their leave of the scene of a traffic accident. Their vehicle may have been unusually well silenced, or perhaps combined shock and fear rendered me clinically dead for a few merciful moments in a manner science has yet to understand. Perhaps I was deafened. Whatever the reason, it took me a while fully to grasp that the slug of a broad-gauge weapon had penetrated the dirt a few inches from my prefrontal lobes, and that Dr Arroyo's anonymous companions from the car behind had left me on the beach for dead.

THREE

20

I SAT IN a white plastic armchair drinking and watching the light show on the pool. Each time the blonde girl from number 9 disturbed the water, galaxies exploded through my eyelashes until I had to check the highway to rest my retinas. Sometimes a breeze from the Sierras came past the bungalows and hustled up a spangled wonderland, bringing scents of grape must, earth and pine. And when the water-skin settled, a few huge highlights blazed languidly here and there, as if I could be coaxed back to life. Northern California was having a freak December, and I was part of it.

The girl from number 9 was about sixteen, a woman, knew how it was, and moved around the pool with eyes averted. Now she was bouncing to the end of the white dive-board and stretching her fingertips ahead, staring down them to infinity, with scarlet-varnished toenails hooked over the rim. She was long-limbed and newly filled out, with the fresh glow of life on her belly. As I watched, the woman-power inside her reached out, grabbed me by the racial memory and clenched, churning up memories of Peppi. Maybe I'd win yet, but something had to be done about being so confused when sober. I looked away towards the peaks and the girl dived with a clean *kaplosh*. Once we'd all been like that; then we got to be like the girl's mother, who made a living working tour buses in the low season, went back to Tacoma in summer and worked keyboards. I'd bought her the one drink the night before, rehearsing my identity fresh from hitching up the coast after my little fall from Arroyo's car.

121

The girl from number 9 tugged her body up a chromium ladder in front of me, streaming water. Past her shining shoulder, beyond a parade of aspens, a purple and white Napa County sheriff's patrol car was coming south on US 29. I lifted my highball of iced champagne to scratch an eyebrow with it and looked away, in spite of the distance.

Another couple of inches of champagne flowed down me and I pushed the Ray-Bans up into my new college cut – like everything else, fraudulently obtained on a BankAmericard found in a pocketbook lying on the shoulder of Highway 1.

The girl had high-slung haunches, built to run far, making trouble all the way. Again I scanned Route 29; it was getting to be a nervous habit. The armrests helped haul my skinful a long way up onto its feet and I stayed testing the posture for a while before walking carefully to the pool's edge to fall in and float on my face. This phase, this mourning ritual that I had to go through for Peppi, and for myself, shot through the head the night before but missed, meant that the shocked skull had to be wrapped in a comforting bandage of C_2H_5OH and the body laid down by cooling streams. If I was good, very good, I might be able to figure out something by nightfall.

The girl crawl-stroked up and down, her rolling face lost in the bubbly pounding of her arms. I paddled to the side, armpressed myself out in case she was watching, and emptied the glass in two deep gulps, with water dripping from my bermudas. The key to my bungalow was under the shade on the white plastic table, beside the ice bucket. On its outsize fob was engraved *Chalet 13 Noble Grape Motel, Box 149, Napa, CA92004*. I took it and walked purposefully along the empty mid-afternoon off-season poolside, stopped abruptly, making a noise in my throat, then turned and headed off in the other direction. It meant too many bottles if I'd lost the way thirty-five yards from home.

A fresh white bathroom towel felt good around my waist after a long piss, and I gave my ghost-walker self the blankly staring look people use in bathroom mirrors.

It was better than I made out. Body firm. Waterproof makeup hiding scuffs, bruisings and the purple blush under one eye. Pecs hard, the act plausible. Pass for thirty, thirty-five. A bum, but a legal one, who's built up a little credit, using it to look for something to do in the valley. Thousands of law-abiding drifters the same in California.

In the bedroom, I opened the closet and surveyed the garments on the rail. A loose-cut Italian cotton suit in light khaki, natural cotton shirt with Western poppers, pigskin loafers, plus an ankle-length Burberry. All items changed in different locations round the Oakland bus station area.

Somebody knocked, and I looked up at my valises shelved overhead. Address unknown. No one invited back. I crossed to the door and opened it an inch.

It was the girl, wearing a candy-striped beach towel, rainbow-soled thongs and a wise look. She was trying to turn from a fertility symbol into a neighbor, the tour guide's daughter, down from Tacoma for a visit before school went back.

'Hi, Shelley.'

I said it without expression, moving the door back an inch.

Her lips had a way of hanging open like fuchsia petals.

'How come you know my name?'

'Answer to it, doncha?'

Crestfallen.

'Yeah, right. My *mother*.' She shook off the horrid thought, remembered what was in her hand and arched an eyebrow, showing me my shades, which I took back in silence.

'I dove for them.'

'Fine.' I nodded slowly, reaching round to massage the back of my neck in a gesture meant to say: I'm bored and smashed.

Which seemed to suit her. She leaned a shoulder against the jamb, pressed the door and peered in past me.

'This a two-room suite, huh?'

I eyed her coldly. 'Wanna foam-clean the rugs?'

She went on inspecting. Her hair smelt damp and warm and animal.

'You live better'n my mom. All this side two-room?'

'Just give me the question sheet, I'll fill it in later, huh?'

I took a step back and she sighed, letting me have a look

into some of the brazen wickedness she had available in her eyes.

'Shame, maybe I could've fixed that floor.' She leaned off the house and wandered away, swinging the lower chassis. The catch clicked, I laid the shades on the TV and palmed brow. Keeping Shelley at bay for thirty seconds drained a man.

Going back to the pool was off. Bed looked better, but the telephone buzzed, setting me cursing softly. I went to the fake-walnut bureau and halted it.

'Mr Gilberto?'

A woman, the motel desk woman. Sherrill? Sheree? No, Shuleen.

'What about it?'

She was embarrassed. I listened while she outlined the problem.

'Credit terminated,' I echoed brightly when she'd finished. 'That's strange. How d'you explain it?'

She couldn't. Could I?

With an easy chuckle I told her I usually kept American Express Gold for items like shopping, eating out, but – would it do?

The response was gratifying. In a cutesy voice: 'That'll do nicely, sir!'

'Ha, ha, ha!' I overlaughed. 'Be along in a while, okay? I'm standing here in my towel.'

The discomfort of grinning went away as I got rid of the handset and stared unsteadily at the white plaster wall. So it's over. Flying saucer's out of gas. Time to make a move.

21

MY CALL TO Frank Delius brought back ugly memories of Cody Wallace. Calls from the police. The *Times*, TV stations. Even my mother from the ranch. The poker game and its stakes had come to light with the deposit of the deeds at the divorce attorney's. Frank was expecting a call from insurance adjusters. Nothing firm, but the flies were gathering: shit would happen. I told Frank I was hiding. The men who'd done the house job were after me, ruthless, possibly insane. He said to turn myself in for police protection. I said if that was as safe as the federal witness protection program they could forget it, I preferred to stay incognito until things blew over. I asked him for a favor, he grudgingly agreed, and we signed off uneasily. Abe was not available; more than two rings, he was out at his winery. Ray Mandel told me the Toronto area sound stages were dead for the holiday week and nobody'd heard of Reska DeWoers coming – it'd be news if she was. Later I was showered, shaved and shirted, sitting by the pool at the usual table, very brittle.

The management came. Shuleen. The way Shuleen walked, stood, talked, reminded everyone what she told them within thirty seconds of meeting her, how she'd performed downbill from Jefferson Airplane in the Sixties, an era when she'd lived in a mist of potential and pot, wasn't in the slippery-slope forties, voice smoked husky, scarlet frizz losing its crackle. Customers had to understand that Shuleen, an artiste, had known the Big Time, wanted no truck with petty commerce or credit. I watched her coming, assessing whether cheers from hippie hordes had evolved into beatings from the husband with hair over his collar who came and went in a late-model with dark-tinted windows.

'Another bottle of Korbel, please. Oh, and call Taco Belle for more of those prawns, would you? A basket?'

Shuleen's expression said: first credit trouble, now me laying out cash, and I waited to hear her telling me to fetch the non-existent Gold Card from my bungalow, but maybe she liked the way I sat soaking up champagne, clearly not going any place soon, like some pop music lush from her past.

'Feeling rich?'

I shrugged.

'Why not?'

'Wanna try Doncella?'

A pause, which I hoped could pass for a connoisseur's caution.

'*Real* Doncella?'

'You don't seem to understand . . .'

'Rare, huh?'

'We got connections. One case only left.'

'Look, why pay over the mark? Korbel's fine.'

'You got the card.'

'If you put it on the account . . .'

'Gotta try this. Forty dollars – worth eighty-five.'

'Well iced?'

'I put one in the fridge for you last night. Could tell you were the sort when you arrived I guess.' She left a short pause for the flirtation to caress, then to register her scruples added less enthusiastically: 'Fries?'

'No fries. Hot rolls.'

She turned, caught herself, holding aside her scarlet frizz.

'Mrs Slezak was lookin' fer you.'

Silence.

'Who?'

'Shelley's ma.'

It was fair to assume I knew about Shelley. Shelley in her bikini was the hottest story thereabouts.

When Shuleen came back to the table with the champagne in a bucket Rae Slezak was sitting with me. She had permed curls, used Clearasil, wore Dralon suits and polyester blouses. I'd rubbed my neck quite a few times, but it hadn't helped.

'If this was the first time,' Rae started up again.

'Glass for Rae?'

'Uh, well, okay.'

'Prawns're ordered.'

'Thanks.'

Rae was pleased about the glass.

'Like I say, if this was the first time I'd ride it, y'know? But she did it twice last winter. First time, she fetched up in Prince Rupert BC, fer God's sakes – halfway 'cross Canada. Told me she was headed fer Alaska. Heard there was jobs fer laundrymaids on the pipeline. How d'ya like that?'

I nodded slightly. 'Lotta kids don't know for Alaska you go north. She coulda gone south, got in trouble.'

Rae ignored that.

'Another time she was in Klamath Falls. Least this time she's come here. I gotta take her back or the school board'll dump on me. So the story is I got to escort her up to her father, and there's two days' couriering open if you want it. It's down-season, not many people, and tips're thin, but it'd help me out. What're you smiling 'bout?'

'Oh, I don' know, coincidence. Two days' couriering, huh? How much does it pay?'

'Hunnerd a day. One trip inna morning, one inny afternoon – like, late afternoon.'

'Cash?'

'I take checks, but it's casual shifts – maybe you could swing cash. Doncha have a bank account?'

'Hold it, I have to *talk*? What do I say?'

'Read a script. I got it here. Oh, thanks.'

Shuleen placed a second tulip glass on the white plastic table, took out the dripping bottle and showed off the label.

'Doncella 'eighty-five.'

Too much was happening at once. I examined the label. 'Is there a Lago Doncella?'

'That's the old name for Lake Hennessy,' Shuleen told me.

'The Doncella place is a mission overlooking the lake. Kept the name. Means virgin.'

'Well, *I* sure don't ...' Rae quipped, and the champagne splashed happily to her suggestive grin, which revealed a discolored tooth. Shuleen finished pouring, stayed to watch me savor it and approve, then went away. Rae Slezak pulled dog-eared sheets of typescript out of her shoulderbag and laid them down.

I spied idly through the wine.

'D'you cover Doncella?'

'Innerested, huh? Hey, look, don't get the wrong idea. You don't get to wade in the sauce when you're on the job.'

I got up.

'You going to Tacoma right away?'

Rae Slezak shrugged. Maybe men told her she was attractive. Now this guy seemed repelled.

'Uh, not exactly. There's a night bus outta Oakland, 'leven-forty-eight.'

'Got a ride? Friend o' mine left some kit here. He's checking in at the Napa Holiday Inn tonight.'

'Yeah, a girl friend, lives in Sonoma.' Rae cocked her head, sitting there with a glass of dregs, me holding the half-full bottle.

Script under my arm, I bent and filled her glass, boiling it over.

'Take it easy, big fella,' she murmured, getting her lycra-padded shoulder in the way of my groin.

'Here, put this forty-dollar wine away while I get my buddy's gear sorted.' I eased my mating tackle out of her reach. 'Call your friend, tell her you got a cab taking you to the Holiday Inn and you 'n' Shelley'll see her there. Okay?'

'That'd be nice, but you don't have to –'

I put the bottle on the table.

'Forget it, it was you reminded me about this thing. I gotta get the bags down there. Guess I'll have to go along too, say hi to the guy. Nine o'clock, okay?'

She shrugged and sipped, bucking an eyebrow over the glass at me.

'Sure, that's okay,' she said. 'Shelley likes cabs.'

I nodded.

'Yeah. I'll get the cab to ask for you, huh? Girls need more warning than fellas, y'know.'

Rae kept her eye on me, so I'd see she wasn't fooled.

'That's a'right. Whut's yer name, anyway, us takin' a cab together 'n' all.'

'Gilberto.'

Her mouth dimpled at the corners.

'A'right, Gilberto.'

I went over to the cottage and started packing, thinking how often it seemed to come down to women with me. Me and Gilberto.

22

THE NEWLY PURCHASED Gilberto baggage looked good: crushbag and international valise in slick black webbing emblazoned round the handles with Japanese ideograms in gilt. The factory gleam off it made the lobby of the Holiday Inn look tacky.

The clerk's eye tracked up from my new casuals to my Armani suit, to the haircut and back to my hardest gaze, which bore down on him, warning of strong customer resistance. He sighed.

The bags were deposited in a secure room behind the reception counter pending Gilberto's return and after waving mother and stray daughter off Cody Wallace cabbed it back to spend the night at his bungalow.

Next day I left the key by the door and did exercises in my bermudas on the patch of lawn outside. After a dip in the light show, I put makeup on the eye, dressed and went out for a morning stroll, waving casually to red-headed Shuleen as she stood on the doorstep of the auto-court office talking to a wetback in a blue lab coat.

Half a mile along US 29 I flagged down a cab and returned to the Holiday Inn, feeling a pang as the driver made change from Gilberto's last twenty and I turned to look for Rae's friend Moira.

There she was, sitting in a red blazer at a table covered in white linen behind a showcard saying *Valley Wine Tours*, marking something on a list, cordless phone tucked under her chin – like Rae'd said, you couldn't miss the glossy natural chestnut curls.

Face coming up as she felt me watching, vivacious eyes lighting up as if I were an old friend.

Hand in pocket, saunter over, enjoy the tremendous smile, showcasing pearls and rosy-pink tongue tip.

Her voice is pure happiness. 'Well hi! You're Rae's friend from the motel, right?'

'Lucky bungalow thirteen!'

Yuk-yuk-yuk, with crinkling eyes and wagging tail, the less they know you, the sweeter they play it.

Squeeze the lady-hand just a little.

'Bet *you're* good for business, Moira.'

Moira glowed modestly.

'Got to get along with folks on a job like this, let me tell you.'

'Here it is, breakfast time, you look like a million dollars.'

Moira rolled those eyes.

'Tell ya, I have my problems, hoo boy!'

'When do I start? Bin boning up all night.'

I produced the unread script from my hip pocket, but the heavy clatter of a diesel bus pulling up in the forecourt interrupted.

Moira was on her feet, grabbing papers.

'This is the Silverado Trail early run. There's another at eleven that Rae does, but I'm making switches to get you on the Highway 29 route – it's more straightforward. You check back here at nine-thirty, okay?'

She headed out with her clipboard and was joined by other blazered people. I saw them stepping into the bus, and turned away to find the coffee shop. Coffee smells hit me at the same moment as I felt one pocket empty, the other with a soiled five-dollar bill and a few coins in it, and crossed the lobby.

In a booth I nursed coffee and industrial donut, looking out onto a side street of Napa – nowhereland supermarket America. Over there the struggling sideshows, a loan shop, a chicken takeout, a pawnshop credit jeweler, a barred-up disco. On the sidewalk, a few slouching autoless loners – white trash, Latino, Afro, Indian – enjoying equal rights of losing in the golden state.

A headache forked up my cortex and I sat for a long time in freeze-frame, traffic rolling one way outside, mostly pickups and dusty automobiles, their colors muted by the tinted glass, but the shadows hard in the winter sun. Inside, round the leatherette and fake veneer planes of the booth, the air was refrigerated. Could get depressed again. Could go down there. It's a fine line.

A light blue patrol car with white stripes glided silently past the window, with a fat-elbowed officer talking into his squeeze mike. I leaned away. When I looked out again the patrol car was waiting on a red and the doorway of the jeweler was still grilled up for the night.

'Hi!'

Moira slid her trim can along the bench opposite, knees brushing mine. They were soft, friendly knees. She seemed like a real warm person with no hang-ups. Nice married parents, high school cheerleader, junior college diploma in commerce. My mouth blew the words out.

'How does it feel?'

A little cloud passed across the sunny sky of Moira's face.

'How does what feel?'

No suspicion in her. Looks even prettier confused. Some steady fella gave her the engagement ring with the blob of emerald on it. Probably as decent as her. Won't even know what he's got. On the other hand, some do. Is that it? She's in love? Still happens. Squeezing hands. Saying no. Shower. Church wedding. It's what keeps her soft. No, there's plenty soft whores yet.

'Mr Gilberto, you all right?'

'Huh? Oh! Yeah, guess it's a headache. It'll go away. Get you a coffee?'

'No need, they bring it. Listen, your bus is here now. You do four pick-ups round the hotels, but you won't have many people this time of season. Leaving town you do the introduction – don't hold the mike too close, remember. First stop is Trefethen, then you turn off down Oak Knoll Avenue – it's scenic along there. You read the script marked "Silverado Outline". The driver will stop at Clos du Val and Stag's Leap. You make the people feel at home at set-down and boarding, then you head back to US 29 and do Domaine Chandon. They have lunch there.'

I rubbed my neck slowly.

'Right.'

'The pace kind of changes after lunch.'

'I guess.'

'Robert Mondavi is the highlight, with a tour of the cellars. After that you read the Rutherford Bench outline. Stop at Charles Krug and it's time to go home. If you were a regular you'd field questions during then, but just enjoy the ride instead.'

'Reckon I will. It's time I took a look around.'

The coffee jug came. I refused a refill.

'I don't drink it on an empty stomach.' Pause, Moira watching. 'I ran out of cash and my cards're in the safe at the resort. Would it be okay if I got paid in cash today? Maybe half up-front?'

She only hesitated for a second, but I instantly gave in.

'Okay, forget I said it.'

I had my baggage transferred onto the Rutherford bus and said hi to a driver with a neck nearly as red as his blazer and a badge marked *Valley Wine Tours: Chuck* who gave me a look I didn't like, and Moira started marking on her clipboard that the US 29 route had departed on time, nice Mr Gilberto in charge.

23

I WATCHED THE doors.

'To tell you the truth, Mr Gilberto,' Jay Glimby said, 'my wife and I had this all planned for our grandson, Delmar. You see, it's his birthday today, but he, uh, had to cancel. As we came along the valley this morning and you were giving the talk, Elaine said, "Jay, that young man could just *be* Delmar. Don't you think it'd be kind of nice if we took him along to lunch instead?" I'm real glad we were able to get you to come along, aren't we, Elaine?'

The Glimbys and I were installed at a corner table of a restaurant at Domaine Chandon, next to a window with a knockout view east across rolling earth and vine stumps patched with clumps of dark holm oak to the snow-capped Palisades. The carpets were thick, the silver heavy and the waiters moved with dignity. There was a library-like air of concentration among the tour people, whether they were guzzling up the gastronomic food or sipping overpriced wines.

A waiter in a cutaway jacket, buttoned vest and wing collar with bow tie arrived and licked his pencil. Glimby's wife used her graduated lenses on the menu and ordered stuffed vine leaves, mussels, crab salad and rabbit stew. Jay Glimby said he'd have the same. Mr Gilberto said it was a good order and he'd have it as well.

'We always go with the market and the season,' Glimby said, with Elaine Glimby nodding. 'Whatever's fresh will be best.'

The maître d', swarthy enough to be Sicilian and stooped enough for a gravedigger, was making notes on his book at a lectern beside oak-paneled doors which gave onto a large vaulted entrance hall.

Something about the doors made me restless. I turned back to Glimby, who was handing the bulky tooled-leather wine folder back to the waiter.

'No need for this. I had my secretary order ahead last week. It's Mr Glimby, the 'sixty-nine vintage, for my grandson's birthday. Check with the maître d', would you?' He winked merrily. 'As a wine man yourself, I think you'll be interested in this.'

Glimby looked interested. He'd be paying a lot for the meal. He'd already told me he was an engineer, inventor of the Glimby self-locking bolt, royalties from which had turned the Glimbys into Berkeley Hills idlers and worn their skin sinewy walnut on the links. It was a case of the early stages of being very old. He a shrewd, silvery brainbox, glinty eyes peering over half-rims, the wife a hen sitting on him like a golden egg. Between the pair was a bond, as though experience had shaped them into a team, but the door made me so uneasy I gave no attention.

Elaine Glimby leaned forward and confided: 'Our grandson is at Napa Sanitarium.'

The maître d' moved away from his book, leaving the doors unattended.

'You're visiting?'

Both nodding wistfully.

'We'd never have taken the trip so many times if it hadn't've been for him,' Jay Glimby said. 'He likes it a little. At least, he usually does.'

'You've taken quite a few?'

They exchanged glances, and Elaine Glimby counted off fingers.

'Coming to see Delmar six years, trips twice a year – must be eleven, twelve times we've done the tour.'

'That many.'

I tried to sound surprised, but a man was in the doorway, in mirror glasses and a dark pinstriped business suit, very still.

'You lose count,' Jay Glimby said.

A caricature of a Mafia soldier appeared at the table. Everything about him – gleaming greased hair, dark-honey skin, bulbous nose, unhappy morning suit – spelled shame. The maître d' even muttered with shame.

135

The man awaited him in the doorway, fifteen paces away.

'Your champagne.'

No 'Mr Glimby'. No 'Sir'. His doughy fingers spread towards a junior holding a trolley with a silver bucket on it, out of which poked the mouldy head and stem of a wired bottle.

'A'right young man,' Glimby said to the waiter, 'let's see what you've got.'

Doughy fingers brought the bottle out of slushy ice, presenting it label-first.

'Doncella Grand Reserve,' Jay Glimby recited. 'Nineteen sixty-nine. Y'see? Ha! They say every year is a vintage year in this state, but there's no rules apply to this one. Show the bottle to Mr Gilberto, he knows wine.'

I leaned in, genuinely amazed. The label had a classic French look, plain white, speckled with brown rot and printed in wavy black copperplate. There was a coat of arms with a unicorn butting at a tower which had a little portcullis in it. On a mouldy red choker round the neck of the bottle you could make out the words *Brut Extra Dry*.

The man at the door scanned the room for the management and found the maître d'. He removed his shades. The icy look shattered my nerve. It was Gilberto.

Glimby was chortling as the sad man filled glasses as if with venom.

'This'll come strong, let's get in there. *Gesundheit*.'

The hand that held up my glass needed no guidance to clink. More than clink, it vibrated. Gilberto's nasty expression was directly beyond it, like an olive over the glass. I bowed my head and sipped.

'Very good.'

Glimby chuckled.

'Developed experimentally by Krug, the French champagne people, in the Fifties.'

'The wine boom hadn't happened,' Mrs Glimby said. 'Movie stars drank bourbon.'

The maître d' moved miserably away, relieving me of the view. Glimby prattled on: 'Krug even sold the place to a Russian aristocrat who supplied what champagne was made to Orthodox monasteries and churches in the area. The case this bottle came from must've been lifted off the back of a truck. It's a fluke property which gives superb body and flavor to Chardonnay so long as it's blended right. Of course a while ago some Hollywood character got hold of the place. Such is California.'

I stopped averting my face.

'What Hollywood character? *Who?*'

Glimby reacted to my harsh retort with a smile.

'It's not so bad. The winemasters do all the work. Ownership's not important, you should know that.'

'Yeah, but . . .' I suppressed an urge to grab the old man's shirt and pull him across the table '. . . . Have we heard of this guy?'

Gilberto was conferring with the Sicilian, half-turned.

'Oh, I see what you mean.' Glimby pouted and tossed a hand, sipping champagne. 'Who was it, Elaine?'

'Let me see, he goes back a while . . . Didn't he do that Nazi picture with Richard Burton?'

My mouth muttered the name, with me listening in wonder.

'Saul Kempinski.'

'That's the guy.'

Old wattles flapped, nodding, and toasted again, Señor Gilberto the Second toasting and gulping deeply, with hypercharged heart. Misery-guts was stationing Gilberto at a table for two by the door, ready for me.

The label reared in the foreground, with a name that shouted. I muttered it out loud.

'Lago Doncella.'

Glimby nodded wisely.

'Glorious colonial mission up in the Palisades, perfectly preserved. Overlooks Lake Hennessy. Wild spot, off the wine trail. They know us here, so we get a bottle.'

Using a pretext about the light on my food, I swapped seats with Glimby, devouring hurriedly to kill a persistent hunger, and drinking deeply to deaden my nerves. Arroyo's seat never was filled. I passed it unsteadily, wearing the Ray-Bans.

24

CHUCK EASED UP on the gas and said: 'So who we got for these bags to put down? Where they wannem?'

I was on the jump seat across from Chuck, desperate to get out. The whole prow of the bus was glass and I was looking through it at the approaching main street of little St Helena trying to focus. I picked up the mike and said clearly as possible: 'Mr Chilco? Come forward please?' Danny Chilco sold real estate in Santa Flora.

'Mr Chilco?'

The street clarified; I looked, and let it haze up again. The long dashboard of the bus was much more inviting. Stretch out there, get a few days sleep in this refrigeration. Don't think about it.

Chuck getting pissed with the temporary help.

'Whassup?'

Our chauffeur came into focus. Fleshy guy wrong side of fifty, straw hair thinning on a pink dome, thickset, with the belly that you got from chugging beers in front of many TV ball games. Took leaks during the Stat-Attack breaks. Smug feel about him, as if he had other connections, not of my kind. Gun club connections, barroom friends who were cops. I thought of Dylan's line: *This whole world's a prison yard, some of us're inmates 'n' some of us're guards*. Take care.

'Don't have radio, huh?'

Chuck said, 'No radio,' steering past gas stations, car lots, sports fields, leading into this hokey town. Lucky I'd woken, or I might've ridden back to Napa. But telling Chuck Mr Chilco wanted to stop when there was no Mr Chilco ... I wished I'd thought it out better.

'Guess the guy had the wrong bus.'

Chuck came back: 'Which hotel?', doing twenty now, and there were no marquees, no neon lights, no folksy inn signs that I could pick out.

'Didn't I say?'

'You forgotten?'

'Hey! Watch the road!'

Chuck picking up speed.

'I'll call the office from Krug's.'

'No!' I seized the chrome handrail, craning forward. 'Went clear outta my head but I got it now – the Hacienda! Where the heck is it?' I took my eyes off the sign I'd noticed and jerked my head left and right.

'It ain't far,' Chuck said disgustedly, braking.

The place with the sign on it had a flaky pueblo façade and a black fish-tank window on the street, with Coors and Budweiser signs lit up. An arched doorway had a bead curtain across it. The upper stories had dusty windows with air conditioners fitted over the sills and grimy lace curtains. Above them a row of protruding rafters made a lame stab at old Mexico. Some of the rafters had broken away, revealing plaster bases like rotten teeth.

The bus halted outside the doorway, which had the skull of a Texas longhorn fixed over it. A faded notice said: *Parking in rear*. A young squaw in an unbuttoned blouse, micro miniskirt and stiletto-heeled shoes barged out of the bead curtain, turned uncertainly on the sidewalk and wove away on wobbly ankles towards town.

'Shit,' I said.

It was too late. Chuck pulled the the door lever, pushed past me down the steps and went along to the baggage hold. I followed, showed him my bags, headed over to the curtain and ducked in. There were two heavy black swing doors which I shouldered through.

The barroom was long and dark and a cooler was blowing frigid air. A counter went halfway down one wall and two men were

139

hunched at it on stools. Another man was half-turned, talking with two girls. One of the girls, a Caucasian brunette about sixteen years of age, was perched on stilettos with her miniskirt jacked up to show her pubic tuft. Her unbuttoned shirt revealed hard young breasts. The other girl, mixed race and fully developed but puppy-faced, wore a skin-tight jump suit cut away into a string which twisted through the split in her shaven mound. Behind them, in a glade filled with yellow light and lambada music, another girl was lying naked on a podium of pink shag carpet idly splitting a pair of slender legs in the air. The pale disk faces of a couple of onlookers hung emptily outside the light.

The bartender was a swarthy Caucasian well past his youth, eyes puffed into sloping slits, his black shirtsleeves rolled up to the armpits to reveal two yards of taut tattoos. His bored, slanted look took in the guide badge pinned on my coat pocket (no blazer for me) and bounced up from it. He tucked away the glass he'd been drying, slapped the cloth over his shoulder with a practiced movement and leaned on the bar with doughy hands. I took a deep breath.

'You do rooms?'

He shook his head and used a sponge on the bar. The lambada beat ended and the long-legged girl on the podium got up, stepped down into a pair of stilettos and tip-tapped away, scratching her bare white backside, to sit at a table beside one of the disk faces. With the music off, the idling rattle of the bus engine penetrated.

'Dammit,' I said, tousling my hair. 'End a my shift. I gotta put my bags at the front desk for a few minutes. Till I get rid of the bus.'

The bartender's eyes said: Okay screwball, keep talking. The girl in the chopped jump suit was walking to the podium.

I made a sucking noise with my lips and glanced back at the doors.

'Where's reception?'

He showed me a short, dark look.

'Leave the bags inside the door.'

Out on the sidewalk, in atom-test brightness, I saw the bags outside the closed hold of the bus. The passenger door was closed too; Chuck'd shut it behind him for the air conditioning. Vague shapes sat motionless behind the windows.

Transporting the stuff broke me out in a sweat and when the bags were inside I sank back against the doors in the dark and savored the refrigerated breeze.

There were two bartenders now. 'Riders on the Storm' started up, and bulges of blood batted across my brain, helping things to slide into place. The bags are in the dive. I'm in the dive with them. Elbow the wine wagon.

Outside the light hurt your head. I beat on the side of the bus. The door sucked in, delivering coolness and the sour puss of Chuck, leaning on the wheel, keeping a lid on it till the customers were off his hands, then he'd sort it out with this joker.

I swung up the steps, scooped my Ray-Bans off the jump seat, plastered them over my face and moved the lenses near Chuck's thundery world.

'This Chilco asshole's passed out in the beauty parlor, how d'ya like that?'

'We're due at Krug's two-thirty.'

Chuck reached for the door lever, kicking the floor and getting a distant response from behind.

'No, hold it,' I came back. 'Guy's barfing into a Valley Wine brochure. Swears he got poisoned on the Silverado bus.'

Chuck's hand stayed on the lever.

'How'd he get here?'

'Who knows? Reeks a liquor. I better sort it out. You go onto Krug. I'll get a cab take him outta this joint to a resort and catch up right after.'

Chuck grunted, pulling the lever.

I dove into the bar. The second bartender'd gone. The coffee-colored girl was pacing round a cage of illumination on the pink shag platform.

I locked with the tattooed guy's sloping wolf eyes.

'Lunch hour fer me, and this guy I know showed me some very nice folding paper earlier.' I unclipped the guide badge and pocketed it. 'Seems he'd like comp'ny over at his room. Relaxing from a game.'

I got a looking up and down and a conniving grin.

'We-e-e-ll, first I heard a you tour people hustlin' fer the senior citizens!' The black eyes moved behind their puffy slits. 'Hey! Cigar!'

'An automobile,' I added. 'Need a chick with a ...' My voice trailed off.

The blonde with the slender legs who'd been on her back showing her genitals to St Helena's unemployed earlier was approaching stark-naked but for the high-heeled shoes, picking out a pretty path of her own, hips swaying just right, eyes looking down, a go-go angel. She even had the legendary blond beaver, a little shiny goatee of spun gold.

'Hi, I'm Cigar.' She leaned an elbow on the bar, set one stiletto over the other, and gaped with her fuchsia-petal mouth.

My mind raced and went calm. I forced deadness into my eyes, peeled off my glasses and grinned like she was the kid next door. Which she was.

'Hi, Shelley. Didn't Rae take you to sunny Tacoma?'

With makeup you could make believe she was twenty-one. Where ordinary women often have stubby legs, she had wands. Her hips and torso were sleek, but full enough to get a hold on, and her nipples tipped upwards. Her shoulders and arms had mannequin-school poise and her face was delicately made-up to give a firm mouth and put character in the eyes, which were tigerish against the light blond waves of hair. Tacoma wasn't her.

'Cigar's the name,' she muttered rebelliously.

'Hi, Cigar. Go get dressed, huh?' Rubbing a thumb on a forefinger. 'Got a nice daddy down the highway a piece wants you to dance for him.'

She pursed the lips and said: 'I only dance,' which had me glancing round to see if anyone was laughing. Leaning on the bar stark-naked in her shoes – but nobody was laughing.

'No one's gonna hurt you.'

'Okay.'

She went away, and I pulled out the five-dollar bill and laid it on the bar, watching her go.

'Steam beer.'

142

It tasted like gassy piss after Glimby's vintage wine, but the coldness and the fizziness braced the head-pumping. I watched how the little brown dancer peeled off her jump suit to Jim Morrison, how she moved privately, like a child doing aerobics in her bedroom.

Cigar came down the staircase off the mezzanine before the track ended, wearing a black leather biker jacket with padded shoulders, white hamlet shirt with the collar up, black leatherette miniskirt, and white stilettos. Her long hair, which had near-white sun-bleached highlights, was brushed into a blaze. She had a soft leather pouch slung over her shoulder, and arrived in a wave of patchouli, smiling as if I was her first date.

One mean sonuvagun had got hold of this package.

She led the way past the kid on the podium, who was on her back pulling herself pinkly open by the labia and flexing her puce guts at the lights. We went through darkened tables, down a passage smelling of toilets to a pair of fire doors with metal bars which she pressed.

I pushed the Ray-Bans up and took her shoulder, bringing her round.

'Gotta car?'

'One I c'n use.'

'Tell me 'bout Rae.'

She looked away through the wall.

'Nutt'n, that's all. No way I'm going back to *him*. I got friends here.'

I wondered what her dad did that she hated, and brushed it aside.

'Okay, it's your funeral.'

She put her hands on her hips.

'What about these guys you said were in some hotel? I wanna hunnerd bucks.'

I massaged the back of my neck.

'There's one guy. He's loaded, he'll pay more.'

She checked her Swatch. 'I got an hour and a half. I'm working, realize. You smashed?'

I stood tousling my hair. 'First we got to get my baggage

143

before that asshole bartender strips it. We take the car to the front.'

She led me outside to a powder-blue Porsche Targa.

'Nice car,' I said, and was rewarded with a grin that creased her eyes across her temple way into her hair. *Shame about the driver's license.*

'It's my boyfriend's.'

With beer breaking the wine's grip and jangling my spinal cord, I got gunned round the block onto the highway and into the slot where the bus had been. Each time she worked the pedals barefoot I looked across at her legs. When she turned the wheel I caught the bounce of a skyward nipple against the silky shirt. I watched her face in profile, the way her mouth rested in smiling position, lips pouted a little apart, glistening, and the boyfriend's bucket seat became the electric chair as I got an unwelcome erection.

Under the blue steer-skull, looking at the Hacienda, I flopped a hand about and said the hell, forget about the bags, and she accelerated down US 29.

'Know the Lago Doncella place?'

She flashed me an amused look, evidently getting a power trip out of driving me in this car, in this place, having met me in that bar, working. Labia pulling's work, and there's dignity in work.

'Whadda *you* know about it?'

'Mission. Lake Something.'

'Anything like that?'

She pointed at a ridge of oak scrub. Beyond it, on a shimmering blue slope far away, was a dinky white-arched monastery, roofs red-tiled, complete with mission bell-tower, slopes all round its stripy vineyards. It was beautiful. She said it was Lago Doncella. I felt ill.

'*Turn down there!*'

Porsche zooming, rubber mewing, she made the turn where it said WINE and accelerated us down a side road through gaunt ranks of vine stumps to a parking lot where we laid black stop-tracks outside a low white store designed in stuccoed colonial kitsch. Coins scooped from the bottom of my pockets sufficed to buy a low-grade sparkler from the fridge. I'd flushed the credit card away at the motel and I wished I'd flushed Gilberto away with it. Of course, Gilberto thought he'd flushed *me* away. I was going to flush this bottle instead, and go stick my head in one of the toilets in Lago Doncella ready for Dr Arroyo to work the handle. Back in the car I forced down my heartbeat and eased the cork out with my thumbs. Vapor wafted off the mouth of the bottle. She had her hands on the wheel, watching.

'You drink alla time?'

This was a teetotal stripper. And at sixteen still full of wonder, which was a shame.

'Nope.'

Laying a rug of lip over my lower teeth, I leaned the bottle on it and tipped a steady flow of wine into my gullet, making little clicking epiglottal noises as the contents ebbed steadily down green glass. In about ten seconds half the bottle was gone and she tossed her head.

'You're some kinduva big baby. How old're you, anyway?'

She followed my gaze out towards a snowy-headed eagle circling a crag on the wooded ridge. Its white head echoed the white walls of Lago Doncella on the foothills far beyond.

'You bin there?' she said.

''S where the client is.'

'You nuts?'

Her expression of gleeful reproach begged me to confirm I was indeed nuts, and I was only too glad to reassure her.

'Dr Arroyo,' I said, feeling the words leave me and hang there in the car, so that I hit the bottle again. 'Yep, he's my man. Beam me up, señorita.'

25

SHELLEY FLEW THE Porsche back across US 29, up to Rutherford, where she turned left, speeding through level vineyards towards humps of hillside resembling burial mounds. White peaks on the skyline lent the landscape a hygienic, mortuary feel.

'Bin exploring up here with your friend?'

'He calls it guerrilla fucking. Up in trees, in the gas station john, side a the highway.'

I offered no reply. We did a sloping lane at ninety and popped out abreast of a sheet of water stretching a couple of miles into the distance, a mile or so wide. It was a big, sudden aquatic statement that turned Shelley on; she wanted to pull in and admire it. A stripper who liked scenery.

'For*get* it!'

I curled the bottle out and scored a net in a Parks Commission garbage can, then we made a lightning tour round the south shore of the lake which ended when we came to a signpost marked Pritchard Hill and turned right, climbing through scrubland and woods and turning past a huddle of flat-roofed structures flanked by gleaming zinc tanks: a winery. About a mile past it, Shelley made one of her halts.

'See it better now,' she said as I landed.

She was pointing at a picturesque church and cloisters with adjoining buildings laid out on a ledge on the hillside opposite, separated from us by a ravine. The façade had a dozen rounded arches and windows with wrought-iron grilles, and the bell-tower on the church was capped with curling red tiles. The place stood in lonesome communion with the mountains, where presumably God had once been. Beyond the encircling vineyards were woods of maple, madrone, laurel and redwood and there was no sign of any weaponry or telecoms equipment. No glint of field glasses under the eaves of the belfry. No movement atall.

'Siesta time,' Shelley muttered, staring past me.

'You really do have an eye for scenery.'

She made a blushing admission.

'I wanna study art history.'

'How about art?'

Wistfully. 'Yeah, that too.'

It was a touching and horny moment which prompted me to take a mental snapshot of the scene because I had a sense of occasion about driving into Kempinski's place, and this was the establishing shot. Porsche, late model, dusty, parked on dead-end track on foothills bordering Napa Valley, northern California. In car: one passenger, male, disheveled and flushed of face as if high on wine, masked in Ray-Bans, short hair curly-tawny, dressed in canvas-tone Italian fashion suit with Burberry thrown in back. Driver: blonde, even-featured female with provocative mouth, great legs, whore clothes, about sixteen going on twenty-one. Car and occupants ought to look totally out of place, but the scenery's dramatic, the mission's a dream, and they don't.

'So, you're a friend of Kempinski the movie producer, huh?'

The way her mouth went, you couldn't tell if she was really smiling.

'I know him, yeah.'

'You in the game?'

'The movie game?'

'The poker game.'

'Sure, I'm playing him for the house. Let's go.'

'I only dance.'

'Sure, now drive.'

It wasn't many days past the solstice and the sun was already taking an interest in the hills over towards Marin County concerning a place for the night. I had roughly the same idea, and intended to spend it with my wife. The way I saw it, our marriage was not interfering seriously enough with her career.

I told Shelley to drive right up to the arched gates in the side of the cloister buildings, and she screeched up to within three inches of the studded oak planks, and backed off. Standing at the inset door, I made a series of authoritative rappings and handle twistings and got no reply. At the car, Shelley sank part of her main market product onto the hood, folding her arms.

'Is there a bell? What you smilin' at?'

I wasn't smiling, I was baring my teeth. It was painful to think that Arroyo might have been referring to any old Lago Doncella, or that old man Glimby might have got the wrong Kempinski. There might be many rich Kempinskis in northern California; Poles have done well in places other than Chicago. Maybe I was grinding teeth, too, because of the picture Shelley made, her peachy back end squashed on the hood of the Targa, the sunny front end irresponsibly amused, as if she had countless carefree years of vice laid out ahead. Before I could make any further move an Englishman's voice cut in from overhead.

'Please will you hold your hands in the air in the traditional manner so that I can make sure you don't have any pistols or anything?'

Moving out from under the arch and twisting my neck to ninety degrees, I had a long throat-mike view of a stubbled chin, bristly nose and slab of brown hair.

'Please?' he wheedled at Shelley, who kept leaning on the car. Men did her fighting.

I showed my palms and called up to him, sure of the address now that people were barring doors and telling me to stick my hands up.

'Where's Kempinski?'

'You'll find the door in the gate needs a good twist on the handle. There's a trick to it.'

We stepped into a classic cloistered quadrangle out of old Seville. The late sun was laying a black bell-tower shape across the flagstones, and the pillars of the cloister walks were doubled up in shadow on the mosaic floors. The ploosh of a fountain feeding its tank in the center of the yard was the only sound.

'Fuckin' postcard,' Shelley opined.

'The waterworks are all gravity-driven,' the English voice remarked, and we found a tall, horse-faced man stooping out of the shadows of a spiral staircase. He had a lantern-jawed graveyard look, boyishly tousled hair and big searching dark eyes that glared like craggy murder. He wore a rumpled white shirt, baggy green corduroy pants and sandals. Through his belthooks was knotted a necktie, and his fly showed a couple of buttons. Carried loosely in his hand, dangling towards the ground, was an old service revolver.

'No guns,' I pointed out.

'Good. I'd never dream of carrying one,' the stranger said mildly, poking the one he had deep into his pocket, 'except I'm alone here.' We considered the conquistador architecture he was alone with. 'Lovely, isn't it,' the deep voice said, 'a true soul could get holiness back in this place again in no time.'

I named Peppi's latest picture – *Chi* – and he angled the spooky glare down on me, reciting fussily:

'"A true soul could get holiness back in this place." It is indeed a line from the picture, yes. The whole *theme*, really. First film about healing and cancer ever, you know,' He frowned, seeming to realize what he was saying and who he was saying it to, and looked me up and down. 'May I know who I am addressing?'

I told him my identity was none of his business, but I could figure who he was. It came spilling out unfettered by much sobriety. 'You're Nevil Rayner that wrote this stupid DeWoers picture which is fucking up my life.'

He studied me with interest.

'I don't understand how you recognized me.'

'Sorry to break it to you, but people don't make a habit of quoting verbatim from movies they see in the mall unless they're the anus that wrote them.'

Shelley chirped out a laugh, and I winked at her coldly.

'This the trick?' she inquired, pointing as if he was hard to see.

'Nobody else is here. You only dance, remember?'

'What's *he* do?'

'He's a Limey with artistic pretensions.'

'You're being very silly,' Rayner complained. 'If you're here to deliver something, get it over with and be off.'

'Hey, genius, where's Peppi Harman? She here?'

'I am authorized to take any message there might be for Miss Harman.'

'Authorized, huh? Author-authorized?'

He didn't see the joke and poked his gravedigger face at me, long, spooky and suspicious.

'Do you work for Visionville, by any chance? Because if you do you're in trouble. You're obviously over the limit.'

'I'm not driving, she is.'

For the first time, Rayner took in the girl, without any appearance of interest. She turned to me, suddenly deflated.

'So where do I dance?'

I scowled.

'You don't, you've been conned. I needed a ride here and an entry ticket –' I faced the writer '– but there's no Kempinski and no DeWoers and no Peppi Harman, only this jerk. Where are they, Rayner?'

The writer peered at me.

'You name these names – who *are* you?'

'I'm Nathan Field.'

Naming Peppi's agent cheered me a little, as if it brought her nearer.

He frowned, unrecognizing.

'Do you know Reska DeWoers? Do you have any idea where she is? I'm getting worried to death.'

Shelley stamped a stiletto heel on the flagstones.

'Worried to death? I'm bored to death 'n' I bin ripped off. Gimme a hunnerd bucks' cancellation charge 'n' I leave.'

'Hold it,' Rayner said, tearing his gaze off me and striding after her toward the door in the gate that showed the powder-blue car crouching outside. 'Sign the visitors' book in here first.'

'Wha . . .?'

He took her arm and hustled her unceremoniously into the porter's lodge, slamming the door and turning a big key to the accompaniment of fist-bangings and muffled squawks of protest.

'So sorry about that,' he said, dusting his huge hands off as he came back. 'We don't want the girl getting any ideas – after all, you never know when a fast car like your thing might come in useful. As you may have gathered, we're having one or two problems with the new picture. Would you care for a cup of tea?'

I guess I was staring at him.

'Not much.' I sniffed the air. 'Has Peppi Harman been here?'

One of Rayner's lugubrious eyes got bigger, as if he'd poked a monocle into it.

'What *is* your interest in Miss Harman?'

I let a flush of anger pass, putting my hand to my brow.

'I own the Field agency.'

The other eye got bigger.

'The Field agency! You're her agent!' It seemed to boost his urge to snare me into a tribal drinking ritual, and he whined about it again. I had nowhere else to look, so followed. We went along in the shade of the cloisters, trampling mosaics that were part of Castilian history, to the opposite corner of the quadrangle, where we ducked through an arched doorway into a whitewashed terracotta-tiled office. Two recessed arched windows framed iron-grilled portraits of the lake and Napa Valley beyond. Rayner indicated a high-backed armchair, plugged in a kettle on the bureau and perched on the corner of a period oak desk placed to command the soaring view.

'This is where I've been doing the latest rewrite.'

He riffled heaps of typescript drifting up against a vintage Underwood.

'What's the problem?'

The screenwriter moped with a gloomy stare.

'Oh, nothing, merely the twenty-eighth revision in six months.'

'Take a script conference recently? Greasy guy with a dimpled chin?'

The dark look loosely included me. A slab of hand gestured at the world.

'Can't you hear the sound of axes grinding?'

'Flash character in a limousine? Traveling with the star?'

Rayner brightened up. He gave his weird, jerky, humorless laugh, slapping a yard of femur.

'You mean Peppi? Ah-ha! Ah-ha! She *should* star, she *should* star, only . . .' Pulling a sour-taste face, he swerved back into doubt. 'Trouble is . . . we'd be stretching history a bit far. Nardela Brú, her character, was only briefly the dictator's mistress. The way it stands, she's already paving the way for the Castro revolution almost single-handedly.'

'Was she a Communist?'

Rayner took his floppy lower lip, folded it and sucked. He talked intently, as though resuming a long, intense discussion with an empty cell.

'We portray Nardela as a woman of the people who has strayed into the oligarchy – a result of her looks and her intelligence, in that order. But her loyalty remains to the people she sprang from, and when she witnesses one of Batista's atrocities, she tentatively begins plotting behind his back for a better world. But it's clear the bloodbath that could break out if one-man rule is broken, and she temporarily loses hope. Through a chance meeting, she makes contact with the freedom fighters and finds love.'

'Seems fine. Seems terrific! Let's shoot it! Where's Peppi?'

Chewing the lip again, Rayner glanced darkly at me and back through the wall.

'But it's not fine. Nardela Brú was not a Communist, she was an upper-class flower arranger who never even worked a Catholic soup kitchen, let alone headed into the hills packing a Kalashnikov. No, we're going to write Batista bigger, better. We'll flash back to his early days as a Thirties New Dealer. It's actually quite an interesting angle. The picture will be wider in scope, more meaningful for export audiences. Batista in the Thirties had a fascinating challenge: to reform the remains of colonial Spain in an economic slump, while somehow dealing with the gambling industry in a lucrative way. It mirrors Franklin Roosevelt's dilemma in microcosm. I sometimes think we should use what we've shot so far, simply as the framework for a whole flashback drama – a *rahmengeschicht*. I love that device.'

He snapped fingers with a resounding clack, his mournful mask momentarily lighting up, but promptly groaned and clapped his hands to his face.

'It's no good, though, we'd be loading the story onto Hunker – it'd crush him.'

'Hunker plays Batista, huh?'

Rayner chewed a nail.

'He's okay while Batista's a fairly wooden, symbolic role, and not the love interest. In the current version that's provided by Nardela's closest revolutionary comrade – a part never played straight in Hollywood before. Asking Lenny to carry the love story would be hopeless.'

'Particularly since he had a serious automobile accident day before yesterday.'

Rayner squinted, bewildered. He had a few drinks to catch up, and he must have been pals with Hunker because mention of the accident shook him more than I'd expected. A melancholy stare went zooming past me into memories of lugubrious comradeship with the dusky idol, and his voice dropped to near nothing.

'So.' He looked down and shoved a heap of typescript off the desk, spilling papers across the terracotta tiles. 'Talk about releasing a film – this is releasing a writer. Probably a good thing Lenny's done for.' He nodded, lost in agreement with himself, flopping a greasy bang down over an eye.

'He's not dead. You may still have your picture – but not without Peppi. Where is she?'

Somebody suddenly blew a whistle at my shoulder and I whipped round in a panic, realizing immediately that Rayner's dumb Limey Sixties goodwill-store electric kettle had reached the boil. Something in me snapped.

'Keep your fucking tea,' I yelped, dancing to my feet and shouting over the head-splitting scream of the kettle. 'I've had enough of this script shit. How long've you been here? Did a maniac called Dr Arroyo turn up? What happened?' My hands waved angrily at heaven and I bawled rhetorically after them: 'Most of all, dear God, do you know – *where my goddam wife is?*'

Rayner didn't budge. The kettle reached an ecstatic pitch of tension and started to jiggle around, straining at its cord, threatening brain lesions with its screeching. Glaring at me with ugly resolve, he lurched forward, snatching up a hatchet from the fireplace and bringing it over in an arc towards me, diverting it at the last moment down with a violent thump onto the bureau, where it sank into the veneer, shearing the kettle's electric cord. The whistle mewed and died. The screenwriter let go of the ax handle and brought his eyes round onto me, alight with catharsis. I tried to steady him with sensible advice.

'Call Kempinski. Tell him Arroyo is the Brú woman's son and it's him hiring goons to try to wreck the picture. We can have the guy's visa rescinded.'

Rayner went to the door, leaving the ax handle pointing to the sun, and recited a couple of facts.

'The phone is down; Kempinski hasn't paid the bill for months. The place is up for sale, that's why I've got it.'

'So? We'll drive into Napa. Listen, the guy's got Peppi.'

Rayner looked at the ground, then up from under his brow, the cultured voice striking a new, vulnerable note.

'So you're Wallace, are you? Cody, is it?'

'Yeah, hi, the asshole had me thrown out of his car and shot. It's the only reason I found out about this place – he thought I was set to get a bullet through the brain. It was dark, the goon missed by about an inch.'

Rayner nodded reflectively and moved into the frame of the door, filling it. His voice came over his shoulder.

'Better follow me.'

He led the way out into the sharp chiaroscuro of the quadrangle, across to the cloisters tucked against the hillside, then ducked through another arched doorway and down various tiled passages that got progressively darker as we walked, until we emerged into cool, echoing blindness where he scraped a match and applied its flame to a yard torch, which flickered into life, sending shadows leaping away into high, rough-hewn vaults.

'Cellars. Cut out of the hillside. Power's off I'm afraid.'

He lit another torch for me and went ahead between stacks of wine cases which in the dancing light showed the legend: *Champagne*

LOW MEAN MEN

Doncella, Napa Valley, California, USA. Glass – handle with care. This way up. We passed dusty, antiquated pieces of bottling equipment and two parked pickup trucks, on through a big arch into a further hall and the musty smell of dozing wine and rock-face.

Looming in the shadows down each side of the hall were outsize oak barrels, tall as two men. Rayner pointed to a cable which ran along the ground from the winch at the prow of one of the pickups, and followed it past more tuns to one which lay out of kilter, with a surprise under it that stopped me dead. A shape very like a prone man was stretched out beneath the belly of the enormous barrel. I hung back as Rayner advanced into the shadows and knelt down, his flame highlighting a contorted mask which jerked feebly from side to side, its features unrecognizable. My flame showed where the front chock had been dragged forward by the cable, evidently lowering part of the mass of the barrel onto the tethered man's chest, pinning him down. The rubric *100 hl* was carved on the oak barrel-head over a chalked date from the preceding year: if it was full of aging wine, the tun weighed ten tonnes.

I'd been sobering up fast and my faculties became acute as I tuned in to Rayner muttering imprecations over his victim, threatening to get in the pickup and back it into the yard, talking about the place being deserted and how it would be days, probably weeks before anyone came, how the man's corpse would swell and burst and pollute the wine, because oak absorbed everything. The twisted face thrashed weakly and there was no reply.

I moved forward, and Rayner looked up at me with a long story in his eyes. The prone face was turned away from me. My mind raced.

'Is it Kempinski?'

Rayner replied by pointing under the next-door barrel. I poked my torch. It showed a Persian cat thrown there, shrunken and tufty.

'Jesus!'

The prisoner moaned, rolling his head. I saw the brainy brow, the downturned mouth, the jaw with its dimpled chin. He still had the pinstriped suit on.

'How long've you had him here?'

Rayner glanced down at the prostrate man, like someone considering a difficult engine repair.

'You see, the thing is, I don't speak Spanish.'

'He speaks perfect American.'

'I know, but when he turned up here, came into my office, accepted a cup of tea and started haranguing me about what I was planning to do to his mother's reputation, luckily I put my gun on him. They'd brought both their cars into the courtyard – a Mercedes limo and some Cadillac or other – and he ran to the window and shouted orders. I saw them transferring this tall woman with cropped hair to the Cadillac and, you see, I realized it was Peppi.'

'They took off with her?'

Rayner looked even readier to weep.

'I'm so sorry. This chap's driver hung around outside until I slipped him all the folding money I had and told him to go and wait at the hotel till he got a call. Haven't seen the fellow since. It was a good wad of money.'

'Must've been Gilberto.' I kept repeatedly checking on Arroyo. 'Why's he like this, for Chrissake?'

Rayner patiently explained.

'Because of what he said. He told them to go off somewhere in Spanish, and since yesterday I've been trying to persuade him to tell me where. But Peppi's his prize, you see. She plays Nardela – who *he* says is his *mother*. Can you *believe* it?' There were tears filling Rayner's eyes, huge, horsy tears, and the long gargoyle face was crumpling into a tortured plea. His voice creaked with emotion. 'The bloke's a madman, d'you understand? And now he's got *Peppi!*'

Again, I tried reasoning.

'Yeah, but Rayner, the guy must be half dead. You're looking at a major felony here. Go get a jack from the truck. Get *two* jacks. I'll check his pulse; he seems to be having difficulty breathing.'

Rayner glared, pushed me aside and went away.

I stood alone with my burning torch and what was left of the presence of Arroyo. His face was upside down for me, eyes tightly shut as if concentrating on inner agonies. I bent down to an ear, keeping the voice low, measured and trustworthy.

'Listen, you don't know me, but Rayner just said what's happening. I'm very concerned. He has a history of mental derangement, and I have to break it to you – he's murdered your cat.'

The eyes snapped open.

I groped behind me, picked the thing up by its furry tail and dangled it. The eyes met the face of the cat and bulged.

'Now, unless you tell us where Peppi Harman is being held, Nevil Rayner will certainly kill you as brutally as he killed this sweet innocent little pet.'

I swung the cat a little and the eyes followed.

The voice came in a tortured blurt, like a pothead fighting to hold the smoke.

'*Miranda.*'

Pause.

'Mmmn, yes, well done. I need more than that, though.'

'*El Paraiso.*'

'Ri-i-ght. So far, so good. Now tell me –'

My voice was drowned by the angry whine of a starter and the cavernous roar of an engine revving into life. The cable leading to the chock thrashed.

Throwing my torch and the dead cat aside, I lunged for the chock, but it shifted, forcing me to scramble away from the barrel as it lurched forward, producing a horrible yawn from the darkness as the treasured remains of a man's life were pressed out, and leaving me in the guttering half-light of my fallen flame.

The chock skidded away and halted. I snatched up the torch and sprinted towards the waiting truck. A high wedge of daylight slashed down into the darkness, exploding round the writer as he hauled open the warehouse door. Groping for a few ounces of breath remaining after my dash, I shouted into the dazzle.

'Arroyo talked!'

At the sound of my voice the lofty head came round, a dark skittle haloed with blaze, watching me bending over, heaving for oxygen.

I said: 'Get a jack to him, he might make it.'

'Where's Peppi?'

'Put a jack under the barrel.'

'You!'

'Both of us.'

He left the door and perched on the fender as I accelerated towards the tuns, now thrown into contrast by the shaft of sun. There were rusty bottling tables and thousands of cases of wine, the two ranks of tuns stretching away in their vault, one of them sickeningly lurched askew.

The jack was handy in the box, and I quickly got the barrel moving upwards, inch by inch.

'He's alive,' Rayner announced, staring down with distaste. 'The barrel wedged against this rock.'

I jumped in behind the wheel, pushing the shift to R.

'We get out of here and call an ambulance.' Rayner stayed by the passenger door, lingering vindictively around Arroyo, and I added warningly: 'It could save you from a jury trial.'

He got in, and we went to release Shelley.

'No way you're taking that friggin' car,' she snarled, cutting straight through to the point. 'That's my friend's.'

I held her at arm's length, indicating with my eyes Rayner's hand plunged deep into his baggy pocket. She glared at it and considered me with hatred. I hitched a spare thumb over my shoulder.

'Your friend is small potatoes, Cigar. There's an injured man in the cellars who could buy him about a thousand times over. He's your client, and you have an opportunity to succor him in his hour of need.'

Her gaze brightened, irresistibly delayed.

'Sucker 'im in the hour of need?'

It was a proposition that deeply appealed.

'The warehouse is round the back. Show the ambulance. Hold his hand in the back of it – he'll never forget.'

I chased Rayner to the Porsche. He had the driver's door open and tried to fend me off, but I barged him away.

'You ride jump.'

'I'm not going in any car with a driver in your condition,' he quibbled, wrestling with me.

158

'You think *I* want to ride with a homicidal maniac at the wheel? Get in and bag your head – we need each other.'

When I'd jostled him into the other chair I made a U-turn and accelerated down the loop of road and round the gorge, stopping at the Conn Dam call-box to wise up the operator. Then I used the Silverado back road to avoid meeting any early rescue vehicles and police cruisers. As we headed south I tackled Rayner about locating Peppi.

'Okay, where're we going? All Arroyo said was: "Miranda, El Paraiso". Is that some hooker waiting in a Reno hotel? Is there a town called Miranda? Do we have anything, in fact?'

He lay crumpled in the racing seat, looking over the rim of the door at the eastern fringes of the vineyards, all that bare earth with rows of knobkerries sticking out of it.

'Keep going south.'

'Okay, how far?'

'A long way.'

'How long?'

'El Paraiso is a resort in Indio.'

'Wow.' I drove down a very long road which stretched away in my mind towards scented groves of orange and lemon trees, with soaring date palms waving in the background. 'How come you're so sure?'

'I'm sure.'

I thought about it. About Nevil Rayner and my wife. About my wife and Nevil Rayner. Their knowledge of Indio. And I wondered what Miranda had to do with it. So I asked him.

'And what's this Miranda woman got to do with it?'

There was no answer. The writer's huge, buckled-up frame was still and his pod of a head lolled, slumbering.

The tank said full.

I drove towards Peppi with the sun letting me down in the west.

26

THE TARGA FLEW, and nobody tried to ticket me. Nevil Rayner slept as if torturing the son of Nardela Brú had been hard work. When he woke, he was depressed again.

'Who cares if this picture's another of the thousands, the tens of thousands, that never got made? DeWoers has disappeared, and Carmody thinks he's buying it out. We're into one mob against another.'

'With writers running like hyenas, thrown red meat now and again to keep them bloodthirsty, right?'

He looked hell at the dash.

'I'm getting out of this.'

'That has a familiar ring, Rayner, how many times've you said it? Why not make a video loop and save yourself the effort?'

His hands got to praying, clasped between his bony knees; his muzzle went up and he bayed.

'Oh God, take me back to the BBC!'

'I don't know, a screenwriter like you should be glad to do time: the eyewitness research could give you a top-rating jailbird mini-series. You'll be king of dirty realism.'

He didn't seem to hear, only extracted a couple of grimy capsules out of the bottom of his pants pocket and popped them both.

We made Indio long after decent people had said their prayers and hit the sack. Rayner came to life when I told him where we were but appeared too stoned to know the way to the resort called El Paraiso, so I had to stop at a diner, where they told me to

160

head north into the hills, which was some idea of being located in Indio.

After a few miles we passed signs to County Park, rounded a rocky outcrop and saw the place from about a mile away, laid out at the end of a shallow canyon. It was a colored blur at first, gradually clarifying as we approached to make a blue electronic waterfall, followed by the forty-foot-high legend: EL PARAISO SPRINGS COUNTRY CLUB, whitely streaming like studio snow. Then we were traveling along a grandiose avenue flanked by floodlit date palms, and there was more floodlighting at the sprawling clubhouse, which lay beyond a lagoon with a fountain playing in the center. Considering the scale of the operation and the electric bills, I once more regretted leaving Peppi's Lady Smith .38 in the sweaty hand of Saul Kempinski, not to speak of the drain on the Colorado.

We cruised the downlit drive which swung round the lagoon to low-line, glassy buildings and a cube of porte-cochere where a uniformed commissionaire touched the peak of his dictator hat and ushered us out of the car. We were processed through car-key removal, coat removal, entry-charge removal and – when we reached one of the coppertop bars – eardrum removal. Rayner used the gold card lodged in the breast pocket of his rumpled, formerly white shirt to lease us two whiskeys and we downed them contemplating the holiday crowd that was there, mostly casual singles dressed in singular casuals, milling in all directions round a stroboscopic, laser-beamed intergalactic war of a dance arena, with an overspill of tanned, big-jawed young studs congregating for solace near the alcohol. Supper was a Carta Blanca beer chaser.

Emptying the beers, we exchanged shrugs and wove our way back through the deafening throb, out through swing doors into the quiet palm-fronded reception area, where Rayner angled down like a drinking giraffe for a word with the cashier at the hatch. We hung around the lobby with the clientele coming and going, swing doors flapping.

'Lot of waiting in pictures,' I told the writer. 'Lousy hours.'

Rayner paid no attention, watching the approach of a man whose appearance had been haunting me: a big, swarthy Latino male with puffy eyes, hamburger cheeks, steel-wool hair and a white mustache, coming towards us wearing a baggy silk suit, painted tie and alligator pumps, acting as if he owned the place. I tried hard to look like a quiet, reasonable, six-foot, two-hundred-pound weakling who didn't want to die young and had definitely never seen this person before. He looked at the writer like a gun.

'Okay, what's the story?'

The voice was an extra shock. I'd heard it on a dark night on Highway 1, north of Santa Flora, joking about how I needed a major servicing following my car accident. And I'd heard it laughing scornfully at death.

'I'm Nevil Rayner.'

'So?'

'I work for Visionville.'

The management ignored that information and switched the look onto me.

'Who's this.'

The dead eyes conveyed an electrical charge that stretched my already taut strings to snapping point, and I had to fight to keep the tone of voice business-like.

'My name doesn't concern you. I have a message for Peppi Harman and I give it to nobody but her, in person.'

'We don' know any lady of that name here. Now if you fellas would be so kind as to step this way, we have a fine floor show coming up at one-thirty and the bar is open till —'

I pulled my arm out of the man's guiding grip.

'Where's Miranda?'

The postmortem look held me steadily.

'Who wants him?'

'Tell him we have Arroyo.'

The name pressed buttons. The man with the white mustache said, 'Okay,' and turned away, leading us behind the ticket office into a soundproofed executive suite done out in designer-desert – ochers, olive-greens and potted yuccas – with lavish carpeting, drapes and abstract paintings. The empty receptionist's desk was next to a pair of doors covered with green baize which our guide tapped with a hooked, bejeweled finger. He pushed the doors open and ushered us in.

The first thing I saw was stocky little Carl Carmody reclining on a couch in a safari suit and using a pick on his teeth, teeth which showed gold as his mouth fell open: he knew me from DeWoers's garden party. There was no lanky actress beside him, or anywhere else in the wide room, which had a swanky glass-topped executive desk set before a plate-glass panorama of the floodlit lagoon, the fountain and the date palms. Manning the desk was a fleshy individual who bulged over the arms of his chair. The cotton shirt was sticking to his pork, and the top of his head, slicked with oil like a black garbage bag, sloped directly down into his shoulders. With piggy eyes and tanned face all bulbous and sweaty, he hadn't got to where he was with his looks, but his manner was cordial when he saw Rayner, and he rasped a greeting that jerked his belly.

'Nevil, how's yer knighthood?'

He pumped his bulk out of the chair with surprising agility and reached out two stubby arms for a showbiz shake. When they'd got that over, Rayner presented me Tony Miranda and started to make my introduction, but I interrupted.

'Cody Wallace. I can exchange Dr Arroyo for Peppi Harman, my wife. Bring her in and let's talk a deal.'

Rayner arched an eyebrow appreciatively, the man with a white mustache looked thunder, and Tony Miranda perplexedly turned to Carmody, whose confident, smoky voice came from behind me.

'She's at my place, Wallace.'

'Let me speak with her.'

'She's there for her own security. My wife's a physician, she's in good hands.'

'Fine. She can confirm that herself.'

I reached past Miranda and plucked the handset off his phone, which had two ranks of light-buttons on it.

'What's the number.'

Miranda, still perplexed, turned to me.

'Now wait a minute.'

I starting hitting keys.

'Oh shucks, my fingers seem to be spontaneously picking out the

number of a late-man I know at the *Times* so I can inform him
that a beautiful actress he's interested in's been kidnapped.'

The man with the white mustache took a step forward and Tony
Miranda pressed a chunk of tanned ham on the telephone bar,
giving me a strong whiff of barber's pomade.

'Let's be reasonable about this, okay?'

I looked past the heap of talking meat.

'Where'd Rayner go?'

Carmody calmly took his Gucci loafers off the limestone coffee
table and tossed the toothpick into a ceramic ashtray two-foot
wide.

'Forget him. The picture's in turnaround, we got other people
working on the script.'

I stayed with the phone.

'Anybody tell the director?'

'Sure.'

'So where's the shoot?'

'Toronto, Monday. New director. New script.'

'No shit.'

'There's a distribution deal. This picture has a deadline.'

'Well, whaddaya know.'

'Most pictures don't get made, Wallace. This one will.'

'There seems to be some disagreement about that.'

Carmody replaced the toothpick with a six-inch cigaret drawn
from a green package, and used a doorstop-sized lighter. He spoke
a vapor of peppermint toxics.

'If you know where Luis Arroyo is, we'd like to know too. His
mother recently died, which is one of the reasons the picture I'm
taking over became possible. Unfortunately, he saw a very early
version of the script, misunderstood it, and decided to interfere.'

Miranda took the handset away from me and hung up, coming
to the point.

'Where *is* the crazy fuck?'

'Why should I tell any of *you*?'

The forces in the room shifted. Miranda and Carmody glanced
at each other, and Miranda checked a golden garbage can chained
to his wrist.

'Frankie's too busy to talk movies right now, aren't you Frank, with the one-thirty show coming up.'

The man with the white mustache flared his nostrils and sniffed. The two men exchanged looks like collaborating moray eels, and the face that had haunted me for days backed off expressionlessly. A green baize door folded him away, but the room was left infected. Miranda hitched his wide butt onto the glass desktop, his pile of face and neck glistening with what looked like the habitual slimy coating of a swamp animal. He'd got over being confused, and along with Carmody looked composed and ready to move, as if between them they'd reached some unspoken arrangement about what to do with me. He had whiskey eyes, baked in red flab, bloody red lightning across the whites, and a bleary, fiery energy behind them. They shone, like a kid with a secret.

'Willis,' he opened, and Carmody's voice corrected him from the couch.

'Wallace.'

'Wallace, listen, we're making the ultimate Cuba picture. They've tried it before, but never like this. Castro's going to come tumbling down, and we're going to go roaring up – in lights.' A rumbling, passionate tremor came into his voice. 'I got five mill riding on this. I sold a piece a the golf course.' He left a pause for the information to penetrate, as if I might fall down, and his chubby muzzle jerked into a ghastly rictus as he muttered: 'Carl's last picture grossed forty-two million and I got big points in the new one.'

Carmody's voice said: 'Last but one, Tony. Anyway, forget the money, you're doing this one for the truth, right?'

As soon as I heard the word 'truth' I knew that Miranda was Carmody's sucker. He laid a sweaty paw on my arm and I stepped back from it. 'So?'

'So give us this mad fuck Arroyo back and we'll have the White House ship him back to Nicaragua. His people *rammed* Leonard Kerry Wills's *car*.'

'He had *me* shot in the *head*, and your guy Frankie was there. Where's Peppi?'

Miranda pressed air at me vigorously, wobbling his blubber.

'Frankie went along with it only so far, Wallace. The guy's Cuban like Arroyo. They see things differently from us.'

'Yeah, luckily he sees crooked, puts his gun outta line.'

Miranda clawed at the air again.

'Frankie was along to *stop* that shit, Wallace. He'd never've taken a shot at Peppi Harman's ol' man. Look, to prove it, Frankie was the one brought Peppi back here, to the new owners of the production.'

'*Kidnapped* her back, you mean.'

The fat man stood there in a shrug with his hands open.

'Wadda's it matter? Long's she's okay?'

There was a pause while I contemplated paradoxes: the dreamy lagoon outside, located fifty miles from the nearest natural supply of water, and the scintillating fountain with its visionary lighting, contrasted with the porker who owned them. Considering these absurdities brought me to a decision.

I said: 'Arroyo is in hospital in Napa. I imagine he'll be transferred to Berkeley or San Francisco in the morning. They'll be treating him for several broken ribs, internal lesions, bleeding, lung and heart damage ... the guy was half-dead last time we met. Your friend Nevil Rayner tortured him within an inch of his life, trying to find out where Peppi was.'

Miranda and Carmody glanced at each other and Carmody cursed under his breath, bending forward to concertina his unsmoked cigaret in the birdbath and getting to his feet, which did not make a huge difference to the scene.

'Come see your wife.'

He went to the door and Miranda simpered at him – it was amazing to witness the star-struck narwhal's eagerness to lose his capital.

'Don't forget, Carl, my jet, eight tomorrow night: Toronto via bourbon and blow jobs, pugga-pugga-pugga-pugga-roooo! *Baff*!' He did a blubbery little war dance on the spot and ended up slapping his fist into his hand, making you wonder what dire fate lay in store for those unlucky playgirls five miles high in the prairie skies.

Carmody said: 'Lie down, Tony,' and left.

I followed the short, purposeful shape of the producer out

through the reception office, down a private passage and through a side door into an executive car park divided from the main car park by a wall of palm shrubs. We went under a billion stars to a late-model, open-top Mercedes and soon were accelerating away from the resort, past the glittering studio snow and the bright-blue electric waterfall, speeding towards Peppi, which made me full of compassion and warmth and thankfulness. I appraised Carmody as he drove: he had an Irish dome of a head, salt 'n' pepper hair round a midlife-crisis bald patch, and a decent, rugged face with scrawny eyebrows, battered, turned-up nose and resolute chin that would have looked fine on an impoverished bog-land priest. He didn't look like a renegade. I spoke across the fragrant windshield slipstream.

'Why buy out DeWoers? What's the big thing about this picture?'

He threw me a canny glance.

'I've raised twelve million dollars on a one-word pitch.'

'Oh yeah?'

He grinned coldly down the highway and barked the word at it.

'*Coobah*!'

Again, someone naming the jewel of the Spanish Main evoked a flourish of drums and castanets and scents of rich tobacco. The rushing, perfumed night that smelled of oranges, the smoothly cushioned acceleration of Carmody's Mercedes, the warm anticipation of taking my wife in my arms, swept me into a reverie, and I echoed the idea aloud. 'Twelve million on one word . . .'

With a paw draped over the wheel, Carmody poked a toothpick out of his safari-shirt pocket and tucked it against a canine.

'All I had to say to the right people was *Coobah*! Let them get the script looked at, they came in. Points were sold in three weeks.'

'Was it the strike at Visionville prompted your buy-out?'

He bucked the suggestion off with a movement of his head.

'I did it after seeing the latest edition of the script.'

'Yeah, I heard from Kempinski it was script problems.'

Carmody stared grimly down the tracer bullets of the highway's white line that he was straddling with the headlights.

167

'She sold Kempinski on her version. See, *Chi* made nothing. The studio's broke and the unions know it. They want redundancy insurance. Originally, I personally backed the Cuba picture. After I found out the abortion we were making, I tried to bring her round. Took her to dinner with a coupla flesh 'n' bone Cubans – more than she'd spoken to in the whole of her life. They filled her in on a bit of reality, 'stead of the dream-shit Rayner was serving up, time after time, getting worse and worse as it went on.'

'Nardela Brú single-handedly paving the way for Castro, was how he put it to me.'

Carmody eyed me askance.

'Rayner said that?'

'Uh-huh. After Arroyo'd been to see him.'

Carmody shook his head.

'Jeez, that Arroyo guy!'

'Where'd he come in?'

The producer made a sucking noise past his pick.

'After Reska said to forget it, I invoked my buy-out clause. Showed a rewrite to some of the Cubans who love this nation. Trouble is, you never know who people will get to cover a script for them. One of my investors in Miami showed it to somebody, who showed it to somebody, and a copy got to Arroyo – he's some kind of trade attaché in LA for Nicaragua.'

'And the son of Nardela Brú.'

Carmody muttered bitterly.

'How d'you like that? Some horse's ass comes out of the wood-work, the son of our movie's *heroine*, screaming 'bout suits and injunctions and murder.' He took a hand from the wheel and jabbed it emphatically. 'Get this: he's not mad 'cos we're making his mother out to be a cocksucker and a whore, but 'cos we're dressing her up as a cross between Jane Fonda and Joan of fucking Arc.'

'She wasn't a Communist, though.'

He twisted the rim of the wheel, fuming.

'Yeah, okay, it's true. Historical fact goes, Batista was in love with this woman in the early Fifties, nice kid, plenny potential 'n' that's all. The original treatment we bought off Rayner and

Lemuel used this real-life story of Batista and Nardela to give a taste of the dynamics of Cuba at the time: floor shows, high life, game fishing on one side, pissed-off peasants gathering in the hills the other, with the clashes that sparked off between them. You c'n imagine it: the landscape, the color, the conflict, great production values, and ready to dump on the kids when the shit finally hits the fan, Castro is out – however it happens – and Cuba is turned into part of the USA again, like we're winning a whole new beautiful state that'd been lost. Can you imagine the critical mass it could build? The tornado of dollars'd hit us? All right, that was a year ago. When we started to shoot end o' last month, we were making a totally different picture – a picture that could've been personally vetted by Fidel to use in guerrilla training school, fer Chrissake.'

Suddenly I was angry.

'And you want to buy it out? Shit, man, he's rubbed out thousands of people who bugged him, up to and maybe including the President of the United States. He even pointed hydrogen bombs at Washington. You think he'll worry about getting rid of an indie executive producer like you? You out of your mind? When me 'n' Peppi get outta here, we fly to Europe and don't come back until this whole crazy package is flushed down the toilet.'

Carmody nodded grimly.

'With patriots like you around it's not surprising we're going down the tube.'

'Patriotic! What's patriotic about making a movie about some crummy dictator who turned his country into a whorehouse?'

Carmody flashed me a black look.

'You one a them, huh?'

'Bullshit I am. Castro wiped out anyone in his way – piss on him, too. But he only did it after the Bay of Pigs, which was a goddam invasion.'

Carmody nodded eagerly.

'Yeah? And then what?'

'Well, he threw in with the Soviets. Fuck him. Which would *you* choose, Carmody? Free whorehouses or free tractors?'

The producer took his eyes off the long, straight, vacant road, glared at me with an expression of surprising conviction, and made a speech.

'Forget the whorehouses, forget the tractors, focus on the *free*. The man you call a dictator put Cubans into housing in the Depression, when a lot of decent Americans were living in cardboard boxes. And when a *real* fink of a dictator like Franco declared Spain neutral against the Nazi empire, Batista lined up Cuba with the Allies. When Castro first made trouble, started killing priests and police officers and burning public property, Batista practised forgiveness, gave him an amnesty, let him outta jail – did you know that? And anyway,' he tailed off somewhat sheepishly, looking at the highway again, 'Batista's Cuba was good enough for Hemingway, so lemme tell you, it's good enough for me. We're gonna make a picture that'll blow that commie bore in Havana right outta his clogs.'

I muttered darkly: 'Like you arranged to blow DeWoers right outta her house, huh? Only way to teach a tough lady a lesson, right?'

He shot me a reproachful frown.

'No way I engage in shit like that. I have twelve million dollars gets me my way.'

'Helps to send in a Cuban pit-bull, though, to help the lady make up her mind.'

Carmody's confident manner faltered, the way I'd heard it do on the telephone in a cab in the city.

'You talkin' about Frankie? Tony Miranda sent him after Arroyo, play along with him, keep him from doing too much damage.'

'Oh yeah? So is that why I saw him at Reska's place, waving a gun, the night it was torched?' That scored. Carmody shot an uneasy glance no higher than my waist, and murmured: 'Yeah?'

'There's too *much* fiction flying 'round this production. What the hell happened there, Carmody?'

'Fact is, Arroyo got outta hand.'

'Don't blame it on Arroyo. Frankie was there – I saw him. You sent him in, didn't you, Carmody?'

The producer swung the wheel, throwing me off balance and swerving us into a palm-fringed driveway, pulling up at a guardhouse where the shape of a security man showed in the door and saluted us through, remotely operating a traffic bar. I followed Carmody's gaze to a glade of lights which discreetly illuminated a fronded, low-line condominium complex. He guided the car into a parking space in front of floodlit lawns where sprinklers were doing their nightwork.

I said: 'Really a one-word pitch? How much were DeWoers's paintings worth? Five, six mill? Isn't that about the difference between Miranda's stake and what you need?'

He twisted the ignition key off and draped an arm down the wheel, facing me squarely.

'Listen, Wallace, you're lucky to be alive. Try and stay that way, huh?'

'Is that a threat?'

'No, just I hear you were in very bad condition the night before DeWoers's place tragically burned down. You'd been drinking for weeks, all it needed was to drink through New Year's and you were in dialysis and brain damage.'

'So, you figure I hallucinated Frankie.'

Carmody splayed his hands and gave me sober attention.

'It was only you there.'

'Who told you that? Others saw . . .' I trailed off, thinking of DeWoers on the floor, Lemuel tending her, Hose, Kempinski engrossed in the carpet, Hunker and Peppi too stoned to see . . .

Staring at Carmody, thinking it through, I caught sight of a movement over his shoulder, a sliding window at a balcony over the lawns drawing back, a conservatively dressed woman filling the frame. Her voice snaked eerily across to us, tremulous and strained.

'Is that you, Carl?'

The husband could read the wife's tone, and he blanched, craning round.

'What is it, chip?'

The voice rose to a muted wail.

'I called the club. You'd gone.'

'What's up?'

He was out of the car, with me vaulting the door as he slammed it.

'That Englishman!'

We were loping across the lawn, soaking up spray, making for the glowing glass porch behind a low row of shrubs that lined the pathway. The voice came from above us now, sobbing.

'He took Peppi with him. Oh, Carl, I'm so afraid!'

27

THE APARTMENT DOOR was open, and Carmody's woman was inside, stranded in the middle of a wide, multilevel reception room, clasping her drained face as though it, too, might be violated and taken away. She was long-limbed and elegant, with a string of pearls supporting an ivory crucifix, and the décor matched her style: tasteful French Empire, with moulded bookcases round the walls packed with substantial hardbound volumes, and a short black Bechstein with a book of Beethoven sonatas ready on the rack. The way of the woman and the quality of her surroundings gave an unsuspected new dimension to Carmody. Clearly it paid an educated man to move in plain wrapping in the Hollywood money game. His private world seemed to have everything to offer except my wife. I asked my echoing question, like a priest leading a weary litany.

'Where's Peppi?'

The Carmodys embraced – she was inches taller – and looked bleakly at me. The producer murmured introductions and Tina Carmody broke away, fretfully massaging her brow.

'He came about half an hour ago. Peppi was in my bathrobe, dog-tired, but still looking fabulous, you know how she does. How lucky you are to be married to her!'

I nodded, appreciating the whiff of motherly normality. Good manners felt warm and comforting.

'Did you examine her? How broke up is she? These guys' – I indicated Carmody – 'are trying to make her work Monday.'

Tina Carmody took a deep, shuddering breath. Her Ivy-League accent became more pronounced as she composed herself and adopted a professional manner.

'Considering her condition, she's okay. At this stage she just needs plenty of old-fashioned rest, which she's not getting racing round Palm Springs with that awful man. He's wrong in the head.'

Carmody cut in using a gruffly expert tone, shaking up a menthol tampon and poking it into place.

'Neurotics write better, quote Sigmund Freud. Bad emotions make good movies, quote Aldous Huxley. We're forced to rent people like Rayner. Trouble is, they're dreamers. Give 'em a chance they write dangerous totalitarian shit 'n' you end up with a nightmare. Where'd he take Peppi?'

His wife turned and cast him a scolding look, clicking her tongue, and he sheepishly dumped his unlit cigaret into the fireplace. She nodded at it.

'That's what upset me – he didn't say. I was in and out warming soup for Peppi and preparing her room, and next time I came in here, they'd gone. He didn't even let her dress.'

Through the half-open balcony window, the darkness beyond the lawn sprays took on a new menace. I called out to it.

'She's out there in her robe with Rayner?'

Mrs Carmody's oval, well-bred cheeks flushed.

'He'd already told me she was in danger being here and, well, being English, and a writer, and so earnest, he's got credibility up to a point and I . . .' She turned to Carmody, the professional manner crumbling, her voice tearful. 'He even advised me that I should get away as well . . . I was confused . . . He said terrorists were sabotaging the new picture, said they'd burned down Reska DeWoers's house . . . Peppi backed him up . . . But just to slip out like that . . . I . . .'

She used a handkerchief produced from her sleeve and her words hung in the air as she snuffled, strangely discordant with the lush, illuminated greenery at the window, the gentle hiss of the garden sprays, the culture which graced the shelving and the old-fashioned refinement of this frightened woman's voice.

Carmody made an exasperated gesture.

'There *have* been problems. I've been trying to contain them in Burbank, not bring it all spilling out here. This is my sanctuary. This is my *home*.' He looked pleadingly at his distressed wife, who asked miserably:

'What kind of problems?'

He was candid, almost shamefaced, like a schoolboy being carpeted.

'There was a strike at the studio before Christmas. We took a hard line and started setting up key parts of the shoot on location in Canada. When the unions found out what we were doing, fanatics evidently broke security, used contacts and got a copy of the script to the Cubans. Somebody high up in Havana decided the picture wasn't going to get made. A Soviet guy out of New York flew out and offered Reska a good price. He had a new treatment on offer, which threw shit all over Batista, and when I turned it down these heavies came out of the woodwork.'

I listened to the fluency of Carmody's domestic fiction with the uneasy complicity of a fellow married man.

'Is Peppi in danger?' his wife asked, applying a fine self-denial.

Carmody glanced my way, conveying a plea not to spill the beans here, not in his haven of love and learning, on the thirty-foot Chinese rug possibly paid for by his wife.

'None atall; we've squared it with the Cubans now.' He poked a toothpick from his shirt pocket and jabbed it into his teeth, growling round it. 'Next I make a vampire picture.'

'Dr Carmody, do you have any idea where Nevil Rayner's taken my wife?'

She had pure eyes, dazed by anxiety, that went distant with inner reflection.

'I can't think of anything he said. You know, Mr . . .'

'Wallace.'

'Of course, Mr Wallace, you know, it's distressing the way they've disappeared, but I'm not sure Peppi's life is in danger with him. The opposite if anything.'

She transferred her uncomfortable look to her husband, who gave a gruff briefing that made her blench.

'He's crazy about her.'

I said: 'He's crazy, yeah, and if he's crazy about Penelope Harman that's not reassuring. Was he in the Porsche?'

Tina Carmody frowned. 'A little light blue thing with a rattly engine?'

'That'd be it. Goddamit!' I slapped my pockets and clawed my hair. 'He must've picked the keys up off the bar at Miranda's. No good calling the Highway Patrol, it's borrowed and I've got no idea what's on the plates. There must be hundreds like it in the valley.'

A burbling in the corner was broken by Carmody, who raised a warning hand as he listened.

'Peppi! Where?'

For seconds the world was concentrated in the tiny electronic disk pressed against Carmody's earhole, then he was putting the handset back on its rest and hurrying towards the door.

'She's at Palm Springs airport – she snuck a call from the powder room. Rayner's trying to charter a plane. We may be able to catch them there.' He bridled, looked round at his wife, and went back to embrace her. I saw her high forehead sink against the tousled side of his head as I left the apartment, intending to wait in the Mercedes while he did his husband work. She seemed like a decent person to work for. In the parking lot I groped in my pants for Gilberto's wallet and found by the light of the floods that it contained a bundle of credit-card receipts.

I asked Carmody how much money he had as he yanked the door shut and roared the car into life, throwing us violently into reverse and jack-knifing us out into the avenue amid yowls from the radials.

'If the asshole really is trying to charter a plane,' he shouted, 'that takes a while. We may just make it.'

We cleared the gates, swerved onto a curveless highway and passed other sets of condominium walls and gates and signs to resorts and country clubs which blurred as we picked up speed. I pitched across the rush of night.

'How long's Rayner been in love with Peppi?'

'He got obsessed when she was the sick girl who got healing.'

'In *Chi*.'

176

'Yeah, Rayner wrote it, and the girl he had in mind and Peppi Harman got confused, I guess. Didn't you know?'

I looked out towards the hills behind Indio, which cut a black outline against the stars, as if Earth was keeling out of orbit into the universe. I had an image of the lanky Limey in the darkness, sweating over his script by candlelight, staring haggardly at a vision of all the loveliness he did not possess, and writing it into his tale. *Chi* was the story of a beautiful, conventional woman who learns she has a fatal cancer of the lymphatic system and sets out on a spiritual quest for healing. Peppi had set the character up as chic and beautiful, but reserved, frigid, repressed, and costume and makeup helped her with a superb impersonation of the wasting-away process, so that by halfway through the picture she was a living ghost. At which point she is forced through desperation into self-examination and a search for ways out of death. Involvement with a music-making woman, consulted as a last resort, plus a strange love affair with an unsettling shaman (Hunker), effect the transformation of caterpillar into butterfly. During the action, Peppi had moved from the physical to the spiritual, achieving at the climax a subtle transcendence of gender, before finally succumbing to the cancer, surrounded by her healing spirits, and leaving not a dry eye in the house. It'd been the kind of performance which made it impossible to imagine any other actor in the role, and sitting in Carmody's open car, racing through the Palm Springs darkness, I realized how completely the gargoyle-like writer must have fallen for Peppi's incarnation of his vision. I recalled him, too, earlier in the day, bending over the prone Arroyo, muttering threats and imprecations, and my gut rolled.

'How did he look to you when we came to the club?' I shouted.

Carmody shrugged.

'I guess the usual way – gloomy, weird, half stoned. He was hanging round Visionville from the start, and he's always been like that. All I noticed tonight was how he lit out right away when I said Peppi was at my place. It didn't occur to me he might be headed there, although he knew the way, because we had a couple of script conferences there last fall.'

I said: 'I think he's more than weird, he's having some kind of breakdown. He assaulted Arroyo at Lago Doncella – the guy was crushed under a barrel in the cellars. Apparently Rayner'd been torturing him.'

Carmody punched more gas, and we sprang forward.

'Guy needs help.'

'I called Arroyo an ambulance. My guess is that they could've stabilized him, but he was in a bad way. Nevil Rayner's going to get a close look at a jury trial and I'm going to be the number-one witness.'

Carmody was gathered into a concentrated scowl, straight-arming the speeding car.

'Me too. I'll be on trial if I get my hands on him. Anything happens to Peppi, there's going to be trouble, because the insurance on this picture is all shot to hell.'

'Yeah. That's what I care about too. The picture.'

The producer cast me a bitter look. Barely slowing to take the corner, he steered us onto a section of divided highway and rammed his foot back down. A gale built up over the windshield crest. I asked him how far the airport was.

'Maybe three miles to the Gene Autry Trail, then about two from there.'

I checked the digital clock lit glowing green on the dash.

'It's one-fifteen. Reckon he'll find a plane?'

'Sure. That's supper time for some folks round here. It's what I'm worried about, particularly after what you just said.'

'Where's he headed?'

Carmody shot me a glare of bright anger.

'Mexico. And I don't understand it, 'cos she disappeared three days ago, but somehow he found out where she is.'

'He's her writer – she needs him. Surely you don't need DeWoers any more.'

'I do if she's making the picture.'

He stamped on the gas again, and the liquid-crystal speedo notched up a hurricane against the night.

FOUR

28

ALL I REMEMBER clearly of the flight is the landing – a vicious series of bangs that smashed my pelvis into the seat and wrenched the seat belt across my waist – the furious buzz of the feathered prop, and our choppy progress across what felt like a ploughed field but was desert hardpan scattered with tumbleweed.

Somewhere over the Mexican border Carmody's expert handling of what he called his toy plane had settled me into a kind of prayer for Peppi's safety, and after a long journey through dreamlands I had finally fallen asleep and been interrupted during an angry fuck with a *chava* who was naked except for bulging bags of jingling coins strung around her hips. Our rough progress across the airfield provided a cruel parody of the butting motions of knee-trembler sex and I stared round at the dawn scenery like an extraterrestrial.

'Aguános!' Carmody shouted across the clatter of his prop. 'State of Sonora!'

We deplaned near a shabby hangar in uncanny silence. The only other sign that we were at an airfield was the drab windsock which hung limp against a peeling pole. No customs officer appeared, and immigration control seemed to consist of a decaying five-barred gate which gave onto a dirt highway. Dawn was coming damply, and a haze blurred the sandy crags which fringed the plateau. Struggling holm oak scrub made a rough perimeter round the field, and there was no sign of human habitation, only a strong, gastronomic whiff of thyme.

181

'This where Rayner came?'

Carmody extracted his head from the cowling, where he was immobilizing the engine, standing on a little folding ladder.

'Must've sent his pilot back. This is where he was headed.'

Finding our land legs, we walked for an hour through scrub past mean peasant holdings, then through *barrios* made of corrugated iron and plywood scraps where no one stirred but chickens and dogs, and into genteel, palmy suburbs of barred villas slumbering behind high courtyard walls. From these comfortable slopes we moved down towards the river and the center of town, which was barely beginning to stir. A big fountain was running in the fronded central square, but little else. A few stray mutts were snarling over something torn from a heap of garbage, and somewhere behind the tangle of shutters above the barred shops a baby was giving its mother the primal scream. Near where we stood, water gushed out of a grille and made a rivulet down the gutter at our feet, washing away pieces of fruit box and other market junk. In a corner of the square we found an open bar where two ill-shaven grandfathers with the stature of boys were nursing brandies across a zinc top from an impassive Zapata with bushy black mustache and flowing white apron.

Carmody set the pace with rapid-fire Spanish, and soon he'd learned that a *directora gringa* was set up in a camp a few kilometers along the rail line towards La Colorada. We could find a cab at the station, along the main street.

'She's already famous,' Carmody muttered, 'shooting a picture that's s'posed t'be in turnaround.'

'Rayner knew.'

'Rehired the bastard behind my back.'

'Hope my wife found clothes.'

'She had Tina's pyjamas.'

Twenty minutes later we'd wakened a young driver where he slept at his wheel, fed him a coffee from the station bar, learned his name was Sergio, aged fifteen, and were riding in his improbable 1962 Dodge Coronet with tail fins and chrome-plastic shooting-star gauges on the dash beside the push-button transmission, through a region of tattered industrial sheds and bedraggled brush along the riverbank, approaching a run-down marshaling yard where overgrown rail lines splayed around a derelict freight house. A scattering of army-surplus tents had been pitched on wasteland where rails had been torn up, and there was a posse of horsemen wearing jeans, T-shirts and red bandanas wheeling round a caboose hooked onto pieces of dowdy rolling stock that looked as if they'd been mothballed before Pearl Harbor. Puffs of smutty steam billowed up over the battered roof of the freight building.

Catching sight of our cab, a few of the riders wheeled their steeds and peeled off in our direction. At a perimeter gate of rusty woven wire, two civilians in jean suits and ponchos stepped out of a shack and stood in the path of our cab, leveling shotguns. Before Sergio could say '*Que pasa!*' one of the gunmen had cocked his weapon and loosed a double-barreled volley which clanged against our stout Sixties Detroit steel, sending a quadraphonic echo effect across the landscape and throwing Carmody and me onto dusty rubber mats, shouting orders across a gargle of rubber on gravel.

We crouched and hoped while pandemonium took over, our car made like the Coney Island Whip, shotguns blasted, a horde of hooves pounded, and the long, potent chugs of a departing steam locomotive spoke across the yard.

When Carmody and I ventured our heads above the parapet, Sergio was gabbling about his *madre*, his *creador*, his *patrón* and his collectible *carro*, but he'd managed to get the wheel under control and was speeding beside the freight depot's rusty wire fencing, with the gunmen left behind and the handful of horsemen wheeling back into the yard. Now we could see a vintage express locomotive with its tender clearing the freight house under a cloud of vapor, hauling three ancient passenger cars and the caboose.

Carmody craned out of the window and fell back into his seat pawing dust and sweat off his bewildered expression.

'Jesus fucking Christ I don't believe it, it's the fucking train!' He searched for it again, half-blindly, and fell back. 'She scored a train. She got down here and scored a fucking train, the loco, the whole thing. She's got a crew camped out, hired extras for guerrillas for God's sake. I don't believe it, she's shooting the picture.' Turning to me with a wild stare, he shouted in no more than a hoarse whisper: 'Toronto was a blind. She must've been working on Mexican licenses and clearances and bookings since right after I invoked my clause.'

He seemed to come awake to his own revelations, rediscover my presence, and experience sudden shame, which shut his mouth and set his jaw muscles flexing. Almost immediately he lunged forward, slapping Sergio's head and shouting orders. I looked past him out of the rear window, which made a miniature Cinemascope screen, and found myself viewing the stuff of movie legend: parched tawny landscape with swirling dust, billowing loco in foreground hauling vintage train, tailed by posse of mounted raiders. The image held, with Sergio keeping a just-right distance ahead as if we were a mobile camera unit. As I watched, a rider stood on his stirrups and reached out for a grab-iron at the back of the caboose, swung a leg over his galloping mount and vaulted onto the train. Carmody rounded on the scene and gasped.

'Great take, but there's no camera, no truck, no crew!'

It dawned on me.

'Could be a tryout, but I think DeWoers's got herself a real-life mutiny!'

Carmody stared, his eyes filled with a childlike astonishment which knocked years off his face. Before he could beat me to it, I said: 'We have to nail 'er on the fly.'

He brought the eyes onto me, fascinated, and breathed in echoing understanding.

'Jump it!'

He dug out a roll and thumbed sawbucks into the front seat, explaining fresh instructions to Sergio, who wailed in protest but moved the Coronet near the open rail track, which ran alongside us, although not for long. We had been on a gentle gradient; in a thousand yards our road plunged away down to the riverbank. Sergio braked until the express locomotive was drawing ahead, its pounding shafts and drive wheels blurred a few feet from us, followed by the coal tender and the relative quiet of the trundling Pullman cars. The lead car came by, then another, until you could hear the yips of the horsemen with their red bandanas bent near the necks of their mounts.

We bawled at Sergio to match speeds.

He held steady with a metal balcony, I forced open the car door, tucked a hand under the lintel, breasting the door away, and waved a loafer over the racing track. The shoe hung two feet short of the stairplate. Carmody bawled at Sergio, Sergio jerked his wheel, the car barged up onto the shingle, my foot found the plate, and my hand the post. The car swerved away. I made it onto the railcar stoop and turned to grab for Carmody.

Sergio was yelling about the approaching bend, losing his nerve. Carmody had a hand under the car top, shouldering the door open. His hand came across the blur of railbed and wristlocked with mine. Sergio managed one last barge with the car, Carmody scrambled aboard and the cab swerved on a cambered bend, veering out of sight.

The train skidded to a shrieking, thumping, juddering halt, throwing me against the car's front railing, where I stared down at the connecting hoses and couplings suspended over oak ties and rubble. There was a crashing of china and tipping furniture inside, followed by the stamping and whinnying of many horses and the shouts and arguings of twangy Mexican voices from the rear. I followed Carmody in.

An old-world carpeted smoker ran the width of the car and about a third of its length, furnished with worn button-back couches, side tables and tasseled lamps, all askew. Carmody was at the far corner where a half frosted-glass door gave onto a corridor and cabin doors. We listened. Many boots were tramping on the stoop at the tail of the carriage. The room behind offered no cover, and we were unarmed. Carmody shrank back.

The handle of the nearest cabin gave, and I stepped into shaded gloom, trying to quell the craziness under my ribcage. We'd clearly walked in on a strike which in superbitch style Reska'd whipped into a rebellion. No macho Mexican troop of extras was going to stomach her kind of shit, above all from a *gringa*. The cabin door burst open, its latch smashed by a single booting from a huge man with a dirty red bandana, impassive black Yaqui Indian eyes and a snarling mouth.

'*Pos, que chingados tenemos aquí?*'

My hands reached for the ceiling, prompted by the muzzle of an unbracketed Lewis-type machine gun that the extra held poking into the compartment towards my gut. A belt of shells curled heavily past the oiled gas chamber of the weapon and over his shoulder. It was not worth worrying about whether this movie property contained blanks or not. If the weapon didn't jam, one short burst from anything it had would hack a man in half.

A shriek came from the next cabin, and the woman-fear of it jerked the extra's head. A microsecond opened and without thinking I filled it by kicking the barrel casing against the doorjamb and pinning it there, grabbing an old service pistol out of the Mexican's belt and bringing it up unsafety-catched near the ivory snarl, blessing its miraculous explosion as I squeezed it next to his ear, sending the mouth rearing back with a howl. The machine gun loosed a deafening volley past me into the cabin, blowing one of the plate windows spangling-jangling out.

Firing each way along the corridor, and throwing a shot out of an open window at circling horsemen, I went to the next cabin and halted at the door. Two men in guerrilla outfits were in there, and one of them had his pants round his ankles and his grimy T-shirt rucked up, exposing tawny buttocks vigorously butting against spread-eagled white thighs, with the strangled face of Amaryllis visible past his waist, across the bedside table, being shoved and bumped against the window. Another Marxist freedom fighter was arguing with Peppi about her shirt. He raised a pistol to whip her with it, and without thinking I threw a shot at the back of the curly head, which tore open splashily, and slumped away, leaving Peppi shrinking into the corner, clawing her cheeks, and me gaping at what I'd done.

The rapist distracted me with a shout – '*Lárgate, estoy occupado*' – and I steadied my smoking weapon to train it on the top of the tangled head and fired. A piece of the neck and its spine blew away and the bare legs crumpled like a blasted chimney stack. As he fell he vomited an arc of it, leaving red muck slapped across Amaryllis. She screamed, climbing on her back across the tabletop up against the window shade, her sex crudely exposed. A snarl had me whipping round to face the huge machine gun. The rapist's open, nerveless hand was palming a revolver at me. I grabbed and brought it up firing. The machine gun wavered as the man behind it was punched against scarlet splashes on the corridor window. He went down.

'*Aguas! Agáchense! Quítense de aquí!*'

Scrambling and shouting, Mexican hillbillies veered away from the doorway, downtrain. The corridor was clear, with the connecting door hanging half off its hinges, showing the smoker beyond. Carmody shouted:

'Wallace! I control the corridor from this end. There's cavalry outside, we need artillery! Walrus is up front.'

I looked down.

'I'll bring this!'

It weighed about forty pounds. The gas-regulator snout was a good six inches long. I glimpsed BRNO etched below the bolt. The cartridge belt hung cold as a slave-chain round my neck. I pulled the barrel vertical so I could turn the weapon round in the narrow space, and deeked into the smoker. Carmody was at the far end, flattened against the wall, wielding a smoking service pistol in each hand, with other handguns lying near his twill slacks and Gucci loafers, injured men sprawled around. He ducked under a shattered window and fired over the ledge twice, shouting racial slurs. Peppi shouted and I called back.

'Crawl out here!'

I snaked my way upcar, dragging the Czech gun. Carmody called from under the window:

'They're busy with something in the caboose, could be the payroll. This lot're holding us down ready to take the engine.'

Peppi was crawling towards me with sputum dangling from her mouth, dragging Amaryllis, who looked too shattered to throw up. There was an exchange of fire ahead. Carmody stared round.

'Where's DeWoers?'

Peppi spoke up wretchedly.

'Rayner took off with her right before this.'

'Off the train?' Carmody barked back.

I shouted at him across the trilling in my ears.

'Forget it, we have to get the loco moving or these crackheads're going to wipe us out.'

The women took cover in the lee of the open car door, holding pistols. Carmody eyed the machine gun respectfully and waved uptrain with a thick arm, his face flushed, burn-marked, exhilarated.

'There's a ladder up the back of the tender. I'll need flanking fire. You work that pig, pal, I'm going fer it.' He bent low and plunged out of the door, over the gangway between the cars and into the one ahead.

I hauled up the gun and poked the sights over the jagged glass next to me. A half-dozen rifle-wielding revolutionaries were cantering around on grassland against the climbing sun, hanging low on the offside of their mounts. Bracing shoulders and feet, clutching the weapon under my armpit, I squeezed.

It rattled my brain and chattered my teeth, the barrel battered against the sill, the cartridge belt jerked across my back, and two horses were brought down in the mayhem. I cease-fired.

'*Arríba! Arríba! Muévanse!*'

Other horsemen appeared, yelling.

Arranging belt-slack, I squeezed a burst, and another. It was like breaking rocks: the World War One-vintage gun was for defending a mountain, or unthroning a king. Face screwed up, teeth grinding, I squeezed again. A horse screamed and did a head roll. Gunplay came from further up the train.

Peppi shouted and went out the door before I could grab her.

'I think he's made it!'

Firing a parting burst at the stragglers, I shipped the gun round my back and followed with Amaryllis.

The next two cars were empty. We made our way up to the platform at the end of the front car and I parked a ragged, shivering woman inside the door. Peppi scuttled up the ladder on the back of the tender and disappeared over the rim. It was a jump from the tailgate onto the ladder, and the weight of the gun sling dragged me back from the grab-irons. A bullet ricocheted off the wall with a zinging clang. The last few rungs were made on nerve-power, and crawling along the catwalk over the coal was an invite to get shot in the butt.

Walrus was down in the engineer's cab in basketball jacket and jeans, twirling an iron wheel beside the firehole door. Carmody and Peppi were kneeling over a prone man in coveralls. The producer looked up grimly.

'They clubbed him. He's bad.' He waved over the side. 'Fireman's dead.'

Walrus shouted from the controls in Parisian.

'Feegured it out! *Allez*-op!'

He worked another wheel, hauled on a lever and the loco shifted, sending a reverberating clank down the couplings. Excited protests came from behind, along with volleys of shots.

From the catwalk, I jumped into the coal and scrambled up a scree in the corner, which took me high enough to heft the gun barrel's cheese-grater casing onto the rim with the butt braced. The loco made a slow, humping whoompf-whoompf and picked up speed. Half a dozen horsemen were fanning out each side of the caboose, kicking and whipping and whooping and making plenty of ground.

'*Arríba! Arríba! Arríba!*'

29

THE LOCO ACCELERATED and left the horsemen behind.

Scarfing the cartridges, I hefted the gun on its sling, shinned down the ladder onto the railcar and got my shoulder-blades pressed against the wall beside the open door.

A quick look inside showed Amaryllis had made an upturned davenport into a barricade, and was kneeling with a gun poked over it. I fired over her head, blowing out windows and opening sky in the wallpaper. She stared round, her face with its hooded eyes a mask of horror that brought back to me the panic in DeWoers's basement. Her accent came hysterically shrill.

'Gemme outta here!'

'Wait!'

At the corner, looking downtrain, there was no sign of the horsemen. I darted across the doorway and checked the other flank.

Another shot blasted from inside.

Two men swung down from the overhang and landed lightly, snatching bowie knives from their teeth.

I had time to bring the barrel round and fire into the sternum of one of them, hammering him off his feet and propelling him back over the railing and down under the bogies, but the other, a calm-looking sage with a rabbinical beard, muttered: '*Di tu ultima oracion, pinche gringo,*' and plunged his dagger at my shoulder under the collarbone, aiming expertly for the subclavian artery, hitting me hard. I brought the barrel casing up under his elbow, poked the gas regulator into his wooly armpit and rapid-fired a burst.

Soft-lead slugs angled through the unlucky actor's left lung, sheared the jugular and the windpipe, cut grooves in the cervical vertebrae, ploughed through the cerebrum and punched jagged holes in the left parietal bone of his skull, whacking gray brain matter, tissue, bone, scarlet arterial blood and soggy hair against the ceiling. The warm carcase careened away, astonishment fixed on its dead face. I glanced down at the dull brass buckle and hasp on my gun sling. A bright scratch-mark showed where the knife-point had stubbed against it. I turned to the door, shouting over the chatter of the engine.

'Low on ammunition – get outta here. We ride loco and unhook the train.'

Amaryllis emerged from the car, blotched with powder burns and groggy on her legs. She stared at the racing grassland, keeping her tattered clothing together with a fist, the motion pressing sweaty cotton against her. Coagulating gore was all over her throat, and her face had a look of frozen shock, as though most of her mind had escaped and left it behind.

'Okay, follow me!'

A burst inside to cover us, and another at an angle up through the ceiling, bringing a piece of sun-dazzle through racing vapor.

With the gun slung behind me I jumped over a blur of sleepers onto the ladder, moving aside onto the toe-rail to make way.

She dropped her gun and took my outstretched hand, but still hesitated, grasping the rags at her stomach. I had to bawl over the clattering wheels and the rail-hiss and the huffing.

'Move, *hermana*!'

She stared at the ladder and then down at the coupling and the connecting hoses and speeding track. I jerked her hand. She let go of her fistful of cotton and jumped, seizing the ladder beside me with both hands. Her shirt fell open and her skirt tore loose to luff against the car railing. She clung half-naked to the ladder and sobbed. I bent across the gulf and retrieved a corner of cloth, but as she clutched at it, gore spilled over her lip and she fell away. My free hand scraped uselessly against her sleek black hair and she was whisked down. A second bullet clanged against the tender and I sprang across onto the car platform, pirouetted and smashed my back and the gun against the wall.

Bring the gun up and poke it through the door.

Click.

Retract the barrel casing, jack the wing bolt, and poke it into the door. Squeeze.

Click.

Bring the gun back and jack the bolt again.

Out of the doorway, a pistol, impelled by an extra with crazed eyes and graveyard teeth, muzzle veering toward my face and firing, me in fury jerking my barrel casing upwards, ramming the foresight block against the jean crotch and ripping it back. The diverted blast injuring my right eardrum and cutting a hot parting in my hair.

'*Ay! Cabrón!*'

The man going down, preoccupied.

I picked up his handgun, a Colt-style with four more rounds, and prodded it round the jamb, squeezing off a shot.

Light landings on the platform behind me, a hard forearm latching round my neck, two more pinioning me. The machine gun wrenched away.

'*Adios, campañero!*'

Strangled, I watch a hunting knife as if in freeze-frame, glinting its blade luridly against the smoke, incongruously bright and ambitious, and I croak to somebody up there for mercy, my bladder draining hotly.

The point hovers. I live on the point.

'*Ya me chingaste!*'

As the knife-man yelled, his blade twitched and dropped away and I gazed at my executioner curling up on the iron floor, eyes clenched, teeth and gums bared, noticed Peppi on the ladder, taking a bead from behind a smoky muzzle, understood, and wrenched my captor round into profile for her. The movement brought my better ear towards the gun and I heard it utter, felt the grip on me fail, punched my elbows back and sprang clear.

She fired another shot at the falling figure, tried again, and sent the handgun twirling high out over the racing plain. I bent forward and chivvied the kneeling, buckled-over figure towards the open gangway gate, hustling him with shoves and kicks until he was clenching the gateposts, staring down at skimming track. The butt of the Colt broke each finger's grip and my knee pitched the actor forward across the coupling, where he clung to the connecting hoses beneath. I took up the espadrilled feet, wrapped an arm round the ankles and rammed him downwards. He somersaulted under the carriage. Only two bony hands and taut-sinewed forearms remained in sight, gripping the hoses. One hand released its grip, reached forward and reclasped, bringing part of the upturned, canvas-colored face into view. Dark, shiny eyes stared distantly up and met mine.

I looked past them at the coupling. The two latch hooks were linked with a screw and a tensioning lever. I fetched the Czech gun, held it by the barrel casing and used its butt to pound the lever, which dislodged and stuck out. I hit it again and made it quarter-turn to a position below the screw-bar, where it was invisible.

At the doorway behind me, no movement. I reached for the Colt and passed it across the bogie-chattering gulf to Peppi. Then I bent down to the coupling, noticing that the distant eyes and the straining hands had gone.

It was hard labor, hammering the lever clockwise with the forty-pound bulk of the machine gun. One of my Armani pant legs was sopping, and blood from cuts on my hands made them slither. My ear whistled. Each full turn required five or six butt-blows from varying angles.

Crossing onto the tender ladder, I swung the gun against the hanging lever. Nothing happened. I used all my remaining force to pendulum the gun so that at the end of its swing it knocked the lever upwards. Nothing happened, except the gun slipped out of my grasp and disappeared under the racing bogies of the Pullman car. Somehow I stayed on the ladder. Gripping a rung behind me, feeling the hem of Peppi's jeans brushing against my head, I jabbed at the lever with the ball of my foot, pushing it past vertical and over toward three o'clock. The coupling links parted.

The connecting hoses burst and hissed – and the train drifted away with men dying, one slumped half castrated, on the tailgate.

I looked up at my wife and we exchanged an arcane, exhilarated gaze of darkness before she fitted her feet and hands the other way round and climbed over the rim of the tender. I watched her thighs moving, half fainted with exhaustion, and lost the grip of one slippery hand on the ladder. When I got over the rim of the tender, she was a tangerine-crested butterfly against the valley of coal, moving under a ceiling of vapor towards the loco.

We met at the far end and looked down. Carmody was kneeling with his ear against the engineer's face. Walrus was at the boiler, working valve wheels. Both men seemed possessed by the mana of the engine. I climbed down onto the hot, waffle-iron floor of the cab. Walrus looked over his shoulder, streaked with sooty sweat, and shouted across the din.

'Can't stop ze fucker! 'Ave to un'ook. Carl says ze guy's raving 'bout green fields and his *madre*.'

He worked a wheel one way and then the other, and peered into a gauge. Stepping across the delirious engineer, closer to the heat, I took in the array of iron controls, dismissed the idea, and shouted.

'I already unhooked.'

Carmody got up, eyeing me with a leer, making me vaguely aware of my suit and the blood, urine, coal dust and powder-blast on it. Walrus pulled open a metal chest, revealing a heap of tools, and grabbed Carmody's arm. They rifled through files, screwdrivers and hammers, pulled out box wrenches and knelt down to work on a swivel-plate arrangement in the floor which had securing bolt heads caked with grease and coal dust. I snatched up a wrench, fitted it over a bolt in the plate and shouted to Peppi.

'You make coffee!'

Walrus grunted over his wrench: 'She c'd blow!'

The vast tonnage of iron rocked and bucked as if it'd grown legs. We hauled steel. With an angry squeal, the Wallace bolt shifted. The engine moved into roaring excess, lurching and trembling in its exertion. More bolts squealed and turned. Each was threaded into the swivel-plate underneath so that once dislodged, it wound free of the assembly. As the loco reached a pitch fit to blow the rivets off its boiler and fling off connecting rods, we loosened the last of the bolts securing the tender.

Carmody picked up the engineer by the arms, hoisted him over his back, and ponderously climbed the rocking ladder out of the cab. I used a grab-iron on the wall of the tender as Walrus turned the last bolt to its limit. When it reached the same height as the others, all of them arrayed like a ring of toadstools, the tender eased free of the engine and Walrus jumped across the opening gap to join me. Connecting hoses strained and burst, blowing steam.

We looked over the hurtling track at the engine cab drawing ahead in a trail of wasting steam, taking with it the fury of fire and smokestack, valves and pushrods, the array of spigots and gauges round the furnace.

Peppi took my hand and we listened to the hiss and fuss of the company of coasting bogies. The landscape was a wide, featureless scrubland basin fringed with rocky hills, purple mountains lying far beyond, footing a cloudless heaven. The sun was climbing, glinting dully off the boiler of the unmanned locomotive and highlighting golden billows at its smokestack a hundred yards ahead. I pressed the hand in mine.

'They shot Amaryllis. She fell onto the line.'

In a minute the locomotive was a dwindling shape in the distance and we were alone with the tender's long, tackety-tacking rallentando. Out of the faded thunder of the engine grew a faint mewing of patrol-car sirens. Peppi's brow rested against my shoulder.

'Arroyo told me you were dead.'

'The cat is.'

30

WE COASTED ABOUT a quarter-mile like shipwrecked mariners, listening to the bogies chattering. Ahead, the locomotive had dissolved into a swirling mirage. Behind, empty track stretched away in a long curve to disappear round the shoulder of a hill capped with a tusk of bare brown rock. I thought bleakly of the carnage I'd wrought with the miraculous prop from BRNO. As we waited in stunned silence for our motion to end, I saw a head blowing open, an appalled woman's face, felt the steam-hammer effect on my shoulder. But it had all passed. When I stepped down onto the sandy earth, my body framework had no rigidity left and it collapsed. Peppi staggered from the ladder and fell beside me with a sinking sigh.

Carmody landed heavily, Walrus after him, but spared most of the bloodshed, they had fight left. Carmody paced around, snarling.

'No way I get taken by the cops here. They rob you, lock the cell and throw away the key.'

'I'm illegal,' Walrus said.

We listened to the far-off keening, which echoed from all directions. Carmody halted, cupping an ear.

'Every crooked cop in Mexico's homing in. Let's move it.'

I heard myself say, 'Where's DeWoers?'

'Fuck DeWoers, she's finished. I take over the production from here.' He shaded his eyes, pointing. 'We have to cut out to the highway and flag down a car. When I get back to Aguános I raise hell about those fucking extras. How she ever hired a bunch of murdering thieves like that I'll never understand. I'll sue the state of Sonora for everything it's got.'

Walrus said: 'Zees could be great publeecity.'

Which made Peppi snort into the sand.

'There speaks a future producer,' I muttered. 'Listen 'n learn, Carmody.'

But the little man was staring away past the tender with a visionary gleam lighting his face. Walrus and I followed his gaze. Sensing a revelation, Peppi propped herself wearily on one arm.

Three riderless horses were grazing twenty paces behind the stationary tender, bitted and bridled, with Mexican blankets and saddles on their backs.

'They followed us,' Carmody uttered reverently.

'Try catching zem.'

'I take the Appaloosa,' the producer murmured, moving forward like a sleepwalker, adding: 'Pinch me.'

We watched him walk over, scoop in the reins, each horse placidly allowing itself to be gathered and led.

'They cooled down good with the run,' Carmody called.

I helped Peppi to her feet, somehow mounted the pinto and hauled her up behind the high rustler's cantle.

Carmody announced that the cops could take care of the engineer he'd nested into the coal, then wheeled his horse round, kicking it into a gallop, with Walrus taking off after him, heading off at an angle towards town.

We watched them go, and chose for ourselves a couple of rocky hump-backed hills at the edge of the plain. We set off at an easy canter because our bones had been shaken enough and our spirits were sickened.

We crossed the plain, traversing a two-lane highway that ran north-south, parallel to the railway line, and climbed a slope to a hollow surrounded by saguaro cactus and high brush that offered shade. There we tethered the horse and bellied down on a breast of rock that had a panoramic view back the way we'd come. Right away, toy patrol cars set up miniature dust plumes north and south, turning away from the highway to cut across the plain and meet at the solitary coal tender, which made a little black cube in the shimmering distance. After a delay while the specks made movements we took to be the transfer of the injured engineer, the groups of cars headed off the way they'd come. Stretched out side by side on warm, smooth shaded rock, not eager to go wandering and encounter a police force crazed by killings on a *gringo* location shoot, Peppi and I joined hands and slipped gratefully into oblivion . . .

The stallion whickering woke me, and the sight of Peppi's strong, even-featured face asleep on her stacked hands gave me a dislocated impression of being at home in Santa Flora, reunited. But I was aching from being face down on a rock-face somewhere in the Sonora desert, and the sun had climbed high enough to make my ruined suit damp against the rock. The deep clatter of a chopper resonated in my mind, as though a patrol had flown down the line while I'd been sleeping. And a vehicle was raising dust on the plain about half a mile off.

Coming from the direction of Aguános, a car had left the highway and was cutting a steady route towards the tender where it stood on the rails far away from the blacktop. It was mustard color, matching the hills in the distance, unlike the little blue patrol cars that had visited earlier, which had big white disks and bubble-gum machines on top. As the car approached the tender it became distorted in a curling heat aura, and a truck and double-trailer road train intruded from the north under a steady engine drone, taking a ponderous couple of minutes to pass out of earshot in the south. Shadows crossed the rock; two vultures were wheeling not far overhead, surveying their property, checking whether we were carrion yet. I squeezed Peppi's shoulder and ran my hand over her hair. The lovely eyes came open.

'How d'you feel?'

'Hmmm. Not so good. Puky.'

She rolled on her side stroking her stomach, and the vulture shadows passed over again, with their chilly warning that touches ancient alarms. I helped her off the rock and over to the horse.

'He's thirsty,' I said, patting his withers.

'So'm I.'

'Somebody's down at the tender.'

She screwed up her eyes.

'It's all hazy. Are they cops?'

'It's not a patrol car.'

We stood staring out, me holding the reins, about to untie them from the cactus trunk, Peppi half leaning against my shoulder, and I noticed a canteen tied to the saddle horn, unhooked it and opened the cork. The bouquet lifted my head half off.

'Try a little mountain tequila.'

She examined the nozzle with distaste, and took a sip, screwing up her face and forcing it down. I did likewise, and the firewater burned, but helped. I hooked it back on the saddle. She wiped damp hair off her brow.

'Let's go into town. I don't feel too good.'

'Could be police there.'

'Who cares. We pay.'

'How?'

'Frank Delius. Western Union.'

When we'd ridden down to the plain I asked her about DeWoers.

Peppi told me. 'She was having a bawling match with the extras when Rayner and I got there. Amaryllis took me to the railcar cabin; the idea was I should rest up while they took views along the line. Then the gunplay started and the train pulled out in a hurry. She went up front just before you arrived.'

'Was Rayner with her?'

'When I went off to the cabin with Amaryllis he was. Seemed to think he could help her handle the extras. I assumed he went up the train too, but we didn't see him. Reska just poked her head into my cabin, said there was a labor relations problem and to keep our heads down. I thought we'd left the extras behind, but next thing those two jerks busted in. Poor Amaryllis.'

'We'll search the line.'

Peppi's sobbing prompted me to kick the pinto into a canter and we rode towards the wavy image of the car and the tender, two distant blobs with a blurred figure moving over them.

As they clarified, I reined down to a walk, with Peppi peering over my shoulder.

'What're they doing?'

We could see the mustard-colored car, a compact import model, halted next to the black eight-wheeled tender. One figure, a man in blouson and jeans, was on the ground looking up at a second man, safari-shirted, thickset, who was laboring up in the coal. Something about the scene made me rein in. Peppi tapped my shoulder, pointing south. Out of the roiling distance, a diesel loco was melting into shape.

The man on the tender straightened up and watched it approaching. The domed head with its beetling brows and jutting chin were unmistakable. It was Carmody.

He bent down to work with renewed effort, then threw a bundle of long, thin objects down to the helper – Walrus.

'Hold on, slim,' I said, and she folded long shapely arms round my waist. The pinto, a good mountain horse, sprang forward and covered the couple of hundred yards in a few seconds. We halted in a flurry of powder near the car, which had Walrus in it, sitting at the wheel, watching Carmody, ruddy and sweating, as he swung over the ladder, climbing hastily down with an eye on us. Deep diesel rumbling permeated the atmosphere.

'Wise guys, huh?' Carmody paused opening the car door and jabbed a stubby finger. 'Peppi, you're under contract. You better get down and ride in the car.' He glanced over his shoulder and back at us. The loco was looming downrail. 'You too, Wallace, move it!'

We dismounted and Peppi moved towards the car, but I restrained her.

'Hang around. Don't want him taking off without me.'

I reached under the girth of the pinto and unstrapped his saddle, pulling it onto the ground with the blanket. Then I unstrapped the throatlash and pulled the bridle over his head, dropping it. A slap on the haunch sent him cantering away with his head plunging and rocking. Carmody barked over the mounting grumble of diesel.

'Come on!'

Peppi and I sat hunched in the back seat as we lurched overland to the highway. Once we were speeding south on blacktop, Carmody hooked an elbow over his seat and looked Peppi over.

'So how're ya doin'?'

She zipped her lips and studied the scenery. I found her hand, which Carmody noticed with a bumptious grin.

'You two pals again, huh?'

'Where's DeWoers, Carmody?'

'She's through, done for, all washed up. You won't believe this, but I seen the mayor of Aguános an hour ago. There's no problem 'bout the ruckus on the train, he says we done him a favor – how d'ya like that?' He guffawed and punched Walrus on the arm, making us swerve. 'Those guys wearing the red do-rags were pulling bank raids, hijacking trucks, sticking up mail trains, then Reska rolls into town and hires them to play the Commie heroes in her Commie fucking movie.'

'What was the bust-up about?'

Carmody shrugged, spreading his paws with exaggerated candor.

'Who knows? I guess they figured she had to be carrying a footlockerful of cash to pay the help.'

Peppi said wearily: 'Reska had no money,' and Carmody glanced craftily at her, then back at me with a glittering challenge. Holding his gaze, I asked Peppi:

'Did *she* tell you that?'

'She was desperate. Nobody at the studio got paid for three weeks before Christmas.'

I said: 'It didn't come out.'

Carmody kept looking from Peppi to me and back again with a wary gleam in his eye.

Peppi said: 'They couldn't let it. She had to have a chance.'

I locked with Carmody.

'Is that true?'

He jutted his jaw, half-grinning.

'She brought in Kempinski.'

'Kempinski backed her version of the script?'

He kept his eye on me, nodding. 'Poor sap's over the hill. Couldn't see past the script for seeing Cuba, Castro falling, megabucks.' The grin widened, glittering up his eyes. 'Like I told you. *Coobah's* magic.'

I turned to Peppi.

'What was Rayner on about when you called him from Kempinski's?'

She chewed her lip for a moment, and made an admission.

'Trying to get me to fly down here. You were right about Kempinski, he *was* squeezing her for points. Rayner told me Reska wanted exclusive control, wanted Kempinski and his fancy financing kept out of it, that she'd found another way to raise funds, a much better way.'

Still addressing Peppi, I exchanged a bright glance with Carmody.

'What way?'

She looked out the window.

'I don't know.'

Carmody still had some of the grin left.

'Where is she, Carmody?' I asked.

There was a pause. The producer studied me with his grin fading, and his eyes flickered away toward Walrus, who half-turned his head and did the accent.

'She went up ze train and climb over the ladder to ze engine. I followed to 'elp. She 'ad a fight wiz ze engineer 'bout 'ow 'e was going too slow? 'E poke 'er face and she fell out ze cab. I tried to save 'er, but she fell out. Zere was nussing I could do.'

Carmody brought his eyes off the Frenchman.

'That's the way it was. You heard Walrus. Cops're out looking for the body right now. They got a chopper on it. She'll be found sooner or later; we only covered five, ten miles while the train was hooked up.'

Peppi started to cry. I took her hand and she pulled it away.

'Let's get this straight, Carmody. When me 'n' Peppi got to the cab, DeWoers'd just been pushed out of it by the engineer? Was that before he got half killed by the Mexicans? Or was it after?'

The producer sneered at my innuendo.

'She was stirring shit with the engineer long before Walrus got there, Wallace. The engineer threw her at the Mexicans. Then they got him.'

Peppi smeared away tears, speaking thickly.

'If anything's happened to Reska, I'm through with the picture.'

Carmody fixed her with a shrewd stare.

'You have a contract with Visionville Productions Incorporated, not with Reska DeWoers.'

'If she's through, I'm through.'

The producer leaned towards her, crooning.

'No way, baby. Lookit, Reska handled you all wrong. This picture's shooting right now, with me directing, and it's going to make you a star.'

Her eyes glistened.

'Oh yeah? 'N' what about Hunker?'

Carmody patted air down.

'Lenny Wills is going to be fine. He had a lucky break. Those Cuban assholes couldn't fix a guy like that, not if he was strapped on a gurney ready for it.'

Peppi wiped each eye once, and sniffed hard.

'I gotta have quiet or I'm gonna throw up, okay?'

In front, they lit up a four-paper joint and we fell silent, except for Carmody chortling at Walrus now and again, all the way to Aguános.

31

WE CLOSED THE car windows to circuit the main square, which in sharp contrast to its earlier emptiness was congested with hordes of vehicles, men, women, children and animals. Hands beat on the top and jostled the bodywork as soon as our foreign faces were noticed in amongst the jam-up of disheveled pickups, scooters, trucks, jeeps, beetles and vintage hand-painted US sedans of the type we had hired with Sergio. Teenage boys perched on our hood gesticulating through the windshield, offering calculators, lighters, pot rolled in newspaper. Walrus leaned on the horn, joining in the general pandemonium.

Peppi's head lolled against me, and I daydreamed gushing shower water, crisp white sheets of starched linen, fresh satin pyjamas, and cotton drapes stirring to a gentle sea-breeze. We passed the steps of a crumbling Romanesque cathedral, where crones begged and Indian women crouched among basketwork and gaudy bolts of cloth, the commotion diminishing as we moved onto the main avenue of Aguános, a divided boulevard lined with plane trees.

Here were various picturesque official buildings which had somehow escaped replacement by steel and glass boxes. They culminated halfway down the avenue in a four-story *palazzo* of stone and stucco, with elaborate windows, fussy wrought-iron balconies and a grandiose entrance at the head of a wide flight of steps. Over the door hung the Mexican tricolor, and above it was a double-width bulging iron balcony for dignitaries to take their salutes. Above the balcony and its array of shuttered French doors were fixed white wooden letters which craved new paint and bravely failed to spell out the hotel's illustrious title: RESI ENCIA IMPERIAL.

Walrus went away with the car and Carmody strutted up the steps at the head of his bedraggled party, leading us into a rococo lobby pervaded by scents of steaming fish and stale cigar smoke, and insisting we should join him immediately for a drink in his rooms. Embarrassed about our appearance, and with no indication of where we might find rooms of our own, Peppi and I followed the producer up a sweeping staircase to the first floor, where he ushered us through the tallest, most ornate double doors into a wide, high-ceilinged chamber where the walk-in marble fireplace had been blocked with plaster, much of the exuberant plasterwork on the ceiling had departed, the gas chandelier was hung with two naked bulbs, wallpaper was peeling back in the distant shadowy corners, and the five-acre rug was threadbare. Tall doors on either side of the windows suggested more of the suite, and a white-jacketed boy threw open a set of French doors on the bustle of traffic and overpopulation. Carmody passed him a bill as he left, took up position at the center of the tired carpet and flourished a hand.

'Ladies and gen'lemen, the presidential suite!'

A waiter arrived on cue with a tray crowded with water, coffee, whiskey, tequila, beer and Coke, which he set down on a stained memory of an ormolu table in front of the bumpy plush couch on which Peppi and I had taken anxious refuge.

Carmody paid him off, put blue flame to a menthol long, inhaled deeply and strutted up and down.

'Check it, my friends. The sense of faded colonial grandeur has *exactly* the image we want. We'll be using this as a location as well as production headquarters. It's in period for Batista the youthful liberator – he takes a salute from this balcony right here, returning from a successful pacification program in the mountains and getting massive support from the Havana population. United States officers with him, of course – the new script is a lot more accurate about that.'

I looked up from the shot of whiskey I'd poured.

'Whose new script?'

He waved a hand airily.

'I got five people working on it. Oh, by the way, an inspector of police is dropping by later, but he assured me it's a formality, once I'd outlined the location budget here. Plus they're shitting their pants I'll sue.'

I said: 'Where's DeWoers? Her disappearing could play hell with further film business in this town, not to mention the tourist trade – if they want one.'

'DeWoers is finished. Bringing Kempinski in to try and stall my buy-out was her big mistake. Obviously an old pro like Kempinski was going to start pressuring for control. Soon's she'd got him in, she wanted him out. He's way-back buddies with the union guys, maybe even arranged a strike he could get lifted after he bailed the studio out.'

'I wondered about that.'

'Trust a liberal!'

Peppi was wanly surveying the crowded table.

'Is there any herbal tea?'

Carmody frowned at the drinks tray, the main doors opened, and Walrus came in embracing a tall bundle rolled in newspaper. He followed a threadbare track across the carpet and carefully freed a hand to let himself into the adjoining room.

Peppi stared as he closed the door behind him.

'So what's with Walrus?'

'By the way,' Carmody said in smoke, moving into the open French doors, surveying the street grandly like a little Irish Batista, and turning back. 'I made a few calls. No direct dialing, but you get put through just fine.' He opened his hands, giving a little bow. 'We find that His Excellency Dr Luis Arroyo is on the mend.'

I wiped off my mouth.

'That's hard to believe.'

'My associate Tony Miranda got a call from the Opus Dei Clinic in Palo Alto. Rayner made a mess of him, but he's stable. We finish the shoot long before he makes any trouble again. There's a warrant out for the perp. Attempted homicide. Rayner's gonna get maytagged in Sonora. One crazy writer off the streets. No, there's no herbal tea here – Walrus'll get some.'

Peppi said: 'What's he doing?'

Carmody wandered towards the window, framing a camera angle with his fingers.

'Cleaning the mary jane. You saw him bring it in. He bought a sheaf of it on the way out of town, when we came back to see if that engineer'd been picked up 'n' ran into you. This is the Holy Land for Walrus – Sonora mountain weed's the goods. Guy's a total pothead, but you don't complain any more, they could be into crack.'

I got up.

'Carmody, I've had enough of this shit. DeWoers could be dead and you're acting like it's boys' day out in Tijuana. I'm going downstairs and take rooms for us right now. We're going to rest Peppi up, then we're moving out of here if it takes a cab ride all the way to San Diego. You're bothered about Peppi's contract, call her attorney.'

Carmody rounded on me, shouting.

'You summabitch, you do that and she'll never work in pictures again. We got thousands a feet in the can already.'

Peppi's bell-like voice came as if dragged in from a great distance.

'I work for Reska, not you, Carl.'

Carmody bristled, gathering himself, poised for a strike.

'You dirty little piece a cunt, you bohunk lesbian bitch, you nigger-fucking little pervert, don't you do the high-and-mighty lover girl on me. You're filth with a pretty face fixed on, that's what –'

I didn't sock Carmody, but he never finished Peppi's résumé because the entrance doors opened and a Walther automatic came in, propelled by a shock-haired woman who moved with a limp and wore a bloody and torn jean suit, Ray-Bans masking her eyes.

Peppi cried out: 'Hey! Thank God!'

Carmody turned and said: 'Jesus!'

'No, I'm better'n either of 'em,' DeWoers drawled.

She straight-armed the automatic, keeping Carmody pinned in

silhouette against the bright balcony. Behind her, Della Lemuel, all in black, with her hair in a taut chignon, closed the doors and leaned against them, staring aloofly at her leader.

'Okay. Quit town, Carl. We been down the road a ways. I want to shoot a hole in your head, but Tina doesn't deserve to be widowed.'

Peppi stood half way up and sat down.

'What happened?'

Keeping the automatic steady, the director replied towards Carmody.

'Making movies is a lousy business, but if I ever need to turn a buck, now at least I can get a stunt job falling out of moving trains.'

Peppi gasped.

'You fell?'

DeWoers kept her shades trained on the producer.

'With a little help from Walrus, after he caught me burying some valuable canvases in the coal up front so the art-loving Mexican help wouldn't get their hands on them. Trouble was, Walrus saw me instead and got creative French ideas. I guess this guy caught him gloating. Where're my pictures, Carl?'

Carmody spread his hands, moving a crafty expression from side to side. DeWoers suddenly lunged forward, switching gun hands, and smashed her fist into the producer's turned-up nose, sending him cawing and reeling against a French door, shattering glass.

'Oh God,' he groaned, dabbing palms furiously against his face and checking them. 'Oh Goddamidey.'

The director barked over him.

'Talk!'

She chopped at his ear with the butt of her gun and he went onto his knees.

'I'll teach you to loose a bunch of Marielitos on me, you cocksucker. They went and rammed Hunker and damn near sank the picture.'

'Hey, bullshit!' Carmody countered, clutching his head. 'It was that fuckin' Arroyo.'

DeWoers poked the barrel at his forehead.

'Oh yeah? Sorry, Nevil twisted Arroyo's arm 'n' he sang it all out, buddy. You lent him the psycho that raided my house –' she jabbed the gun '– the heavy that took off with Peppi so none of us knew where she was.'

Carmody cringed, yapping back at her.

'Rayner's a goddam Commie liar, like the rest of 'em. I got a backer employs Frankie as floor manager. We sent him along to keep check on that fruitcake Arroyo. Treat like with like. Y'know they were out at Kempinski's winery? Well, d'ya know the guy told Frankie to take Peppi out in a field and shoot her in the face?'

Peppi sighed, and Carmody pushed DeWoers's gun barrel away from his head.

He said, 'Frankie fuckin' saved her life!'

DeWoers made an exasperated noise in her throat, moved back, pulling off the glasses, threw them aside, and squeezed the bridge of her nose. When she spoke again it was suddenly more reasonably, a switch I'd seen her make before.

'Nevil's not a Commie, Carl, he's an artist – a cultural worker. When are you money people going to understand what that means? Here you are, stealing the last of my paintings, which're all I've got left from *The Slave*. They were to let me make this movie *my* way. *Nevil Rayner's* way. And yet, you think any form of independent creativity or objective drama – really, *any art atall* – is subversive.' She shook her head, shoving the gun into her belt. 'You're not civilized, know that? I'm sorry I hit you. Give me the paintings the Mexicans wanted and blow.'

With an effort I managed to break her spell on the room and moved a step forward, aching all over, with a whistling ear. Peppi spoke past me.

'Walrus took the canvases in the other room.'

DeWoers groaned.

'You better get them, Della. Can't face the little fink myself.'

Lemuel pulled a silver ladies' .22 automatic out of her tight black purse, crossed to the bedroom doors and went in.

DeWoers turned to Carmody.

'Nevil Rayner's facing a jury trial now. He's lost everything thanks to you and your Mafia pals in Palm Springs.'

Peppi asked: 'Where's Nevil now?'

DeWoers brought a folded paper out of her breast pocket and handed it to her.

'Research in Havana. He scrawled you a goodbye-for-ever, baying like a bloodhound as if he was never coming back.'

Carmody snarled, nursing his head.

'He shouldn't. He'll be happy with Fidel.'

The director sighed.

'They rammed Hunker, Carl. What would've happened if they'd got Craven? Huh? Did you think about that when you loaned out your mad dog?'

'Frankie fucked up,' Carmody muttered.

Walrus came out of the bedroom, paused and looked at DeWoers, tugging on his mustache, then hurried to the main doors and exited. Della emerged, fork-lifting rolled canvases across her pointy chest.

'They're all here – at least I think they are.'

DeWoers went over and squinted down the rolls.

'Picasso, de Chirico, Mondrian, Kandinsky, Hockney. Five million reserve at Sotheby's next month. The rest were mortgaged, but your goon was too dumb to realize.'

Carmody's head came up.

'He knocked off pictures? Which ones?'

DeWoers's lip curled.

'Didn' I tell you?'

I interrupted.

'What about the house insurance?' There was a pause.

DeWoers kept addressing Carmody.

'That's a maybe.'

'Sure is, considering it was you that had the place torched.'

DeWoers could control the temperature of a room, and she turned it cooler. Carmody felt it and unfurled, getting onto his feet.

Lemuel looked up from checking the canvases on the floor.

The director kept dead still, her painted lips open and the tip of her tongue pointing out at one corner. There was a moment of something like meditation.

I said quietly: 'Arson and fraud. Quite serious.'

The director replied, almost tenderly: 'No witnesses, though.'

I said: 'Only me.'

She looked at Peppi.

'But you wouldn't make a stir. You're Peppi's hubby.'

'Yes, I am, aren't I.' Peppi's hand snuck round my thigh. 'And you left me to fry.'

DeWoers's voice hardened.

'Listen, I had no idea you and Amaryllis were in the house. It had to be Arroyo's Cubans who doped you both and dumped you down the chute. Peppi told me about it.'

'And where were you?'

'In a car, waiting for Carmody's genius and his Cubans to get through searching the place. Arroyo paid him to make a little call on me and my attorney, put the scare on. He saw the pictures and decided to make himself a windfall profit.'

'The paintings.'

'Most of them. When I came back, you 'n' Amaryllis'd gone – run for it with the others, I assumed. He'd cut all the pictures out of their frames. I asked to keep a few worthless mementoes, which were these, and gave the rest to him, all itemized and photographed and spoken for at First American.' She glared at Carmody. 'That's what a dumb klutz he was.'

'Frankie.'

'Fuck Frankie.'

I broke in, in case she started hitting the producer again.

'You should thank Frankie – after all, he suggested burning the place and collecting, although you never will. Provided a contact too, right? And thinks he'll get a share?'

Considering me balefully, the director allowed herself a shadowy grin, and murmured in a dreamy way, 'Mmmm. He *has* left a message or two.'

'I like emptying it. Scab labor from the studio? Emptying it shows a tidy mind.'

'Mmm, yes.'

'There's only one problem, DeWoers. When I was lucky enough to wake up in time, it was Amaryllis who tipped me off the place was going to blow. How come?'

211

DeWoers looked past me. I turned to look down at Peppi, who was holding Rayner's love letter, her eyes overflowing. She said: 'Burning the house was originally Amaryllis's idea, in my dressing room at the studio before Christmas. She must've guessed what Reska'd done.'

I looked from Peppi to Della Lemuel and from Della Lemuel to Reska DeWoers, and back from one to the other again, and a peculiar intimation of lawless witchcraft made me tingle. Maybe Carmody felt it. Dusting off, he came to the table, sloshed bourbon into a tumbler, gulped at it, slammed the tumbler back down, said: 'I'll make my own picture. You may like to know I just saw Hunker get out of a cab downstairs,' and let himself out of the suite.

Somewhere in my pocket was a document Frank Delius had faxed me at the Noble Grape motel. DeWoers saw me digging and dragged painted claws through her fright of hair.

'Cody! Tell me you did *not* trail a grubby little legal document all the way across the Sonora desert. Listen, call Munro Craven Monday. Take the goddam property – who cares, it's mortgaged for nearly three mill and I'll be folding the Cayman Island outfit that owns it anyway.' She approached the drinks and picked up a bottle of mescal with a rising sun on the label, unscrewing the cap and fixing me with an owlish stare. 'Listen, dildo, you should put the place in trust and take care of your wife. She says Tina Carmody tested her urine last night. Didn't she tell you? You got a little forever person on the way.'

Peppi welled exultant tears at me that said *It's ours*! and my throat constricted, making me choke on my words.

'Hell, no. Do I believe *this*?'

'Hell, yes!' the director shouted, winking broadly over her shoulder at the deadpan Lemuel woman and gushing mescal into a glass. 'What's more, I got insurance on pregnancy, too. Let's drink to that!'

I held my glass up at Peppi and asked her:

'D'you think that bronze dolphin the water came out of survived?'